About Us

About Us

a novel by Chester Aaron

McGraw-Hill Book Company

New York · Toronto · London · Sydney

ABOUT US

Library of Congress Catalog Card Number: 67-15035
First Edition   00023

For Margaurite and Louis

About Us

About Us

About Me
Winter, 1932

Rachel calls, "Benny! Get up!" and I sit up in bed. The cold air bites my body and I burrow under the blankets again, searching for that warm hollow in which I've lain all night.

The blanket before my face has formed itself into a tunnel. I peer through the tunnel at the square of distant light, the frosted window. It was snowing when I came home from school yesterday; it was snowing when I went to bed. It was still snowing when I fell asleep. Now I watch the shadows of the snowflakes swirling across the white window.

I have to go to the toilet but the thought of fighting my way through the snow and lowering myself onto the icy wooden seat is terrifying. I'll force myself to wait until I get to school, where the floors of the toilets are clean white tile and the bowls are polished enamel and the seats are always warm.

After collapsing the tunnel I picture to myself where, on the floor, my shoes will be, where my underwear and my pants and my shirt will be. I memorize my movements so that I'll have to spend the absolute minimum of time in my room and then the hall and then the stairway.

"Benny!"

1

I pull the warm darkness tighter and tighter about me.

"Benny, I'm going down now. You *have* to get up."

"I'm up."

I try to remember if Rachel has been in to kiss me. She must have been in. She never forgets. Well, just a minute more. When I hear her going down the stairs I'll get up.

At the end of the hall, opposite the door to Rachel's room, a flight of stairs drops steeply onto a landing where another door leads into the kitchen. That door is open now in a futile effort to entice warm air upstairs. On such cold mornings as this one the air, by the time it reaches the upstairs and circulates among all the cold rooms, arrives in my room as bitter as the outside wind that claws and screams now at the house.

Suddenly I realize that today is Friday, the last day of school before Christmas vacation. Today, in Assembly, Miss Curry will announce the winner of the poster contest. I leap out of bed.

Naked, I rush about the room. The cold floor stings the soles of my feet but I continue gathering clothes until my arms contain everything except my underwear. Beginning to shiver now, I drop to my hands and knees. My underwear is not under the bed. As I start to check the closet, to see if Max has played one of his tricks, I recall that Momma told me last night that she would have a clean suit of long underwear for me this morning.

I dash down the hallway, my bare feet slapping the wood floor. I leap down the steps, my clothes held high so none of the dangling sleeves or strings can trip me. A shoe falls. I cry out in pain and frustration but I turn and scramble back up the stairs, hesitating only long enough to grab the shoe. I run down the stairs again.

One final leap carries me from the landing into the warm kitchen. I drop all my clothes to the floor and hold out my arms to the coal stove. For several seconds I remain in that position, all but embracing the stove. Then, slowly, I turn to let some of the warmth be smeared across my back.

2

Rachel sits at the kitchen table, eating her toast and coffee. She's reading the *Pittsburgh Post-Gazette*. "It's supposed to go below zero tonight," she says. "Gee, I hope Reuben doesn't have trouble with the buses."

"A good night for hot soup," Momma says. She is at the gas stove, stirring a pot of oatmeal. She wears a heavy sweater over her dress and a pair of Jacob's wool socks over her cotton hose. She is beautiful, despite her rag-picker appearance. In profile she reminds me of the head of the Indian on the nickel. I've often tried to convince the kids at school that my mother really is an Indian. After all, if she is, so am I.

I hear Momma describing the food she's making for dinner tonight to celebrate Reuben's being home. The heat of the stove drains my energy and I stand there, idle, smiling at the way things have turned out. Tonight's dinner will be special for two reasons. Not just because Reuben will be home from college but because I'll win the prize. Everyone will be proud of me. Rachel will sit beside me, hugging me. Poppa will grin, his face beaming, and he'll brag about how this will show *them*. Momma will hover over me, offering extra cake. Jacob will punch me, in play, and will tell me he's always known I'm a better artist than I am a boxer. Reuben . . . well, Reuben's been praising me, no matter what I do, ever since I was born. Even Max will have to find something special to say.

I revolve very slowly to prolong the warm, drowsy fantasies. My belly is a bright red from the heat.

Although I'm only eight years old my eyes are on a level with Momma's. She seems taller because she carries herself so erect and moves with such assurance and dignity that I often feel no matter how old I might be, or how tall, she'll always seem taller.

Rachel walks the same way. Like everyone else in the family, she has brown, almost black, eyes. And black hair. Once this winter, two or three weeks ago, after both Rachel and Momma washed their hair, they sat in front of the coal-

3

stove. Poppa had stoked the fire for them. The walls of the stove were cherry red. I was doing my homework at the kitchen table. Looking up, I watched as they took turns combing each other's long black hair. On the page in the book before me was a picture of a siren on an ocean rock. I sat very still. Poppa, sitting across from me, was stirring strawberry preserves into his tea. He stopped stirring and he watched too. Jacob has taught Max how to play chess. They never talk when they play. For once they stopped concentrating on the board. They stared at Rachel and Momma; each a reflection of the other; each, though small and delicate, strong, not at all fragile. On the radio, on station KDKA, Marian Anderson was singing *Ave Maria*. In spite of herself, Momma, unaware that we were all staring, smiled with pleasure as she listened to a Negro sing the salutation of Gabriel to the Virgin Mary. Rachel began to braid her hair. It was Poppa who first realized that he was smiling. He dropped his spoon. The spell was broken. I went back to my book and Max and Jacob went back to their chess game.

I leap out of my reverie as Momma shouts, "Benjamin! Hurry! Your underwear! You want the bus should go without you?" She interrupts her stirring of the oatmeal to point at the chair near the stove.

To warm the underwear I take it from the chair and hold it close to the stove door, which is open. It is long underwear. I step into the legs, then the arms. For an hour or so the underwear will be tight about my calves and thighs but then, around noon, the cloth will begin to sag. From now until I change underwear again, in three or four days, several minutes every morning will be devoted to the careful folding of the cuffs each time I put on my socks. I button the front, feel behind for the drop-seat, find it and close it. While I tuck my heavy plaid shirt in my trousers I say, trying to sound casual, "The winner's announced today."

"Winner of what?" Momma asks. "Will you hurry, Benjamin? In fifteen minutes the bus leaves and you ain't washed yet."

4

"The poster contest?" Rachel asks.

"Yeah." I feel the blood rush to my head at the thought of the crowded auditorium and Miss Curry on the stage and the kids turning to admire me.

"Benjamin, Max is already left. All the other kids, they're on the bus already."

"Miss Curry says I'll be a great artist some day. She says she'll be able to say she knew me *when*."

"Better you should be a great eater first," Momma says. "Last few days what you eat wouldn't keep a bedbug alive. Hurry up. Wash. Eat. Mr. Griswold's in the bus, growling like Yenta. I can hear him. You want one or two toast? You'll have two."

"Just oatmeal. I want to hurry."

"Take time. Eat. It won't take long, some toast, a cup cocoa." She drops two slices of bread on the gas burners.

I go to the sink, stand on the stool reserved for me, turn on the faucet, hold my breath and push my hands under the icy water. Tonight, to keep the water in the pipes from freezing, Poppa will let the water run all night. Off and on, until morning, he will get out of bed and place hot towels around whatever length of pipe is accessible. I pull my hands out of the water, rub my cheeks and reach for a towel.

"Soap," Momma says.

"It's cold."

"The cocoa's hot. The oatmeal's hot. Hurry up."

I roll the brown soap in my hands, push and pull my hands through the water, rub my face, rinse it once, quickly, and then grab the towel. I dry my hands and face, rubbing them briskly, and I bend forward to receive the heat from the fire directly on my cheeks. Warm now, and hungry, but anxious to be at school, I sit at the table and begin wolfing my cereal.

"You have to eat like Yenta?" Momma asks. "She's a dog she eats like a dog. You're a *mensch*."

"Momma, if I win I get ten dollars and a medal. And my picture in *The Summer Eagle*. Everyone, Miss Curry and everyone, says my poster's the best."

5

"Is *everyone* judges?" Momma asks. "You'll take my advice, the eggs, they're hatched, then count your chickens."

"I saw Mary Schneider's painting," Rachel says. "It's very good." She hurries to add, "Not as good as yours, but good." She takes my hand between her own. Her hands feel as if they're sheathed in velvet. "But Momma's right. Don't be disappointed if you don't win. There must be a hundred students in the contest. From all over Summer County. Ninety-five are going to be losers."

"Reuben won a scholarship. And he won a gold medal at college."

"We aren't all Reubens," Rachel says. "And some contests he enters he'll lose. He has to."

I find that hard to believe.

Momma, who's nodded and smiled at her daughter's support, wipes butter from my cheek. She removes a tortoise-shell comb from her own hair to try to fix some order to my curls. "Hair like his," she says, "black sheep's wool." She rarely refers to Poppa as *Chatzkel* or *your father* and she never calls him *Al*, as everyone else in Sundown does. It's almost always *him* or *his*.

I continue eating, knowing it's useless to try to communicate my optimism. Poppa and Momma, both from the old country, are always skeptical of anyone getting anything for nothing. And *drawing*, or *painting*, is nothing. Rachel can not afford the luxury of hope. Her anguish, should I not win, will be great enough without having added to it the burden of a long day's anticipation.

But wait!

Wait until I come home and put the ten-dollar bill in Momma's hand. Wait until I open the black box and display the gold medal. (Will it be in a black box?) Momma's eyes will fill with tears. She'll kiss my cheeks. When she climbs the stairs to her bedroom she'll take the medal with her and she'll store it deep in her trunk. Every year she'll remove it, to polish it, and she'll hold it up to the light and will remind me how

6

proud *my* children will be and how grateful *I'll* be for her having kept it. I will not protest when she presses my head against her bosom.

And tonight, when Reuben teases me about my prize, and pretends to scoff at it, it will be evident to everyone that he will be even prouder than Momma.

The door leading from the kitchen to the store opens and Poppa comes in, the black curls on his head indeed like sheep's wool. His black mustachios completely hide both lips.

"Hi, Poppa."

"Griswold's yelling you're late, you're keeping the bus."

"I'm coming."

"You're coming. You're coming an hour now. Tomorrow I'll wake you myself."

I laugh. "No school tomorrow. No school for two weeks." I dance around him, chanting, "No school tomorrow." He makes a grab for me and I dart away. While Rachel laughs and Momma shouts for him to let me eat, Poppa roars. Two white teeth peek out from under the black mustachios. He catches me, locks my head in one arm and rubs my curls with a gnarled brown fist.

He lets me break loose. I stumble around the kitchen, drinking my cocoa and biting and chewing toast and fighting my way into galoshes and mackinaw, Momma following me with her comb, trying to repair the damage Poppa's fist has done to the part she just a few minutes earlier had forced into my hair. No sooner does she succeed than I pull on my red tassle cap. She throws up her hands in despair. Rachel has strapped my books together and is holding them out at arms' length. I spear them on my way to the door.

"Your lunch . . . your lunch."

I return, tuck the paper bag under my arm like a football and run again. Out of the kitchen. Through the dark, narrow passage between the wall and the counter. The showcase door is open and I smell the crisp crusted breads and the five-cent peach and apricot pies. Past the red-bellied coal stove (around

7

which four old men sit, patiently waiting for the peace that will routinely settle once the bus departs). Past the candy-cases. Past the meat freezer. Past the shelves filled with all sorts and sizes and colors of boxes and cans and jars. Onto the store porch.

The wind almost throws me back inside the store. I lower my head and plunge down the steps, which Poppa sprinkled with ashes two or three times before I even got out of bed. The snow crunches under my feet as I walk past the gasoline tanks and approach the bus. The cold burns the walls of my nostrils. My feet are so heavy in the galoshes and my underwear is wrapped so tightly that I can hardly maneuver the first step into the bus.

"Let's go, Benny," Mr. Griswold says, growling indeed like Yenta. "We're late."

I stumble down the aisle as the bus creeps forward over the snow. I sit alongside Roman. "Hey," I say, "poster winners are announced today."

"I'll trade you a cheese sandwich," Roman says. "For a peanut-butter."

Never has Brazil or Argentina seemed more remote.

I hear, as I watch the hands of the clock creep across the face, ". . . beef is the major export . . . Matto Grosso . . . the Amazon basin makes up nearly half of all South America . . . who knows what *export* means? . . ." My mind, like Yenta's nose glued to a scent, remains on the coming Assembly. Miss Curry, short and fat and rosy-cheeked, will waddle onto the stage and—as ten other teachers will be reading in ten other schools—will read, in a voice that sounds as if she's balancing one of her secret candies behind her front teeth: "the first prize—ten dollars in cash and a gold medal—goes to Benjamin Kahn of our own McCluskey School. . . ." The eyes of every student in the third grade, and even of the mighty eighth grade, will turn to seek out my face.

To furnish bulk to this fantasy I pluck out of a familiar niche

8

in my memory the display in the window of Salomon's Shoe Store (*The Finest of Shoes for the Finest of Feet in Summer*).

The snow, already ten inches deep all over the city, threatens to rise another two or three inches as the flakes continue to flutter down. Mr. Salomon's window display is a composition of galoshes, rubbers, high-top shoes and fleece-lined slippers. The window is hung with banners of red and green crepe. Each pair of shoes and galoshes and slippers rests on top of an appropriately gift-wrapped box. In the center of the display, framed in black velvet, held upright by a velvet-wrapped shoe box, is a pastel drawing of snow-covered hills and dark pine trees. From the window of a tiny cabin hidden beneath one of the trees in the foreground spills a golden light. It throws the two bars of the window onto the snow in the form of a cross.

On a piece of white cardboard alongside the drawing two lines of elaborate Gothic print declare:

STILLE NACHT. HEILIGE NACHT.
ALLES SCHLÄFT. EINSAM WACHT.

Three exchanges of letters between Reuben and myself were required before Reuben judged the printing acceptable. It took me as long to draw the skeleton of each of the forty-six letters, and then to fill in each skeleton with India ink, as it took me to complete the drawing itself.

Under the Gothic letters, and off to the right, in ordinary and slightly smudged print, are the words:

Benjamin Kahn, Age 8
Third Grade
McCluskey School

Mr. Salomon is very flattered to have Momma in his store. He knows how to impress her. "Benny? *You* are the Benjamin Kahn painted such a masterpiece? I should have known. Could any other family produce such a talent?"

I try to remain nonchalant as Momma, who's performing

9

very well the role of the humble mother, assures Mr. Salomon that I did it all alone, printing and all. Not, she knows, like some of the other children whose paintings are displayed in other stores. I am glad she mentions nothing about the cross on the snow and the argument we have had about it. "It *has* to be there," I'd said. "There's light shining through the window." "So there's light. A cross is a cross. *You* have to paint a cross?" "It's a window," I said. "A window has bars and bars throw a shadow like a cross." "Since when there has to be a window in every house? Believe me, I lived in houses there wasn't a window. Not one. You're spoiled, all of you, raised in houses with windows. You don't know." Rachel and Max and Jacob support me but Momma shrugs off their arguments. Soon, she says, they'll be eating bacon.

Mr. Salomon brings up his hand to pat me on the head. Remembering the knuckles of that same hand thumping my skull those times I've fallen asleep in the synagogue, I wince. "Don't pull away," he whines. "Why do you pull away?"

When Momma and I leave the store Mr. Salomon accompanies us as far as the sidewalk. He hunches his blue-serged shoulders up about his pink snail-shell ears.

"Go in," Momma says. "You'll catch cold. Say hello to Fanny."

"Hello to Chatzkel. When you going to move in town and live like civilized Jews? A family like yours . . . any community'd be proud to have them."

"Please," Momma says, holding up her hand to terminate a conversation she finds too intimate to engage in even with her family, let alone with an acquaintance.

In Geography I'd not been called to answer a single question, so my freedom to dream had helped to speed the sixty minutes. But ten minutes after I sit at my desk in Civics, Miss Kennedy snaps her fingers at my left earlobe. My hand leaps to soothe the injured ear. I hear Roman's laughter above the buzzing in my temple.

10

"Do I have to get a megaphone," Miss Kennedy asks, "and shout it in your ear?"

"No."

"No what?"

"No, Miss Kennedy."

"Then answer my question."

"I . . . didn't hear the question."

"You mean you weren't listening to the question. Isn't that correct? You weren't listening?" She feints a blow at the right ear and when I reach to defend it she deftly catches me on the left ear again.

"I wasn't listening."

Miss Kennedy nods and walks to the front of the class, considering aloud the quantity and quality of my punishment.

During recess, in the hopes that it might prove distracting, I ask to join the kids who've been given permission to play outside.

The snow is perfect for Fox-and-Geese. The six boys stamp out a circumference of a circle and then two diameters.

When I'm the fox I pick Roman to be my victim. I chase him around and around the circumference and up and down the diameters until, tripped by Goose, Roman steps into the snow beyond the circle and automatically becomes It. But he leaps on Goose. I leap on him and three other boys pile on top of us.

Back in our homeroom we meekly accept Miss Grossman's promise of disaster if we behave this way again. We can thank our lucky stars, she tells us, that it's so close to Christmas.

Compelled to stand near the heaters until our pants and stockings are dry means, as we'd hoped it would, that we are to have a reprieve from blackboard work.

I lean against the heater and gaze out through the window, watching the snow fall. I wonder if I should give all the prize money to my mother, or only give the bulk of it and keep a small part for myself. I decide to offer her all of it, knowing

11

that my mother, in turn, will suggest I keep a dollar or two for myself, to spend as I wish. Such a decision satisfies both stomach and conscience.

At lunchtime Miss Grossman will not permit any of us to play outside. "Some of you," she says, "performed disgracefully at recess. Unfortunately, you all have to suffer now for the sins of the few."

It is more fun inside at lunchtime anyway. We can sit in any seat in the room and we can talk or sing, or play quiet games or read. I go to the board. Miss Grossman, welcoming the distraction always offered by my drawing at the board, produces a box of colored chalk-sticks. The children scurry to find seats in the front row, shouting out their requests. "Draw cowboys, Benny! . . . horses! . . . Buck Jones . . . Rin-Tin-Tin . . . draw airplanes, Ben . . . Santa Claus . . . the Manger. . . ."

I choose the Three Wise Men.

I sketch in the figures of the Wise Men first. They advance, arms outstretched, gifts in their hands. I am very good at drawing upturned hands. For the moment I leave vacant the circles which will eventually be heads and faces. The kids are always impressed at the speed and facility, once I turn to the faces, with which I detail the eyes and noses and mouths. Three camels plod behind the Wise Men. Using five full sticks, I cover the stretch of blackboard with sand-colored chalk. Then, after I color the robes blue and red and yellow, and add depth to the many folds in the robes, I set myself to the faces. As usual everyone, including Miss Grossman, sits transfixed as I quickly mark off eyelids and nostrils and teeth and lips, and then add turbans and beards. Finished, I return to my seat, serene in my glory.

Miss Grossman admires it, her head shaking in awe or disbelief or both. "I won't erase it," she says. "When we come back January third it will still be there. It's beautiful, Benjamin."

I brush the chalk dust from my shirt and trousers. I glance at

12

the clock. Two and a half more hours. Then they will toast me, the way they toasted Jacob when he was *Bar-Mitzvahed*. Reuben will hold the medal high, its gold face reflecting the candle lights. Momma will beam, tears in her eyes.

A movie in History class cuts the wait to one and a half hours. For fifty minutes, as I watch the movie about the American Revolution, I forget about the contest and I think instead about Valley Forge and General Washington and Patrick Henry. *Give me liberty or give me death . . . I regret I have but one life to give for my country*. I try to compose an acceptance speech for the prize, but no matter how I word it, it seems to lack the grandeur and the passion of the orators of 1776.

The last class is English. Mr. Uram reads a short story called "The Gift of the Magi."

After he finishes reading the story Mr. Uram closes the book and leaves the room. The children remain silent for a moment and then, since there is little likelihood he'll return, they chase each other up and down the aisles. I sit at my desk, trying to decide why I'm so shaken. The terrible melodramatic ironies of O. Henry's story have struck a blow at my easy sense of victory.

Mr. McPhee, the principal, welcomes the students and then Mrs. Titleman leads the Senior Chorus in the singing of three carols. Miss Grossman recites a poem by Walt Whitman. It is about a noiseless, patient spider. It has nothing to do with Christmas. Everyone giggles at first because it is meaningless and we are embarrassed for her but suddenly I, like everyone else, sit quiet. . . .

> It launched forth filament, filament . . . out
>   of itself
> Ever unreeling . . . tirelessly speeding . . .
> And you O my soul where you stand

13

Surrounded, detached, in measureless oceans
   of space,
Ceaselessly musing, venturing, throwing,
   seeking the spheres to connect them.
Till the bridge you will need be form'd, till
   the ductile anchor holds,
Till the gossamer threads you fling catch
   somewhere, O my soul.

The rustling of the pages in her book crackles like pistol shots in the silence. She reads "A Winter's Day" and then "A Winter's Night" by Whittier. Betsy Griswold plays a Beethoven sonata on the piano. She's in seventh grade and has red hair. While she plays the sonata Mary Schneider, who sits beside me, leans over and whispers to me that a lot of girls say Betsy dyes her hair but she, Mary, knows it's very, very natural.

As always I sit between Mary and Roman. Roman keeps talking about how he is going to double the number of traps he now has set at the Connequenessing Creek, so that by spring he'll have enough pelts to buy a shotgun. While Mr. McPhee goes across the stage to talk to Miss Curry and Mr. Uram, I watch them very carefully to see if they glance in my direction. While they discuss something, Miss Curry gestures with a white envelope she holds in her hand. All the while Mary is describing the details of a party she is planning to have on her birthday. She asks me twice if I'll come but I do not reply. I am hypnotized by that white envelope. When Mary leans forward and looks me in the eye, her head blocking out Miss Curry, and asks me again if I'll come, I swallow several times to lubricate my throat so the words "Yes, I'll come" can find their way free.

Mr. McPhee thanks Betsy Griswold for her beautiful sonata and then he introduces Miss Curry, who, he says, "Has some information about that poster contest in which five of our students were finalists." He looks in my direction. I'm sure it is intentional. Both he and Miss Curry have raved about my

14

talents and I'm sure they're both as anxious to inform me, as I am to learn, that I have won.

Give me liberty or give me death. I hear Patrick Henry's ringing voice. All I'll say, I decide, is "Thank you."

Miss Curry waddles across the stage. She adjusts the height of the microphone and says that first of all she wants to thank all those students who submitted posters to the contest. Next she wants to especially thank those five students who were selected as finalists, whose work had such merit, who were credits to McCluskey School. She calls out the names of the five and when she says, "Mary Schneider," Mary giggles and blushes. When she says, "Benjamin Kahn," I feel my chest grow hot. I don't know what to do with my hands but when Roman nudges me and mutters, "Halfers if you win," I jab an elbow into his ribs and he grunts. Miss Curry says she will open the envelope, just as the envelopes are being opened right now in six other schools in Summer County.

I think I am going to faint. My face burns and I can hardly breathe. Miss Curry opens the envelope and pulls out a sheet of paper. In a quiet voice she says something about, "The winners of the third annual . . ." Mr. McPhee comes over and says something to her and re-adjusts the microphone. My heart is throbbing so hard I'm sure Roman and Mary can hear it. Mr. McPhee leaves and Miss Curry speaks again. This time her voice is loud. "The winners of the third annual poster contest of the Summer County School System are as follows: First prize to Dorothy Vogel, Meridian Township School; second prize to Rita Nietrezeba, fifth grade, Lyndy School; and third prize . . . third prize goes to our own Mary Schneider, third grade, McCluskey School." Miss Curry pauses long enough to permit the Assembly to applaud. When the students turn to search Mary out, I continue waiting for Miss Curry to say, "Oh, wait. There's a mistake. Here's . . ."

But she says nothing. She folds the letter, puts it in the envelope and walks off the stage.

I know that if I dare let my lips move to say one single word

15

to Mary or Roman I'll cry. But I want to shout, I need to shout, "It's a lie . . . a mistake . . . *I* won!"

In the bus, on the way home, I sit with my cheek against the cold glass. Everyone is singing *Silent Night*. Even Mr. Griswold.

Instead of going through the store, where one of the miners, or Poppa, might ask about the contest, I fight through the snow in the yard and enter through the back door. Yenta, in the tarpaper-covered house that Reuben and I built when she was a puppy, comes out to greet me. Her shaggy yellow head is warm and soft as a mitten against my hand.

Somehow, when I see Reuben, I manage to jump into his arms and pretend nothing's wrong. I even manage to laugh when he says I'm growing so fast I'll soon be the biggest man in the house. Before anyone can ask about the contest I rush upstairs, pretending I want to change clothes. After an entire day the heat seeping up the stairs has had some effect. I stay in my room as long as I can, coming down when Momma finally calls me for supper.

Everyone is sitting around the table. Reuben is talking about college. Then everyone stops talking and waits, indulgent, as Momma lights the candles, waves her hands across the flames, then throws her hands across her eyes and prays. And weeps. I know enough Hebrew to understand the word *sister* . . . *brother* . . . *mother* . . . *father* . . . *death* . . . *Paradise*. . . .

She stands before the candles, her body jerking with sobs. Finally, after several minutes, she calms herself and turns to serve the food.

Everyone eats. No one asks about the contest. Reuben talks about the news from Europe, about Russia and Germany and Italy. He studies history in college and when he says that war is inevitable, I know it's inevitable. Momma begs him to stop talking like that. Max, who's in the first year of high school, and Jacob, who's in his fourth year, have been absorbing every

16

word spoken at the table. Jacob says that Reuben is simply stating facts. Poppa says no one knows anything, wars come no matter who does what. That's the way things have always been and always will be. Momma bites her lip and gazes fearfully at the small remnant of candle.

Poppa has closed the store so he can enjoy Reuben's first night home without being interrupted. He opens a bottle of elderberry wine and even permits Yenta to come in out of the storm.

The kitchen is packed with the aromas of a better-than-usual Friday night dinner. There is kasha soup and roast and home-made bread and boiled potatoes and tomatoes stewed with bread. There are beets and corn that were grown in our garden and canned in our kitchen. They're heated now, along with green beans that Rachel canned. There are kosher pickles from a barrel in one of the back rooms of the store. There will be sponge cake for dessert, and coffee and tea. Simmering on the stove are the bits of chicken fat which, late in the evening, will be rendered with onions and served as a final grand delicacy.

I pick at my food, swallow some and push the rest of it away. I avoid Rachel's eyes, and Reuben's, and I wait for Momma to ask me about the contest. She never does.

Late in the evening, after the table is cleared, everyone continues sitting in the kitchen. Poppa has a great roaring fire in the stove and Yenta is asleep under the cookstove. Except for Momma and Poppa, who sit there sipping tea through sugar cubes clenched in their teeth, they talk about politics and literature.

I sit beside Yenta and then I lie beside her, my head on her shoulder. The room seems to roll and tilt under the assaults of voices, cigarette smoke, the odors of food.

The wind screeches in the chimney, pries at the frosted window, pushes down on the roof and up at the floor.

17

In the winter I often fall asleep like this, on the floor with Yenta or curled up on two chairs. About midnight Poppa always lifts me and carries me upstairs to bed.

"Look," Rachel says. "Look at Benny."

I do not open my eyes.

"He asleep?"

"He's asleep."

"I saw all the others," Jacob says. "They were *dreck* compared with Benny's."

"Poor Benny," Rachel says. "He was so sure he'd win."

"Everyone told him," Momma says. "Remember?"

"They didn't believe *he* did the painting," Reuben says. "Either that or they didn't want to give a Christmas prize to a Jew."

"He'll learn," Poppa says.

"But not now," Momma says. "Eight years old? He should learn now, he's only eight years old?"

"Since when," Poppa says, "they save their hate for old people?"

I want to leap up, I want to hide, but I lie there, pretending I'm asleep.

"Now it begins," Poppa says. "It hurts, you're eight years old, you're called such things he'll be called. The bastards! They take it in with their mothers' milk. I better bring him up."

When he lifts me I let my arms and legs flop to give the impression I'm sound asleep. Poppa carries me up the stairs. He undresses me and pulls the covers around me. I smell his sweet-wine breath; his rough cheek scratches my lips.

After he goes down the hallway and down the stairs I lie there, watching the snowflakes swirl across the glass. Is it true? If it's true, if what they said is true, what does it mean? If I did not win the prize just because I'm a Jew then all the rest of my life I'll never win. I'll always lose. If they're wrong . . . if the prize was not kept from me because I'm a Jew, then my

18

picture just did not deserve the prize. I'm not the best artist. I'm not even second best. I'm not even third best.

Someone is climbing the stairs. They come down the hall. It's Rachel. She drops on my bed beside me and she slides her arm under my head.

She tries to soothe me but a worm of a thought is chewing at my mind, distracting me.

None of them, not even Rachel, has considered the possibility that I don't deserve the prize, that my painting might be inferior. For all of them the fault, the responsibility, the source of evil belongs to someone else. To that mass ambiguous *them.* Could it belong to *me?*

No!

I *do* deserve the prize. My painting *was* the best.

Rachel, barely seven years older than I, with a precociously maternal instinct that is destined to suffer for no other child but me, whispers, "Oh, my poor Benny."

I yield to her need to comfort me and herself.

19

About Roman
Autumn, 1933

" . . . Let's put Archy Finnegan's swing up on the telephone pole . . . let's bomb the big guys with tomatoes . . . let's put a skunk in Nietrezeba's smokehouse . . . let's put rotten eggs under all the hens in Armstrong's chicken pen . . . let's write a dirty note to Olga Hallahurich and sign it Ellsworth Cotton . . . let's call Brick Shiptick and the city cops and the state cops and tell them a guy with a gun is shooting people . . . let's pound potatoes up the tailpipe of Bud Hardt's car . . . let's tell McNary's Funeral Parlor there's a dead baby at Bednarick's house and they should come pick it up . . . let's put axle grease around the seat in Charley Conners' shit-house . . . let's tie two cats' tails together and throw them over Millie Krepenivich's clothesline. . . ."

We've not done any of these things before, but the big guys have. We've been hearing their stories for years This Hallowe'en we're determined to begin to collect our own stories.

But first, for required energy, we'll raid Kennedy's apple trees at the top of the hill, in Summer. The apples are Northern Spies, crisp and delicious.

Though he's only eleven years old, two years older than I

am, Roman deploys us about the yard with the assurance of an experienced combat commander.

He sends Goose up the locust tree, from where the interior of the entire rear half of the house can be seen. If any of the Kennedys come outside Goose will see them in time to warn the rest of us, so we can escape.

Kenny Beach and Johnny Trebuka and I . . . the three fastest runners . . . are to collect the apples. Roman and Adam Pulaski, the best climbers, crawl out on two of the limbs and bounce up and down. For several seconds there is a hail of apples. They thud against the ground. Kenny and Johnny and I have been standing close against the trunk, so as not to be hit on the head by the apples, but now we go to work.

We've already stuffed our trousers into our socks and while Roman and Adam climb down from the tree we plop apples through our open flies. They roll down our trouser legs and as we scurry about in the darkness, feeling the cold moist earth, searching out the newly fallen apples, the bruised apples in our trousers and the crushed apples on the ground compose a thick, intoxicating aroma.

A cat meows twice: Goose's signal.

We all dash for the fence. Adam goes over first. Kenny and Johnny and I perform as we, and Roman, have often rehearsed. Roman kneels, one knee up. First Johnny, then Kenny, then I step to his knee, set one foot in his hands. We're lifted and thrown through the air. Over the fence. While in the air I catch the top of the fence in my hands and correct the flight of my body so that I'll land on my feet.

Mr. Kennedy turns on the light and steps onto the porch. He comes down to the grass and peers into the shadows. "You're hearing things," he calls to someone inside, and he goes back in the house.

We walk down the road to Sundown, celebrating another victory over the rich people on the hill. Each of our crisp Northern Spies is consumed in two or three bites. We throw the cores at each other or at the streetlight (the single streetlight in existence between Summer and Sundown and which, thanks to previous demonstrations of our accuracy with apples and stones, is now protected by a cup of wire mesh). Or we sail the cores far out into the vastness of the ocean of darkness that rolls about us.

Bud Hardt, whom almost everyone in Sundown calls "the Mayor," has a swing on his front porch. In the summer his wife, Emma (who is Ellsworth Cotton's sister), sits on the swing, her legs up and straight out as she glides back and forth. She never wears underpants. Cosco and Step and Stash, and a lot of the other big guys, often sit in Cosco's kitchen and take turns snatch-watching, as they call it, through a pair of binoculars Cosco's father brought back from Fort Dix.

At Hallowe'en the Mayor always removes the swing from its hooks on the ceiling of the porch. He stores the swing in the cellar until three or four days after all the tricks have been played.

This year, intent on asserting our independence of the big guys, we start playing tricks a week before Hallowe'en, before the Mayor decides to store his swing in his cellar.

While Adam and Johnny and Kenny watch, Roman and Goose and I sneak across the front lawn. We stay off the gravel path. (Being students of Indian lore, we know how to scout the stockades of our enemies.)

We tiptoe up the steps and across the porch. Through the window we can see the Mayor and Ellsworth Cotton and Emma. They're sitting at the table with a fourth person, drinking beer and playing cards. We can hear the radio. It sounds like Spencer Keane, Tracer of Lost Persons. Rex and Shep, the Mayor's two German Shepherd dogs, are asleep near the radio.

I climb to the banister on the porch and then onto Roman's shoulders. Without a sound. The dogs don't move.

The link of chain lifts up and off the hook very easily. I let down one end of the swing. Goose catches it and eases it, gently, gently, to the porch. Roman, with me on his shoulders, slides across the porch to the other hook. I free the chain and lower the swing to Goose. I step from Roman's shoulders to the banister and then to the porch. Without the slightest tinkle of chain we carry the swing across the porch, across the lawn, down across the B. and L.E. Railroad tracks to the Conequenessing Creek.

The water's too cold for everyone except Roman. He takes off his clothes and leaps. He swims around, snorting like a walrus, inviting us all to come in.

We hand him one of the chains and he tows the swing through the water.

There's a dead tree in the creek, lodged there by some ancient storm. In the summer its branches are filled with the bodies of boys chirping away like a hundred sparrows. We dive from the tree, we swing on it, we rest on its thicker limbs, we play tag in its tangled black branches. Often, in the late summer evenings, we sit in the tree, high above the water, watching night glide down over the hills to surround the three or four hundred houses in Sundown and then advance on the creek to search for us. We sit in the tree in the darkness and we talk, our voices suspended at various levels in the air, some from a few feet away, some fifty feet away, some above, some below.

Roman drags the swing behind him as he makes his way up the tree to the highest branch. He secures the swing and then performs a swan dive into the water, his body glistening in the moonlight.

The Mayor, of course, is furious. He threatens to shoot the next kid that comes near his house.

It doesn't take him long to discover where the swing has been hidden. He and Ellsworth Cotton row a boat out to the tree but neither man dares to climb to the height of the swing.

23

The limbs are too fragile, they're sure, for their weight. They try to rope it, they try to knock it down with long poles, but the swing doesn't move.

The Mayor announces that he'll pay fifty cents to anyone who'll bring his swing back to him. There are no takers. He offers seventy-five cents. No takers. A dollar. "Oh," Roman says. "I'll do it for a dollar, Mayor."

Roman retrieves the swing and Goose and I help him carry it back to the Mayor's house. We walk up the gravel path to the porch where he's waiting for us, a dollar bill in his hand.

Roman, his hair still wet and matted, his eyelashes still glued together from the swim, holds out his hand for the reward.

"Will you boys carry it down to the cellar for me?"

We do. We place it alongside several cases of bottles filled with whiskey and beer and wine, contributions from his brother-in-law. On the porch Roman holds out his hand for the dollar bill. The Mayor slaps his face, twice, whirls him around and kicks him in the ass so hard that Roman sails out onto the gravel.

That night the Mayor chains Shep, one of his German Shepherds, to the front porch and Rex, the other Shepherd, to the back porch.

Roman calls a meeting at our shanty.

This is war.

Even if Bud Hardt, the Mayor, hadn't slapped and kicked Roman, we'd have enough reason to hate him.

For one thing his house is where the township police always stop when they're in Sundown, to have "coffee." For another thing, he's forever threatening to put the cops on us or sic his dogs on us whenever we play games that include running up and down his street. He makes fun of anyone who speaks with an accent. His friends and relatives, who are not Polish or Russian, make up the majority of Sundown's voting population, so that no matter who runs against him in the elections, he always wins. Not only does Bud Hardt have the ideal

24

temperament for a petty bureaucrat, he is the breed of petty bureaucrat who does not endanger his superiors by seeking to climb to their offices, and so he receives constant support from any superior he appeals to.

"We oughta soap all his windows," Goose says.

"Let the air out of his tires."

"Move his shit-house."

Roman agrees to this last suggestion. "But there's something else we can do, too."

The Mayor's house is a two-story clapboard on Valley Street, the only paved street in Sundown. Two sons, both married to cousins of Ellsworth Cotton, live on either side of Bud Hardt's house.

A thick hedgerow surrounds each of the three houses, separating each from the other. Right now, however, construction's under way for a large cesspool that will service the new flush toilets being installed in all three houses. The pit is in the Mayor's back yard but ditches run from the other houses to the pit. For these ditches openings have been torn in the hedgerows. Until the installation's completed everyone has to continue using their outhouses.

We surround the Mayor's outhouse and tilt it to one side. Three of us slide our hands between the board bottom and the ground. It's tilted toward us and three others, on the other side, slide their hands under the bottom. We lift and ease the entire building about twelve inches back. Anyone coming to use it tonight will not notice it's been moved. They'll step where they've always stepped and they'll slide down into the hole, up to their shoulders in shit.

We do our work in absolute silence, successful in not alerting Rex, who's chained to the back porch. Shep, we know, is chained to the front porch. The lights are on at both the front and the back porches.

We lie behind the hedges, near the opening made for the ditch. Goose meows like a cat. Rex barks and rushes at us. The

25

chain pulls him up short but he continues barking. Bud Hardt opens the back door and comes out, a shotgun in his arms.

"What's the matter, Rex? What is it?"

Rex continues barking. Goose meows again. Bud Hardt laughs. He goes back to the house. Rex follows him. While they're both moving away from us, Roman runs forward, drops a large beef bone on the grass and runs back to join us again behind the hedges.

The Mayor goes inside and Rex settles on the top step. He sees and smells the bone. He comes down, sniffs it and then snatches it between his jaws and carries it back to the porch.

While Rex is occupied we sneak along the hedgerow to the front of the house. At one point, where the roots of the hedges are not so close together, and where Rex and Shep have dug for bones, there is an opening large enough for Goose to slip through. He goes just far enough to assure the success of his job. Aiming carefully, he hurls a bone out into the front yard, near the gate, where I've been posted.

Shep hears the bone hit the ground. He rises, comes down the steps, sniffs his way to the bone and grabs it. His chain is fully extended. Roman has not only planned what we've already done, and what we do next—he's predicted what Shep would do when offered the opportunity I now offer him. Holding my breath, I swing open the gate.

Goose, the only one small enough to get through the opening in the hedges, has sneaked up behind Shep, while the dog is preoccupied with the bone in his mouth and the open gate. Goose frees the chain from the hasp on the front porch.

And Shep does it. Apparently deciding that his bone will both taste better and be more secure the farther he is from Rex, Shep bolts through the open gate, his chain jangling behind him.

We all wait for a few minutes to make sure neither the Mayor nor Rex have been warned by the noise of Shep's chain. They haven't been. So we all gather near the front gate and watch Roman carry the heavy paper bag, in which all of us have shit, onto the front porch. He lights a match and sets it to the top of the paper bag. When the flames have reached their fullest glory he knocks loudly on the front door and he walks (he does not run) down the sidewalk and across the street where we all stand in the darkness.

Rex, barking ferociously, comes the full length of his chain. He continues barking as the Mayor opens the door. The Mayor, howling louder than Rex, leaps into the air and comes down on the burning paper bag with both feet. His wife, Emma, joins him. They stomp furiously at the flames. Then Emma stops, rears back her head and bawls.

We're sitting around the stove with all the big guys when the Mayor and his two sons, Clair and Terry, come in.

We've been playing Ghost, a game in which Reuben has gotten the miners interested. Everyone contributes a letter toward the formation of a word. When the word ends on a player he is G, then H, then O, then S, then T. Only Reuben and Jacob and Rachel used to play it, with the miners as an audience, but now the miners join in. They themselves often laugh at their own bizarre talents for spelling. Even Momma and Poppa play, and their spelling is more bizarre.

The Mayor strides over to Roman and grabs his shirt. "You little sonofabitch, you did that, didn't you?"

"Did what?" Roman asks, with the purest innocence.

"You know what!" The veins on the Mayor's neck are swollen and his face is dark purple. His eyes bulge out so far I'm sure they'll pop free of their lids. I can't help but look down, to see if he's changed his shoes.

One of his sons, Clair, sees my glance and he grabs me. "Ah-hah! It was you, wasn't it, you sheeny bastard!"

Jacob brings the edge of his hand down across Clair's fore-arm and Clair bends over, holding his arm and howling. Terry, the Mayor's oldest son, hits Jacob high on the cheek, knocking him backward, into Stash and Cosco, who shove Jacob forward just as Jacob swings, so that the punch has added impact.

27

Terry goes down. Poppa, agile as a high-school boy, leaps over the counter. He grabs the Mayor in a bearhug, pinning his arms at his sides, then he lifts the Mayor off his feet and hurls him against the wall.

Cans tumble off the shelves. Rachel and Momma are screaming, pleading for everyone to stop . . . stop . . . stop. But the miners, standing on benches and counters, urge everyone on.

Max, who's been in the kitchen, comes running into the store. If Momma and Rachel didn't grab and hold him he'd probably be swinging too, though he's often teased for *talking* his way out of every fight.

While Jacob is wrestling with Clair and Terry Hardt, Poppa again picks the Mayor up, holding him again in a bearhug. He carries the Mayor outside and throws him off the porch. He comes back and wades through the flailing fists of Terry and he lifts Clair off the floor and he squeezes. Clair screams in pain, while Poppa carries him through the store. Outside, Clair continues screaming after Poppa throws him into the bushes. Terry, breaking free of Jacob, runs out of the store and off the porch under his own power.

Momma and Rachel are weeping but after Poppa and Jacob, and Max and I, sweep up the debris, even they join us all in toasting (with soda pop that Poppa distributes) our victory.

"What the hell did you do?" someone finally asks me.

Before I can advise Roman not to do it he proudly describes what it was that we did.

Momma and Rachel gasp, and they say I ought to be ashamed (and in a way I am), but when Poppa, and then Jacob and Max, join the miners in their raucous approval, I'm almost proud. Now the miners, instead of telling their stories every year at Hallowe'en, will be telling our stories.

The Mayor and two township policemen, led by Brick Shiptick, arrive about eleven o'clock. There is still an air of celebration in the store when they arrive.

28

Brick, the township chief of police, steps up to the counter. "Al, I'll have to place you under arrest."

"For what?" Poppa asks.

"For assault and battery."

Jacob laughs. "How's that for distorting the law? Bud Hardt walks into our house, he assaults my brother, who's a juvenile, we throw Bud Hardt out of our house and who gets arrested for assault and battery? We do. You must be kidding. We could sue all of you for false arrest. By God, maybe we ought to."

Brick Shiptick takes a moment to consider Jacob. He nods his head, as if what he's just heard confirms stories he's previously heard. "You're sort of a troublemaker, you and your big brother. You're Jacob, right? Yeah. How old are you?"

"What's that have to do with it?"

"You and your brother, you read books. Right?" His repeated nod serves as an answer to his own question. "I suppose you've read things in books about assault and battery. And false arrest. Right?"

"That's right. Most people who've studied American History have."

"Uh-huh. Maybe you'd like to read the things on the walls of our cells, down at the township jail. A boy can get a better education down there than he can in high school." He smiles, or rather he twitches his lips. A gold cap in the front of his mouth casts a yellow glow over all his other teeth. He turns away from Jacob and he faces Poppa again. "Tell me something, Al. What do you think of the trick your little son played on Bud Hardt, an elected public official?"

"Hey," Cosco says, "that was a pretty shitty trick, wasn't it, Brick?" The Mayor and the cops wait until everyone stops laughing.

One of the two other cops whispers in Brick's ear. "Nah," Brick says, "don't worry about him. We'll get him sooner or later." He places his left hand on my shoulder. "I guess we better take this one down to the station."

29

Momma jerks me behind her. She shakes her fist in Brick's face and shrieks at him in shrill, rapid Polish. Brick's body jerks and he looks as if he's about to slap her, then he just smiles and shakes his head. Rachel tries to pull me into the kitchen but one of the cops darts behind Momma and catches my shirt. He and Rachel tug at my clothes. Momma kicks at the cop's shins and stomps on his feet but Brick lifts Momma up and sets her down on a bench, not gently. Cursing in Russian and Polish, Poppa comes hurtling over the counter again, this time with an ax handle in his hand.

"What?" he cries, in English. "This Russia? This Cossacks all over again?"

A large, dull black revolver appears in Brick's fist. I hear Mamma and Rachel wailing. I'm terrified, not so much by the gun as I am by the expression on Poppa's face. I know he's about to swing that ax handle. And if he does, Brick, I know, will shoot him. Will kill him.

"No, Poppa . . . please . . . I'll go. . . ."

Roman steps in front of me, between Poppa and Brick. He pulls back his shoulders and he says, without the slightest fear or regret, "I did it. It was my idea. I put the bag on the porch. I lit it. I knocked on the door. It was all my idea. No one else's."

Judge Kilpatrick, in Summer, assures us that he's taking pity on us only because it's the first offense for any of us. If we appear in his court again, however, may the good Lord have mercy on us because he, Judge Kilpatrick, won't.

But his sentence is as cruel as if he'd jailed us. We're each fined twenty dollars. There are six of us. That's a total of one hundred and twenty dollars.

Max, who has a paper route, and who's been saving money to buy a suit, has more money than Poppa. He's not asked to pay for me but he knows it's expected of him. He manages to spend a great deal of time in town the next few days, reducing the chances that someone might confront him directly for a loan.

The other kids are doomed. It's been years since there's been twenty dollars in cash available in any of their homes.

And, the judge informs us, if the amount is not paid in full, in seventy-two hours, each boy who is delinquent will be sent to reform school.

Momma just can't understand my refusal to permit Max to pay for me if none of the other kids have their fines paid. Jacob says he understands. In fact, he says, he's proud as hell that I've decided this on my own. Momma says Max just doesn't want to spend the twenty dollars. Jacob says that isn't it at all. After all, he says, if I'm freed and all the other kids go to reform school it will just be proof of all the lies these bastards have been preaching all their lives, that Jews have all the money and exploit everyone for their own profit. Max says he thinks we ought to take care of ourselves and not worry about what other people say or think. Rachel just bawls and says, over and over, it's not fair, it's not fair. Poppa agrees with Max, which is the first time they've ever agreed on any-thing, but then, after much cursing and soul-searching and shakings-of-head, he says, well, no, it wouldn't be fair for me to be the only one to be spared. But he pounds his fist and reminds us, again and again, that by God, if the shoe was on the other foot, do I think these *anti-Semiten* pigs would do the same for me? "Remember this!" he tells me, holding me firmly in his rock-hard hands. "Remember this! This is what's differ-ence between them and us. Remember!"

Roman and Stash and their father and the families of all the other kids gather at our store. We spend hours computing the amount of money that can be collected. Though every man, woman and child in Sundown donates every penny they have, it is never more than $42.77 no matter how many times we add it up. This is for the five other kids, not for me. Since we need $100 for them we're $57.23 short.

31

Stash, Roman's brother, suggests that Poppa loan them the money. "We'll pay it back," Stash says.

Poppa, fuming, lifts the package of receipt books that contain several years of itemized debts still owed him by various families in Sundown and he shakes the books in Stash's face. "What do you think? You think I'm a banker? I don't have such money. And if I did, what? I should loan it to you? You'd pay me back? Like you pay me this? And this? And this? And this?" He flips through the pages, reading off the amounts still unpaid.

There's a great deal of shouting, a great deal of name-calling, but suddenly Roman's father stands up. He pushes back the bench he's been sitting on. It strikes the stove and sparks fly out of the open door. "I know how to get that goddamn money." He shoulders his way through the crowd and leaves the store.

Everyone settles down to quiet despair. In an obvious, and not entirely successful effort at repentance, Poppa passes around bottles of soda pop.

I come home from school with Roman and Goose. When we're halfway down the hill we see a crowd on the store porch. We run the rest of the way.

Everyone is standing around Roman's father, who is counting money on the top of a milk crate. He has $56.04. That, plus the $42.77 already collected, makes $98.81.

Everyone waits until Max comes home. He walks up the steps, his empty canvas carrier over his shoulder. Yes, he'll pay my $20 and the remaining $1.19.

The next day, seventy-one and one-half hours after the trial, Poppa and Roman's father and three other men, and the six of us kids, ride in Poppa's truck to Summer, to the courthouse.

The money is delivered to Judge Kilpatrick. The judge orders an aide to count it. Assured the total is correct, the judge pounds his gavel. None of us move.

32

"Well, what is it? That's it!" the judge snaps. "You expect me to dismiss the charges? And give the money back?"

"We want a receipt," Poppa says.

The secret remains a secret for three hours.

When Roman's father left the store the night before, he went directly across the street to Ellsworth Cotton's house. Ellsworth was at his brother-in-law's house, celebrating.

Roman's father removed a case of whiskey and carried it, on his shoulders, all the way to Summer, to the Alexander Hamilton Hotel, where he once worked as a janitor. He sold it for $56 to the chef. Emptying his pockets the chef found four pennies. He tossed them in, too.

"And," Roman's father tells us, "that fart Ellsworth can't report it stolen because it's against the law for him to even have it."

Roman calls a celebration meeting at our shanty. He arrives with a bottle of whiskey.

"Where'd you get the whiskey, Roman?"

He grins. "From Pa. He stole *two* cases. He'll be so drunk tonight he won't remember whether he drank this bottle or not."

We all try to drink it. Only Roman and Goose can get it down. Like Johnny and Kenny and Adam, I pretend to swallow, making very impressive gurgling sounds in my throat. Before long, to match Roman and Goose, the rest of us are reeling about too. We sing every song we know two and three times before Roman and Goose pass out.

It's Hallowe'en night. Ellsworth and the Mayor and the Mayor's two sons patrol their street until dawn.

It's the most uneventful Hallowe'en night in the history of Sundown.

All those who would perform any mischief are at Roman's house, working on the final bottles of that second case. Cosco

33

lies, unconscious, in the grass at the base of the back stairs. Stash sits in the kitchen, his head in his arms on the table, his snores obliterated by the snores coming from the front room where Roman's mother and father lie, their arms and legs tangled around a lamp that has fallen between them. The lampshade, a mottled, muddy new hat, rests on his mother's head.

Roman and Goose stumble erect now and then to rush outside our shanty to vomit among the trees and over the ferns and blueberry bushes. Adam and Johnny and Kenny are, like me, at home.

In the kitchen, I watch Max and Jacob and Rachel play parcheesi. Momma has made fried egg sandwiches. They're stacked on a plate on the table. Poppa eats a sandwich as he reads the newspaper. Yenta growls beside the stove, in which a fire crackles and to which Momma now turns her bare bottom.

"Hallowe'en," Momma says. "You'll notice, please, there ain't such a holiday in our Jewish holidays. Ech! Only the *goyim* . . . only the *goyim*. . . ."

About Poppa
Spring, 1934

For Poppa the entire population of the world has been machined by a cynical God into two classes: Jews and anti-Semites.

We are the only Jews in Sundown, Pennsylvania. Most of the men who work (that is, most of the men who have jobs) are miners. Some are railroad men. A few walk the three miles through the woods to Summer, where they catch a bus to the northern edge of the city, a section called Lyndy, where the steel mills are located.

Though Poppa has a very discerning eye when it comes to evaluating things like wild mushrooms or chickens or tomato plants, he has difficulty distinguishing one man from another in Sundown. He thinks he helps himself by applying additional characteristics to each of his enemies. For example, there is *that fat, goose-lipped anti-Semite* (Milo Yerkovich, the truant-officer); *that pimply-nosed anti-Semite with one ear* (Noyes, the old Welshman who's worked in the mines since he was twelve); *that thieving anti-Semite who sold me the truck* (Oscar Tilko, from whom Poppa bought an ancient truck, with

35

which he now makes his deliveries). And there is *that Polack anti-Semite of a toadstool-expert.*

Like most of the men in Sundown, *that Polack anti-Semite of a toadstool-expert,* George Chupek, works, when there is work, in the mines.

Except for their ages George and Poppa have very little in common. George is, as Poppa pronounces it, a *Cadillac.* George's tiny china-blue eyes and square pink cheeks—despite a sand-colored walrus mustache—convey an impression of irrepressible adolescence. Poppa's dark-brown eyes are flecked with green and always serious, and a perpetual crust of beard exaggerates the roundness of his face. He also has a mustache but, like his hair, it is a collection of shaggy black curls. To my father's Slavic ancestors, I'm sure, there would be something of the ferocious Cossack about George's mustache, and to George's Slavic ancestors there would probably be something of the peddler, the moneylender, the ghetto, about my father's mustache.

George smokes a corncob pipe, using as fill the tobacco he chewed several days before and which, ever since, has lain in the sun to dry. Poppa does not smoke. He used to, thirty or forty a day, all of which he rolled himself. When he started to play the numbers he decided to save all his spare cash for that.

Perhaps because of the traditional conflicts between Pole and Russian in the Old Country, perhaps because of the legendary Polish pogroms and ghettos, Poppa, in his more charitable moments, announces George Chupek to be a liar, a thief, an idiot and a braggart. As well as an anti-Semite. He delights in challenging George's claims each autumn that he, George, has the finest little garden in the state. No matter what George selects as evidence, Poppa always manages to produce redder and firmer and larger tomatoes, sweeter corn, more succulent apples and pears. Poppa's Rhode Island Reds are always heavier than George's Plymouth Rocks and no

36

pullet George selects can out-lay Poppa's prize White Leg-horns.

Though the people in Sundown, men and women and children, admit Poppa's superiority in garden and poultry knowledge they all continue a special respect for George's knowledge of mushrooms. That anyone can consider George his superior in anything, and especially in the knowledge of mushrooms, fills Poppa with terrible resentment. That Momma and Rachel and all my brothers secretly and cautiously agree with the enemy helps keep that resentment aflame. Once, when he learned that Momma had me take some mushrooms he picked to George Chupek for analysis, Poppa notified all of us that if he was ever again so humiliated he would take his belt to whoever carried the mushrooms, even if it was me—his favorite.

After a cold and dreary winter the spring's crop of mush-rooms promises a tonic for the people in Sundown. Normally, they wait for Saturday nights for excitement, and then they have to journey three miles through the woods to Summer to collect it. But here will be excitement at home, due any hour.

The men who lounge on the store porch or around the coal stove when it rains (even though the stove, several weeks ago, burned its last lump of coal until next fall) conceive elaborate tactics to bring the crisis to a head. Mixing their instincts for profit and fun, they establish a pool, a kitty, into which any gambler may contribute fifty cents. The one who selects the date closest to that on which the explosion comes will receive all of the cash. Smiley, the bookie for the numbers racket, holds the kitty.

The men write abusive notes to George and sign them with Poppa's name. Similar notes to Poppa are signed with George's name. They pick mushrooms along the tracks or in the fields around the mines and they bring them to Poppa. When he judges certain ones safe to eat and others dangerous the men,

37

with mock surprise, exclaim isn't it odd, George says just the contrary. Momma and Rachel and my brothers know, of course, that the men are being equally deceitful with George. When they try to convince Poppa that he is being victimized he refuses to listen. He charges everyone in the family not only with betrayal but with cowardice. They can sell their family pride, he rages—a father expects that—but the least they can do is respect a Jew, regardless of who he is, in his wars with the anti-Semites.

His own faith unshaken, Poppa continues his early-morning trips to the woods, to those secret caches that have supplied him so faithfully for thirty years or more. Occasionally he returns emptyhanded but more often his basket is filled with hemispheres of red and brown and pink, their blue and gray gilled undersides whispering aromatically of moist and shaded glades in the woods.

I am the only person he ever asks to go with him. At my age—I am ten—I am old enough to be fair company but not yet old enough to be a distraction. On those mornings when he decides to take me he comes to my room at dawn. It is usually a Sunday morning. His breath warm on my cheek and smelling of creamed coffee, he shakes my shoulders and whispers, so as not to wake Max, with whom I sleep, "Hey, mushrooms. Want to go for mushrooms?" I leap out of bed. I carry my clothes downstairs and dress in the kitchen.

In the blue light seeping through the windows I pull on my socks and shoes and then, at the sink, I dash cold water on my face. If Momma were up I'd have to use soap but Poppa does not take notice. I gulp down my steaming coffee and two or three slices of home-made bread spread with butter and jam. Poppa, in the meantime, has made several cheese or jam sandwiches, which he packs in a bag and places in his basket.

Though Poppa feels no special affection for Yenta, our mustard-colored mongrel (who weighs as much as I do and whose only role in life, so far as Poppa's concerned, is to guard

38

the chickens and the garden and our house and store), he never refuses my request to bring the dog along.

About two weeks after Momma threw out those mushrooms that George Chupek condemned, Poppa asks me if I want to go with him again.

As we walk across the fields and along the Connequenessing Creek, Yenta, barking and howling, darts after the ghostly figures and voices in the cattails and the elderberry bushes. Each time a rooster crows I wonder if it might not be some secret and dangerous signal from one of those apparitions Yenta is challenging. I fall behind to collect Yenta and then hurry after Poppa, shouting to him to wait. But Poppa hurries on, his trouser legs wet to the knees from the dew and his mind fixed only on the distant woods.

He has long ago learned to pace his travel so that the sun rises above the horizon almost at the exact moment we enter the woods. This morning, within twenty minutes after we pass the first outpost of birches and willows, it is light enough to distinguish grass from ground and stump from rock. While Poppa goes swiftly to work I go just as swiftly to play.

Yenta chases rabbits and quail and I chase Yenta. Under crabapple and chokecherry trees, through huckleberry bushes and groves of elm and maple and birch and up and down mud paths carved, so the old men of Sundown say, by tribes of Algonquins and Delawares two hundred years before.

I find the tallest birch and climb it. Fifty or sixty feet above the ground I lean into the wind. I sway back and forth, picking out the creek, the railroad tracks, the highway going to Slippery Rock, the Kearnsey farm and the Gornick farm and the Chernik farm, the mouths of Number One mine and Number Three mine, the slag dumps, the reservoir, the woods nearer home and then the few houses in Sundown that I can see. I pick out our store. There is my world. And high above it I lie in the wind that has just passed over it on the way to the other

39

parts of other worlds I'll someday see just as now I see my own. This is how it must feel to be God.

Searching below the tree, I finally locate Poppa moving in and out among the trees and patches of sunlight and shade, bending or kneeling at stump or stone or log, holding his specimens to the sun or to his nose. When, all too soon, he finds my tree and waves me down I obey.

We walk down one of the paths to Indian Springs, a small pool surrounded by dark, dank and mossy boulders. It has the clearest and coldest and sweetest water I will ever taste. There is a house-sized rock with steps cut in its walls. We help each other to the top. The flat surface there is covered with deep pockmarks in which humus has collected and which now sprout a dozen different shapes and sizes and colors of wild-flowers. We eat our sandwiches. We climb down to drink the water and then climb up again. We toss pieces of sandwich to Yenta now and then and in between bites she too drinks from the spring. The robins and blue jays and catbirds and wild canaries flash in the trees and call to each other and the flies begin to appear, buzzing in the few rare pockets of sunlight high above our heads. Poppa lies back and motions me close. I lie beside him. With a sly grin on his face he draws a May apple from his basket. I slide it into my mouth, popping the cold sweet fruit out of its skin and letting it glide down my throat. One after one my father draws ten more from his basket. He eats a few but I gladly and gratefully eat most of them. Then we lie on our backs, watching the birds and the already lazy flies. Poppa reaches out his hand, almost absently, and squeezes my fingers. A sudden surge of love nearly bursts my heart.

We return the way we came. Yenta darts in and out among the cattails and elderberry bushes. I wait for her and then the two of us run to catch up with Poppa.

We arrive home before anyone else is stirring. Anyone except George Chupek.

40

George, too, knows that dawn is the ideal time to gather mushrooms, before the sun can destroy them. He has his own secret sources. This day, certain of his good fortune, he has returned home before Poppa and waits on the store porch, disappointed, probably, that there is no one else on the porch to witness his victory. He sits on a wooden milk crate, his basket, uncovered, at his side. As we come onto the porch, George, his pipe belching smoke, bends to the right, presses a finger to the side of his nose and squirts a pearl into the dust a few inches from Poppa's feet. He looks at Poppa's basket, which is covered, and chuckles.

Poppa, though he can be an impulsive and terrible-tempered man, chooses this morning to be charitable. He lifts the basket lid, as if by accident, just enough to disclose his fine collection, and then somehow manages to spill from his mouth a fart sound that would do justice to an elephant fed a month-long diet of nothing but beans.

George, as astonished as I am at the power of the sound, sits stiffly upright, clamps his teeth, and snaps the stem of his pipe. Poppa laughs and goes into the store and I follow him, very proud.

I was too involved in play to notice that Poppa had collected a basketful of the very same mushrooms Momma sent to George Chupek for analysis. The mushrooms George claimed to be such deadly toadstools were bright orange lumps ripped from the undersides of rotten logs. Three slices carved from one such lump fill a skillet.

The first time Poppa brought them home (when George had condemned them and Momma had thrown them away), Poppa announced with great ceremony that he'd not seen such mushrooms since his boyhood in the Kafkhaz. Because they had the density and texture of steak and because he had not even the most elementary knowledge of Latin terminology, he referred to them simply as *beefsteak mushrooms*.

Momma recognizes them immediately, but this time she says

41

nothing. She agrees to serve them this evening. But the moment Poppa leaves the kitchen to open the store (which composes the front half of our home), Momma gathers Max and Jacob and me around her. She explains her predicament. I can't help feeling it all some sort of conspiracy against Poppa. My memories of our trip are too fresh in my mind. I don't want to be a part of this plan. But something in my mother's voice alarms me. I linger in the doorway that opens from the kitchen into the store.

Max, who is sixteen, volunteers to take one of the mushrooms to George Chupek. When he returns with the grim information that the mushrooms are exactly the same as those George warned us about before, Momma bursts into tears. Jacob pulls me into the kitchen and closes the door so Poppa won't hear the commotion.

Momma rocks back and forth at the table, wondering if she shouldn't call Rachel, who's working at Fleischman's Meat Market in Summer. Or maybe we should even call Reuben, at college. "What can I do? What can I do?" Momma chants.

Jacob and Max, like myself, aware of the dangers, are horrified. But we are children. What can we do? We sit in silence, waiting for Momma to direct us.

We know that we can not tell Poppa that we took the mushrooms to George Chupek again. But, obviously, we can not let him eat the mushrooms, which he will certainly insist on doing once he learns that he's been betrayed by us. Remembering his threats to use the belt, Max sits in his chair, trembling.

Momma rushes to the phone, which hangs on the wall near the sink. She calls Fleischman's Market. She tells Rachel everything. Rachel, as upset as Momma, says she'll come right home. We should not do anything until she gets there. She'll have her boy friend, Naty, drive her home. She'll be here in ten minutes. In the meantime, she'll ask Mr. Fleischman for advice.

We sit. The ten minutes pass as if each minute is an hour.

Then it's eleven minutes. Twelve. Fifteen. Momma, at the kitchen table, covers her mouth with her hands, covers her eyes, covers her mouth. A half hour after the phone call Rachel comes onto the back porch. When she opens the door Yenta races in before her. I run to Rachel, weeping, but she tells me to be quiet. When Momma begs her for advice she says she talked to Mr. Fleischman and also to the three butchers. Desperate, she'd also called Reuben. Mr. Fleischman said she should use the store phone, he'd pay for it.

Fortunately, Reuben was in his room. He . . . as usual, only he . . . had a plan. Everyone sighs, relieved. If it's Reuben's plan, no worry, it's bound to work.

"What . . . what?" Momma begs. "What's the plan?"

Rachel points at Yenta, who is stretched out at my feet, her chin on my shoes.

"Now listen," Rachel says. "We serve some of the mushrooms to Yenta. She'll die and it will be sad but then Poppa can't argue. He'll have to admit they're poisonous."

Max and Jacob, though never as fond of Yenta as I am, can't help but look stricken. Momma, wringing her hands in desperation, says George Chupek and everyone else in Sundown will laugh and things will be worse than ever. Rachel asks what they're to do then. Are they to let Poppa eat? Should they sit by and let him kill himself?

Only now do I understand what is being planned. I start to howl. Max pushes me, telling me to stop being a cry-baby. Momma comes to me and kneels on the floor in front of me. She says she hates to see Yenta die too and I tell her she never liked Yenta. She's glad to see her die. She hugs me, sobbing, but I pull away and try to run into the store. Rachel holds me. She hugs me to her. "Benny," she says, "it's the only way. Isn't it better to sacrifice Yenta, a dog, than have Poppa killed? Don't you trust Reuben? Reuben says this is the only way."

I return to Yenta and sit on the floor at her side, clutching

43

her head, shocked and sick at such cruelty, and trying hard to resist admitting to myself that what Reuben and Rachel say is the truth.

Jacob, trying to solace me, puts an arm around my shoulders. "We have to do it," he says.

"We'll get another dog, as soon as this is all over," Rachel says. "A puppy. You can pick it out yourself."

I go to a corner of the kitchen and throw myself on a pile of clothes gathered there for the next day's washing. Yenta trots after me, and lies beside me, her muzzle at my ear.

Jacob asks how we can feed Yenta mushrooms, since she will eat nothing but bones and Sweet's Dog Biscuits. Rachel says, "Don't you remember what Yenta loves? And almost never gets?"

"Salami. Kosher salami."

Rachel nods, trying hard not to look at me. "We can wrap a chunk of toadstool in a slice of kosher salami. Come on, Benny, please. Let Yenta go."

I wrap my arms about Yenta but Momma, in a sudden burst of determination to get this over with, jumps up and jerks me away from Yenta. "Come," she says, hauling Yenta to the center of the room. "Come, Yentila."

For the next hour all four of them feed slices of kosher salami to Yenta. Inside each of the slices is a chunk of toadstool as large as my thumb. Yenta accepts it, greedily, but each time she swallows the salami and then spits out the toadstool. She consumes a quarter of a roll of salami before they admit they're failing.

Next, they chop the chunk of toadstool into small pieces and fold the salami slice over the toadstool filling, but Yenta manages somehow to separate the salami and swallow it and then to spit out every piece of the toadstool. Ears sharp, eyes alert, her muzzle wet, she sits and licks her chops, baffled by Max's and Jacob's unusual generosity. But willing and eager to profit by it.

44

They try feeding her the toadstool alone, they try holding her jaws closed, they try petting her, caressing her, they try scolding her, but they can't get so much as a tiny fragment of toadstool to stay down her throat. Jacob lies on the floor and holds Yenta between his thighs in a scissors grip and Max bends her head back and Rachel pries her jaws apart and Momma shoves her fist down Yenta's throat. Yenta gags, struggles to her feet, and spills out over all of them and all over the floor, everything she's succeeded in getting down until now. Max and Jacob and Rachel and Momma are soaking wet. So is the floor. They, and Yenta, slip and slide. Yenta tries to escape and Max falls back against a wall and Jacob releases his legs and Rachel drops in a chair and Momma sits on the floor, her face in her hands, her loose and tangled hair spotted with bits of salami and toadstools.

"What in hell's goin on?"

Poppa looms in the doorway. When he sees the floor and Momma and Rachel and Jacob and Max, he knows what has been going on. Outraged, he marches to the table and grabs the knife that has been used to cut the toadstools. His heavy black brows form a solid line of anger across his forehead. His dark skin is almost black. The mustachios seem to bristle, erect, like the fur of a cornered, crazed animal.

Momma screams as Poppa grips the knife. "No . . . no . . . they're poison! . . . George Chupek swears . . ."

The house is adrift in a sea of forbidding silence. Poppa gasps. He looks at each of us, trying to identify the traitor. He fingers his belt. Max sits, trembling, expectant. Momma stands, her smooth dark chin jutting out. "I took them. He told me. They're toadstools."

Max and Jacob, in a gesture more of fear than chivalry, manage to stand erect on the slippery floor and go to stand with Momma. Yenta, released, leaps at the back door. She knocks it open and races out of the house.

For one horrible moment it seems to me and to all the others that Poppa is about to rip off his belt and whip Momma. I run

45

to her, pushing myself between Max and Jacob and against her legs, burying my face in her skirt. Rachel takes Momma's hand and stares at Poppa. Momma never moves, but she seems to tower above us all in her courage. She is the only one now who is not trembling or sobbing or whining.

Never has Poppa been confronted with such unified rebellion. It's not fear of us that motivates him now . . . he could lift all four of us at once and throw us out of the house . . . but whatever it is grants him the power to behave as if we were merely an audience of strangers.

Poppa carries what's left of the toadstools to the sink. He washes them. At the stove he shifts a large skillet over a burner and drops a piece of butter onto the iron. He then places three thick slices of the toadstool into the skillet, sprinkles them with salt and pepper and, hand on hip, a spatula between his fingers, he waits.

Rachel goes to him, pleading with him. Momma does the same. He ignores them. Sneering, he brushes Momma's hand away. Jacob tries to grab the skillet but Poppa, with a roar, whirls on him and Jacob retreats.

A customer who's been waiting for service in the store comes into the kitchen to complain but Momma ushers him back through the store and onto the porch. She locks the store door.

Within minutes the word has spread. Every man, woman and child in Sundown arrives at the store, crowding onto the porch, pushing at the windows. They wait, murmuring, with solemn faces. Someone suggests that someone ought to call Brick Shiptick and the township police and someone else runs to comply.

Momma, weeping, kneels on the floor, her head on the seat of a chair. Jacob sits across the table from her. Max stands with his face against the wall, crying softly. Rachel is on the phone, begging the student with whom Reuben shares a room

46

at college to find Reuben immediately and have him call home.

Jacob steps behind Poppa. "Poppa," he begs, "don't eat them. Please don't eat them. We love you, Poppa."

Poppa ignores him and continues frying the toadstools.

The telephone rings.

"Poppa," Rachel shouts, "it's Reuben. It's Reuben. Talk to him, Poppa. Please."

Poppa ignores her.

Reuben's voice can be heard calling all the way from Chicago. He is shouting, screaming, cursing. Rachel holds out the telephone as far as the cord will permit. Poppa does not even look at it. We all hear Reuben say, "Goddamn it, if he wants to kill himself, let him. Stubborn . . . vengeful . . . let him. . . ."

I sit with Momma, thinking that this is the last day we will all be together. After today, Poppa will be gone.

Several people have come onto the back porch. They offer advice to us and even try to convince Poppa that he's being foolish, that they meant no harm, that they all know he's a better man than George Chupek.

Rachel has put up the phone and sits at the table, weeping. I go to her and she takes me on her lap.

More people gather on the porch. There's a larger commotion and George Chupek himself appears. He pushes his way through the crowd and into the kitchen. He talks to Poppa in Polish, pleading with him. Poppa says nothing but reaches a plate down from the shelf above the stove and empties the contents of the skillet onto the plate. He lifts one slice with his fingers, bites, chews, tastes and then shoves the entire slice into his mouth. Momma screams and topples backward to the floor. Max and Jacob, in a fit of tears and screams, rush to Momma's side. Poppa continues eating.

George Chupek, spouting Polish, stomping his feet, his cheeks not pink now but flaming red, calls out "Schtop!

47

Schtop!" It is the only time he's ever been known to try an English word.

The people on the porch surge toward Poppa, who's now well through his second slice of toadstool. He sets the skillet down and raises a chair above his head. The crowd pauses. He swallows what he has in his mouth and with one hand grabs and stuffs the third and final piece into his mouth. His face is covered with grease. The juices running down his cheeks and jowls have stained his shirt. He puts down the chair and sits on it. George Chupek falls back against the sink, his hand making the sign of the cross, over and over.

"Not in this house!" Poppa bellows. He stands, ready to fight should George describe the sign again. But George, meek and mild, submits. He nods his head and folds his hands at his chest and mutters. "And no Cadillac prayers!" Poppa orders. George's muttering stops.

Rachel and Jacob and a few men lift Momma and carry her to a chair at the table. Jacob supports her while Rachel forces water between her lips. She groans, opens her eyes, closes them again, groans again and then sits erect, conscious. "You!" she says, pointing at Poppa.

Poppa nods. "Me," he says. He looks at her and then at every single face in the room. He sits back and crosses his arms on his chest. Everyone in the kitchen stands now and waits.

By the time the police arrive it is obvious that Poppa is going to suffer nothing more serious than indigestion from having eaten so rapidly.

The police move everyone off the porch and drive back to town. Rachel does not return to work. She sits with the rest of us in the kitchen, humble and penitent. When Reuben calls she tells him that Poppa ate the toadstools, and they turned out to be mushrooms. Poppa, sitting at the table and drinking coffee, says, "Tell him *beefsteak* mushrooms. He should look up in one of his fancy books. Tell me them in Latin."

48

That night at supper, we are all very quiet. Poppa does not lord it over us. In fact he cracks jokes. When Yenta returns he lets her in the house and pats her head. "You didn't believe either, huh?" He playfully pushes Yenta away.

After supper, in the store, all the men sitting on the benches confide their pity for poor old George Chupek, who's brooding away at home, unable to understand how he could have made such a mistake.

Poppa enjoys it all. "All these years," he says, "he sees beefsteak mushrooms and don't pick them. Oy, and such a delicacy. I pity him, too." Then he turns to Smiley, the bookie for the numbers racket, and with whom Poppa bets a dollar or two every day. "Give me my money," Poppa says.

Smiley nods. He takes $15.50 out of his pocket and hands the money to Poppa. Smiley turns to the other men. He shrugs. "He put fifty cents in the kitty, too. He picked today."

Poppa counts the money, nods at Smiley and puts the money in his pocket. Except for a dime, which he tosses at me. "For Saturday," he says. "Go buy a double feature."

About Aunt Molly
Summer, 1935

Jacob: "They have class. Real class. You're with them one minute and you know they have money. All kinds of money. All colors, all sizes and plenty of it."

Reuben: "Momma and Aunt Molly are sisters but look at them. They're twins practically. But poverty's made Momma suspicious of every person she knows, even herself. Wealth's spread Aunt Molly's love across the world. She trusts everyone. Believes every man's story. She's as good an argument *for* capitalism as Momma is *against* it."

Rachel: "Sarah's my age. Well, three days younger. What clothes she has! Gorgeous clothes! And her bedroom . . . it's right off a magazine cover. She used to have her own maid. Not any more, but she used to. I ought to feel embarrassed when I'm there but I never do. Everyone's so comfortable."

Momma: "Since I was three, four years old Molly takes care of me. Everything she's got she gives me. And such a beauty! A young girl, rich families in Warsaw, in Prague, in Berlin, they'd ask her come live with them

50

like their own daughter. I say, 'Molly, you grow up you'll be rich.' She hugs me. She says, 'I have a million dollars it's all yours.' She don't got a million any more but she got plenty. I'd ask her, she'd give it."

Poppa: "So ask her." (He laughs, to assure us he's kidding.) "Of the whole *mishpoche* Molly's the only one don't look at me I'm a criminal."

Me: "Momma, why are they so rich and we're so poor?"

Momma: "Us? Poor? You got a sister like Molly you're rich. You get older you'll see."

Max: "Their store: *The Goldsteins*. A store like that . . . just one. That's all I want. Wow!"

Aunt Molly's letter said they'd be here today, Sunday, one week after July Fourth.

Poppa's swept the floor of the store, washed the windows, polished the glass in the showcases and removed the overripe fruit from the three flat crates at the front window. He's even shaved.

Momma and Rachel and I have worked all Friday night and Saturday and Saturday night mopping the kitchen floor, dusting furniture, washing windows, cleaning bedrooms and getting the back yard and back porch in order so we can sit under the grape arbor if it gets too hot in the house. I've scrubbed Yenta's doghouse and I've bathed her. Then what does she do but flop down in the dust under the cherry tree.

Using hickory nuts and butternuts saved from last autumn, Momma has made three cakes. She used dozens of eggs and two pounds of butter. Eggs and butter are the two foods that are constantly available in our house. (Our chickens lay more eggs than we can eat or sell and so we trade them . . . with John Prebula, who has two cows . . . for butter.) The three cakes are resting now under a canopy of newspapers which protects them from the flies. Also from Max and me.

Rachel sits on the back porch. She's wearing a sailor's middy blouse and a long blue skirt, both of which she's made herself.

51

For two years, on Saturdays, she's been working at Fleischman's Market, in Summer. They let her have yesterday off. As an advance on her next three checks she brought home slices of salami, slices of corned beef, slices of cheese, kosher pickles, kosher green tomatoes and black rye bread.

"We have plenty what to eat," Momma says. "But who can eat? Everywhere people beg food. And look what we have to eat. It's a crime."

"Well," Max says (and he's right), "you don't want the Goldsteins to think we're *welfare pishers*, you have to set a table like they do." *Welfare pishers* is what Momma calls those who receive relief, or county welfare. Which means everyone in Sundown is a *welfare pisher* except us. One more criterion to distinguish the competent from the incompetent, the proud from the humbled, the Jew from the *goyim*.

Aunt Molly and Uncle David . . . "The Goldsteins," as Max always calls them, since that is what their famous store in Philadelphia is called . . . lost a great deal of money in the crash six years ago. But, unlike most businessmen, Uncle David refused to declare bankruptcy. And he and his store are surviving. "We're not breathing," Morris, their son, says, "but we're alive." Reuben says they have money with which to pay their debts only because Uncle David, with a congenital distrust of paper (a hatred of stocks and bonds and checks), had hoarded much of his wealth in the form of the actual metals, silver and gold. Other relatives, unwilling to grant him such wisdom, insist that he still lost his shirt. ("I should lose such a shirt," Poppa says. "The shirt he got on . . . I'll take a dozen.")

They arrive . . . Aunt Molly, Uncle David and Morris, who's Jacob's age . . . in their black Buick limousine. While the Buick's parked near our gasoline tanks people pour out of the hills to surround and admire it. Poppa keeps reminding them that if they touch the car and ruin the polish he'll cut off their *schmucks* with a dull sickle.

52

The hugging and kissing and exchanges of tearful greetings goes on and on until we end up around the table under the grape arbor. I don't say a word. I only wait, praying silently to myself for the words I've been praying for ever since the arrival of Aunt Molly's letter. Soon, when everyone is eating, Momma says to me, "Benjamin . . . you want we should go back with them? You and me and Rachel? For two, maybe three weeks?"

Aunt Molly draws me into her arms. "You want to come, *mein hertz?* Morty and Ruthy, they're waiting."

Managing to act as if I'm really undecided, I finally agree to go.

Kittanning . . . Indiana . . . Ebensburg . . . Holidays-burg . . . Mount Union . . . Lewistown . . . Clark's Ferry . . . Harrisburg. I've traveled the route every summer, with Momma and Rachel, for as long as I can remember. Sometimes we stay at Aunt Molly's for two weeks, sometimes for three weeks. Once we stayed for a whole month. It's become a ritual . . . Aunt Molly's inviting us and our accepting . . . and yet each time I'm as excited as if each invitation were the first.

Pity may have been Aunt Molly's original motive but now for both Momma and Aunt Molly the summer visits have become essential for survival. They are reminders and assurances that the life they shared as children continues. Each summer their childhood and their youth is revived; memories call back in keen detail their own ancient *Yiddishkayt,* the Jewish life they knew and loved. Buried so in the past, they can more easily and comfortably ignore the present.

As we ride in the Buick, Rachel, who received the highest grade in her class in Pennsylvania History, and who's always telling me stories, nudges me whenever she sees a building or a town about which she's read.

We pass the foundries and coal mines and brick and clay works of Kittanning, stretched out along the eastern bank of

53

the Allegheny River. "There," Rachel says, as we pass the Alexander Hotel, on Market Street. "That tablet on the wall? It tells how a colonel named Armstrong destroyed the town and killed Chief Jacob and forty-two of his braves." . . . "Did you know that Indiana was an important station on the Underground Railroad?" . . . "Do you know why Nolo is named Nolo? Because it's on a mountaintop and doesn't have any low ground." . . .

We move through the valleys and up over the sloping, rolling green hills, through grimy, sulphurous coal towns with their lean men and lean women and lean and grimy children killing the long hot hours of one more day by standing alongside the walls of their broken houses, waiting patiently for the night. We race along the highway through fields of rippling golden wheat and tall green corn, past thin herds of grazing cattle, through towns that are quiet and idle not because it's summer or because it's Sunday but because the foundries and clay works and mines and stores have been deserted for years.

"What will come?" Momma asks. "People starve every day. What will come?"

I want to slide down in the seat to escape the silent, hate-filled stares of every man and woman we glide past. I want to open the window and whisper to every man, "This isn't our car. We're not rich. We're poor too, just like you."

Driving over the Allegheny Mountains, Uncle David, attempting to distract us from our brooding, snorts, "Mountains? These are mountains? Ha! The Carpathians. *They* are mountains. These? These are *bubkas.*"

On huge gray barn after huge gray barn are signs advising us to chew Mail Pouch tobacco. ("Such a habit," Momma says. "You don't find a Jew chews tobacco, I'll guarantee." And Aunt Molly says, "On such farms like this you don't find a Jew." Apparently that's very funny because they all laugh, even Rachel.) On barns and silos and fenceposts and billboards are gaudy posters inviting one and all to the Ringling Brothers–

Barnum and Bailey Circus. ("You want to go, Benjamin? All right, you and Morty and Ruthy . . . you'll go.")

Morris drives too fast. Uncle David . . . balding, gentle, easy-tempered . . . uses his limited fund of English to supplement his vast store of Yiddish to constantly restrain Morris. Morris' duty, Uncle David reminds him, is to only get us as far as Philadelphia. The rest of the way to heaven, please would he let God do the driving.

Aunt Molly's and Uncle David's home is in a residential area called Fox Hills. Built of brick and stone, it has porches at the front and rear wide enough to contain swings that a dozen children can fight over, on and under. Besides the five Goldsteins there are two maids and three of us. Still there are rooms and closets and corridors that remain uninhabited, perfect haunts for dozing ghosts that wait only for the minds of Morty and Ruthy and me to touch them alive.

Morty and I sleep on a second-floor sun porch that is larger than our entire house in Sundown. We have our own bathroom, a chamber of tile so pale blue as to be almost white. There are antique washstands and gleaming enamel bowls and toilets and a shower that dispenses a Niagara which I can regulate from icy cold to steaming hot by turning a single control. During the night I visit and revisit the bathroom, to sit on the cheek-shaped toilet to flush it and feel the tickling splash of water against my buttocks. While from the shelves of the closets come the aromas of soaps and powders and perfumes.

Back in my room I sit on my bed near the window and look out over the blue-green lawns and blue-black rows of poplars. The moon rides high. It is a different, a kinder and richer moon, than the one peering down on Sundown, on all the Sundowns through which we passed yesterday and today.

I think of Poppa in his bare and not too clean room, I think of him sitting on the wooden toilet seat while the flies and wasps buzz above his head, I think of him peering into the icebox to discover that the last bit of salami has been eaten so

55

that, again, he'll have to fry some eggs and potatoes, as he'll fry them tomorrow and the next day and the next.

Something is wrong. Poppa should live in a house like this. He deserves it. Not just for a week, or two or three or four weeks. He deserves it forever.

Something is wrong.

I see less of Rachel now than when we're home. She's with Sarah all day, playing tennis, swimming, riding in the car, visiting Sarah's friends. One evening, when they take Morty and Ruthy and me to the movies, we're close enough behind them to hear Rachel say, "I think I'll marry Naty. He's going to make lots of money. We'll live in a house like yours. With maids."

And what about Poppa? And Momma? Will they remain in Sundown?

I promise myself that if Rachel does marry Naty and if she does have a home like Sarah's, I won't visit her.

Most nights Morty and I lie awake until Momma and Aunt Molly arrive to tuck us in. We close our eyes and pretend to sleep. They take turns kissing us and rearranging the blankets and when they turn out the light and leave we wait just as long as has proven safe in the past. Then we sit up. We pound our pillows into firm back supports and we talk.

Morty envies me the rough and (to him) the adventurous life of Sundown. He has never been in a fight, he has never slept in a shanty in the woods, he has never fired a gun, he has never ridden a line of birches across the horizon.

I'm flattered by his insistent questions, as I have been every summer. But now, as I have not done before, I find myself creating fables of courage and daring that romanticize Roman and Goose and myself. It's as if we live among the Mohicans with Uncas and Chingachgook. There are stories about shooting deer and trapping muskrat and fighting marauding gangs from town.

56

Sometimes, when one of Ruthy's friends spends the night with her, Morty follows me as I cut my way through the jungle of lamps and doors and corridors, past the sentry posts of sleeping uncles and aunts and cousins and into Ruthy's room where, with whispers and flashlights, we play strip poker. Ruthy and her friends pretend to be angry each time I spray the light—accidentally, of course—over a small white breast or milky thigh.

Ruthy has soft downy fur between her legs. One of her friends, Rhoda, complains about not yet having any. "And I'm a year older," she whines. I already have a nice thick black bush, which convinces Morty all the more that I live the life of rugged manhood.

During the day, at Morty's request, I play tennis and cro- quet. In the afternoons we're driven to a private swimming pool.

No one in Sundown has ever heard of croquet. Tennis is considered a sissy's game.

I never feel more outside Morty's world than when I try to play tennis. Morty thinks it's only a matter of instruction, so Aunt Molly arranges for me to take lessons. I would much rather sit on the grass, in the shade, and watch Morty play, but I have no choice. I begin my lessons.

Even the youngest, most untutored in the class has a poise on the courts that I don't have. I feel more and more an im- postor. When asked by someone where I come from I never say "Sundown," which would give away my background. I say, "Pittsburgh," knowing there's a good possibility they'll assume I'm from one of the wealthy districts. Or else why would I be here?

After scraping several rackets on the ground and breaking the gut on others, and fighting a kid named Allen, who says he could beat me with one hand tied behind his back, I'm taken aside by the tall, sun-tanned instructor. "Tennis," he informs me, "is a gentleman's game."

57

The implication is that (as I, myself, have led myself to believe) I'm no gentleman.

From then on, while Morty plays tennis, I lie on the grass and watch him. I also watch the bleachers. There is a woman who comes every day to observe her children and who is very careless about how she crosses her legs.

Everyone dresses for supper at the Goldsteins. In the past this has always been the most impressive part of the day for me. The hot play, the cool shower, the clean clothes, the quiet dining room, the elegant china and silver and floral bouquets, Rachel and Sarah powdered and perfumed, Momma and Aunt Molly catered to like royalty by the two black-uniformed maids, Uncle David and Morris in polished shoes and neatly pressed jackets, the tinkle of ice, the exchange of controlled and congenial conversation . . . it all seems unreal now. Unreal, almost evil.

It's temporary, I know that. In another week or two I'll return to the gray and dusty house in Sundown where the air smells of sulphur and not of roses. I resent more and more having been introduced to all this. Why couldn't they have left me alone?

The transition from resentment to scorn to superiority is quite natural. And quite swift.

"Momma got us tickets to the circus," Morty tells me.

"She paid for them?"

"Sure she did."

"I never pay for circus tickets."

"You don't? Then how do you get in?"

"I work."

"For who? How?"

"I carry water for the elephants and stuff like that."

It's a lie, of course.

Roman and Goose and all the other kids from Sundown

58

work for their tickets. If they didn't, they'd never have the money for admission.

On the day the circus arrives they all rise before dawn and walk to the railroad depot, in Summer, to watch the circus train pull in. They sit on the grassy banks while the trainers and roustabouts unload the wagons and cages and animals. When the whole caravan starts for the fairgrounds the kids follow behind. Soon they're at work. They work all day and receive, as pay, one general-admission ticket, worth fifty cents.

For the last three years I've wanted to work, too. But Momma would never let me go. "That's for *goyim*. All day for fifty cents? Oy! What *sechel!*"

I decided that when I'm thirteen or fourteen I'm going to work, like Roman and Goose do now, even if Momma says no. Then, when I stand and cheer an elephant or a lion tamer or a clown they will be *my* elephant, *my* friend the lion tamer, *my* friend the clown.

"Work for the circus?" Morty asks, his eyes dreamy. "Gee, do you think I could?"

"You have to be tough. It's hard work."

"You know I'm tough. Let's do it."

The next morning, before dawn, with twenty-five cents between us, we tiptoe out of the house. Morty knows where the depot is and where the circus will be staged.

We follow along behind the elephants, basking in the color and confusion, joining with the hundreds of other kids who have the same hopes that we have.

We mingle with the hoarse-voiced, marvelously muscled, beautifully tattooed roustabouts. We run from one to another, begging for a job. But we're ignored or shoved aside or laughed at. Finally, a mountain of a man called Tarzan orders us both to run . . . "Run, goddamn it!" . . . and give him a hand. We're hired.

For hours we . . . Morty and I and dozens of other kids (and some men) . . . run . . . run . . . run from trailers to bleachers, carrying armloads of folding chairs. We

59

stagger under their weight. Our backs ache. Our bodies are soaked with sweat. All the while Tarzan bellows, "Come on . . . run . . . hurry, we're behind . . . run, you little farts." The man's everywhere. Directing trucks, gouging elephants, calling for elephants to push trucks out of mudholes, tying ropes, swinging a sledge . . . always bellowing and promising the most terrible of fates to anyone who shirks his duty or gets hurt. "Run . . . watch out for that pole . . . pull that goddamn truck in closer . . . bring that stake here . . . get that bull on that wagon . . . you get hurt, you little bastard, I won't give you your ticket. . . ."

The animals are roaring and snorting and screaming and hundreds of men and boys scurry about like drunken ants, but, slowly, the canvas tents begin to take shape.

By one o'clock Morty and I can hardly drag one foot after the other. My fingers are cut and bruised, my body burns with scratches spiced with sweat. During the twenty-minute break we share three nickel pies. For a few precious minutes we lie in the grass that smells, not so enchantingly any more, of elephants.

"C'mon, you farts . . . up and at 'em . . . we're behind. . . ."

By three o'clock Morty's tongue is hanging out and he's staggering even worse than I am. I'm frightened. He looks sick. Is he hurt?

I want to quit. I want to suggest we go home, but I know there can't be too much work left to do. Maybe we can stick it out.

"One last job!" Tarzan shouts. "Let's go. Over here . . . run, for Chrissake!"

Morty shakes his head at me. He can't do it. He crawls behind a tent and falls on a pile of canvas, waving me to go on.

The last job is the raising of a center pole. At the moment it lies on the ground, about fifty feet long. At various points along its body are heavy grommets to which dozens of ropes are attached.

60

"Here . . . heave, you bastards . . . farther away over there . . . in closer, you idiots . . . watch out for those cables . . . heave! heave! . . . back up and heave! . . . heave! . . ."

The top of the pole lifts off of the ground. It rises higher and higher, and with it rise the canvas walls.

"Don't stop now . . . heave!"

The pole is almost vertical. A few more tugs and it *is* upright, fully upright. With one edge of its base resting solidly on my left shoe, across the tips of my toes.

"O.K. . . . now fix those ropes! hurry! . . . get those sledges over here . . . run, for Jesus' sake, run! . . ."

Everyone runs. I stand where I am.

I'm afraid to budge. I'm afraid to cry out. The pain is severe but I know if Tarzan sees what has happened he'll do horrible things to me. He'll probably rip me away from the pole, leaving my shoe and my foot behind. Tonight the tiger act will be performed here and my amputated foot will be stuck under the pole and the smell of blood will attract the wild beasts and they'll go mad and grab at my poor foot and the trainer will lose control and . . . and I won't be here to see it. I'll be in the hospital.

"Get the hell away from that pole. You . . . damn it! . . . you with the black curly hair . . . get away . . . "

"I . . . I can't. The post's. . . ."

After the screaming curses and wild threats and cries of exasperation, Tarzan calls for Toby, the largest and strongest of the elephant bulls. It advances toward me, puffing and snorting, the trunk extending through the air, its winkled gray-black feet whispering across the ground. It hovers over me, its tiny eyes peering at me from a mile above my head. I feel the breeze stirred by its waving ears, behind one of which its master jabs an iron hook while shouting orders I can't understand.

Toby curls his trunk around the pole and lifts it . . . gently, slowly . . . several inches off the ground. Tarzan jerks me free.

61

Morris drives down to pick us up.

Tarzan, for some strange reason, gives both Morty and me our tickets. He pats my shoulder with a muddy, hairy paw. "Don't say nothin' to no one about gettin' hurt," he says. He even grins, displaying about seven little puppy teeth behind his thick, moist lips.

Momma and Aunt Molly wrap our clothes in paper bags and have them taken to the garage. Then Morty and I are plopped into a bath.

We fall asleep in the bathtub. Uncle David and Morris carry us to bed. We wake up the next morning.

The tickets, we discover, were good only for yesterday's performance.

Aunt Molly sits on the bed beside Momma, who's been changing compresses on my foot.

"*Amorets*," Momma says. "You're proud you're a working man?"

Aunt Molly hugs me. "He *learned* more than he *earned*."

"Yes, I did."

"I tell him," Momma says, shaking her head. "I tell him a hundred times. He ain't big enough, he ain't strong enough. But no. He knows."

"*Schwester meine*, he's a boy, a little boy." Aunt Molly reaches over and tucks her hand under Momma's chin. She lifts Momma's face. "You don't remember Momma *putsch*ing you in *tuches* you did such naughties? Huh?" She laughs. And Momma laughs. They're apparently remembering several such naughties.

Momma, still chuckling, turns her head away. "You'll spoil him."

Aunt Molly lies beside me. "Go," she tells Momma. "Maybe fix us some tea. I'll come down. I want *mein hertz* and me, we should talk."

Momma brushes my hair back from my eyes and gives me a bright, forgiving smile. "You think we're poor now?"

62

I shake my head. No, we're not. I don't add what I know Momma to be thinking: "*You got a sister like Molly you're rich.*"

I snuggle down in bed after Momma leaves.

"Momma gets mad," I say. "You never get mad."

"It did someone good, I'd get mad."

"She's sad a lot, too. You never are."

"I am, I am. I win prizes sometimes. I'm sadder than anyone. Big medals with *sad* on them, here, like this: S . . . A . . . D."

I laugh and so does Aunt Molly.

"You talked to your momma, you're poor?"

"Yes."

"You wish you were rich? Like us?"

"I just wondered why you're so rich and we're so poor."

"I knew, I'd tell you. Some things, there's no reason. The smartest men, Einstein, can't give a reason some things. You know something?"

"What?"

"Your momma, she had lots of money she'd like it, sure. But something else, other things, she'd like better. Better than money. You know what?"

So this is why Aunt Molly sent Momma downstairs.

"You . . . Rachel . . . Max . . . Jacob . . . Reuben . . . you all be good Jews . . . that she'd like better than money. Your poppa . . . your momma too but your poppa . . . oy! what a *shayner Yid*. He was a *baal toyreh*. You know what this is? It's . . . the smartest, the best student. Men studied the *Talmud*, from far away, they'd come hear your poppa he was a young man. What happened who can say, who can blame, who throws the first stone? You don't know, *kinder*, before you were born . . . ach! such good days. Suddenly they're not so good. And they get worse. For everyone. . . ."

She throws up her hands and pretends to be astonished at the things she's told me. She fluffs up the pillow under my foot. She kisses my cheeks. "You'll make me happy, you'll make your

63

momma happy, you'll make your poppa happy, you know what?"

"What, Aunt Molly?"

"You'll be a *shayner Yid*. A *shayner Yid*, no matter what."

I'm never to spend another summer at Aunt Molly's house.

A few weeks after our visit they sell their home. During the next year they move three times, each time to a smaller house.

Knowing all the while what was about to happen, Aunt Molly held off the catastrophe just long enough for Momma and Rachel and me to have one more summer of luxury.

Three years after that summer Uncle David lies down one night. He kisses Aunt Molly and reminds her that he loves her beyond all women, beyond all love. They find him the next morning, dead, a serene smile on his lips.

For a very brief time . . . perhaps a month . . . Aunt Molly broods in dark rooms. Momma goes to stay with her.

She appears again, her head fitted with a few more gray hairs, but she's the old Aunt Molly, trusting the world.

About Rachel
Summer, 1936

It is 1936. I am twelve years old. Today is Friday, early morning, October.

Rachel comes into my room to waken me. She kisses me on the cheek as she does every morning. "It's seven o'clock," she says. "Time to get up. If you don't get right up Poppa will pull you out of bed."

I leap from beneath the blankets, not because of the threat but because I suddenly realize it is Friday. Rachel has promised to take me to a movie tonight, in town.

Rachel used to take me to the movies every Friday night but lately, since she started going steady with Naty, she rarely takes me anywhere. To remind her and to verify it for myself, I say, "Remember, we're going to the movie tonight."

She's been sitting on the edge of my bed, molding the chignon at the back of her head. Her hands stop working and the rose-bronze color fades from her face and then returns, very red. She murmurs something that sounds like, "Forgive me."

"Forgive you for what?"

"I can't take you. Not tonight. Naty and I have to go some-

65

where. We have to. I'll probably stay overnight in Summer with Harriet Salomon."

I ask if we can go the next Friday night and she promises me, crossing her heart, that we will.

I'm angry. Not at Rachel but at Naty. Tonight, I promise myself, I'll have nothing to do with him when he comes to supper.

On the way home from school Roman and Goose and I plan how we'll play in the woods this weekend and eat in our shack and maybe raid the lumber piles of the company that's building the viaduct across the Connequenessing Creek.

I go through the store on my way to the kitchen. The miners sitting around the coal stove are laughing at one of the men who, until now, had been unaware that he was drinking soda pop out of a bottle in which one of the miners had pissed. I go into the kitchen, light-hearted, and the remnants of anger for Naty are washed away by the aromas of chicken and soup and pie. The linoleum floor, newly scrubbed, gleams, and the white tablecloth gleams and each dish and each glass gleams. Everyone sitting around the kitchen table is talking and laughing. When Naty grabs me and hugs me to him and says, "Boy, are you getting muscles," I laugh and snuggle up to him.

We haven't had a Friday night like this for a long time. In fact, not since Reuben went back to college. In August. With Reuben gone and Jacob working the night shift at the tire factory and Max in town at the furniture store every evening, our Friday nights have been no different from other nights. Except for the candles and Momma's prayers.

But Max is home tonight. He admires Naty, who has quit medical school in his third year to go into business with his father, in Aliquippa. They exchange stories about strange customers and novel business techniques and consider the quickest and easiest routes to enormous wealth. Poppa just shakes his head and snickers at their pretensions and dreams.

66

Jacob doesn't have to leave until eleven and, because everyone's here, he's decided not to take a nap, as he usually does. For the occasion Poppa has brought two bottles of dandelion wine from the cellar.

At dusk Momma lights the candles. The laughter stops and the talk dies down. As always, Momma cries a lot while she prays. Poppa, despite his determination to give up his share of the Friday night ritual—"What good's prayers one night a week? God's in heaven only Friday nights?"—Poppa half-closes his eyes and he sways slightly back and forth and his lips move and he keeps his head tucked under a nonexistent shawl.

After supper Poppa tells me to watch the store for a while so he can have another piece of pie and a cup of coffee.

I leave the kitchen and walk through the corridor to the store. There are no customers. The miners are either home or at Shorty's beer garden. But Roman and Goose are sitting on the porch. I go out and pull a milk-case over to them and sit with them and we talk again about eating in the shack tomorrow night and maybe even sleeping there.

I complained when Momma told me to put on a sweater but I'm glad I'm wearing it. Each night now is colder than the night before.

When Poppa comes out on the porch he taps me on the shoulder. "I got a proposition," he says. "They delivered a ton coal today. Dumped it in back. In the alley. Tomorrow's Saturday. Shovel inside tomorrow all the coal and I'll give you"—he thinks a moment—"I'll give you two dollars."

The first thing I believe is that he must have hit on the numbers racket. Every time he wins he sees it as a signal from God that very soon now all of his financial problems will be solved. So he can afford to squander.

I feel that if he's going to spend money he ought to spend it on Momma, who's sad about Reuben being away. She's also sad that Naty has quit medical school. ("Oy! It could have been a doctor for a son-in-law!") Or he could spend it on Jacob and Rachel, who always give him money to keep the

67

store going. I'm about to say I'll do it for nothing but Goose and Roman yell that they'll help. Poppa says in that case he'll give us seventy-five cents each. Goose and Roman agree. There isn't much I can do.

After Poppa goes back in the store Roman and I decide that when we finish shoveling the coal tomorrow we'll go to town to a movie. Goose says there's a double feature at the Majestic, with a Dick Tracy serial. Roman says there's a movie at the Capitol Theater about big-game hunting in Africa. He's always more interested in hunting and fishing and trapping than he is in playing cowboy. I side with Goose because both of the movies at the Majestic are Buck Jones movies. He's my favorite. Then comes Tim McCoy and George O'Brien and Johnny Mack Brown.

A coal train rumbles along, on its way to Pittsburgh, and though the tracks are a good two hundred yards away we can see each car as it passes through the lights from the switch-man's shanty. We count the cars, not even coming near the record sixty-seven I counted last Sunday night.

Roman says, "Here comes a bum." He nods toward the rail-road tracks. There is a telephone pole in the field between the store and the tracks. A tall bum in jeans and denim jacket is walking through the light from the pole, aiming himself to-ward the store.

As the bum crosses the road and comes up the steps I notice his hat. It is straw and shaped like a cowboy's.

The bum flops down on the porch. He asks if we've seen any fried chickens flying around. I tell him Poppa will probably feed him and he goes into the store.

He comes out about twenty minutes later and sits near us and leans back against one of the porch posts. He looks up at the sky, which is dark now, and filled with stars. "Boys," he says, "if you hit the road, go south like the little birdies." He pulls a sack of Bull Durham out of his jacket pocket and says he wonders if that old Jew would break down and give a man a pack of cigarettes.

68

The words, and the tone, make me bristle. "That old Jew just fed you."

He looks at me a moment and then he nods. "Chosen people," he says. "That's what the Jews are. The chosen people. You can see it the way Jew kids are always so loyal. I like that. I sure do."

Goose says, "Hey, are you a cowboy?"

"Well," the bum says, "I ain't a cow*girl*." Even I laugh at that. "What makes you ask?" the bum says.

"The way you walk and talk. And that hat."

The bum takes off his straw hat and twirls it around the tip of his finger. "Yeah," the bum says, "I'm a cowboy."

My heart sinks. Here's a cowboy . . . not on a movie screen, not in a magazine, but just four feet away . . . and I've made an enemy of him. I know, deep inside, that his admiration for Jews is sham, but in my delirious need to win his real respect and friendship, I soon convince myself that since all cowboys are honorable and virtuous and ethical, he will soon respond to my needs and treat me with the same consideration that Roman and Goose will receive.

"You ever break broncos?" Roman asks.

"Yep."

"Ever wear a gun?"

"I always wore two guns."

"Two guns!"

"That's right. Two guns. I'm a better shot with my right hand than I am with my left, though."

"Did you ever shoot anyone?" Goose asks.

"Yep."

We don't talk as the cowboy—no one could consider him a bum now—looks at the stars. We wait.

"I sure could use some cigarette papers," the cowboy says. Roman and Goose turn to me and I get up and go in the store.

Poppa is bent over the cards he uses to help pick the numbers he'll bet on the next day. Smiley, the bookie, sells the cards for ten or twenty or fifty cents, depending on whether you buy the orange "Hot Dream Numbers," or the green "Otto's Numbers Tips," or the blue "Crystal Ball Winners." Poppa subscribes to them the way people subscribe to magazines or newspapers. He has about twenty spread all around him.

While he concentrates on the cards and writes on his own slips of paper I feel with one hand among the Marsh-Wheeling cigars and the Mail Pouch chewing tobacco and find the box that holds the packs of cigarette papers. I lift one pack, bring it slowly down to my side and then nonchalantly go outside, to the porch.

I sit on my milk crate and hand the packet of papers to the cowboy.

"You're a good kid," he says. "I'll remember this. A cowboy never forgets a favor."

I relax, convinced I'm deeper in his good graces than either Roman or Goose.

"I might as well tell you," he says. "My name's Texas Jack." He leans back against a porch post, smoke curling out of his mouth. The light coming through the window from the store seems to focus on him as he tells us about the man he shot. The man was a gambler in Galveston, Texas, and a cheat. It is a breath-taking story, gory and factual enough to thrill and impress us. I have no doubts that he is a cowboy, and a rough, tough one at that, with the best features of Buck Jones and George O'Brien and Johnny Mack Brown combined.

Goose, who has always been opposed to sharing the cabin in the woods, now suggests that we show it to Texas Jack. Roman tells Texas Jack he can sleep in the shanty that night if he wants to. I say that if he wants to he can sleep there the next night, too, and as many nights after that as he wants.

Texas Jack says he knows what it means to boys to have their secret hideouts and he wouldn't want to horn in on anything. But we insist and he says, well, all right, he'd be obliged. But this one night only. We lead Texas Jack up the alley past the store and up the hill to the woods. Since Roman stole the

70

lock for the front door we always let him open it and go in first to light the kerosene lamp.

Texas Jack goes in next. He tests the old table and the nail kegs we use for chairs. He stretches out, sighs and after a few fake snores, he drops back down to the floor. "I'll tell you men," he says, "I've slept in bunkhouses and hotels and mansions. From Connecticut to California. From the Canadian border to the Rio Grande. I ain't never seen anything homier than this little place."

I dance a few steps, catch Texas Jack's hand and, embarrassed, I let his hand go and I sit on one of the kegs. I remind Texas Jack that he's not to show anyone the secret path by which we've brought him here.

"Boys," Texas Jack says, "believe me. You can trust me. I have secrets could ruin the richest man in Texas. But the man who told them to me told me they were secrets. And you know? Wild broncos couldn't drag them out of me."

Roman stacks paper and kindling in the steel drum we use as a stove. He throws in some coal and in a few minutes the fire is roaring and the room is warm. Texas Jack takes off his jacket and I notice his muscles. Goose notices them too and looks at me and rolls his eyes in wonder and admiration. On the inside of his right arm there's a tattoo of a heart. There's an arrow through the heart and initials that have faded. A shield looks very new. Under it are two crossed sabers and on it are the words "God and Country."

He stretches out on a deer hide on the bottom bunk. "Now," he says, "if we had the makin's of a meal I'd say this was as close to heaven as I'll ever get."

I kneel and lift out a small section of flooring. In the dirt under the floor we have a large tin box filled with all sorts of food. I take a Prince Albert can out of the box, open it and empty seven full-length cigarettes on a crate we use as a table.

Texas Jack smiles paternally at me and selects a Lucky Strike. He lights the cigarette and then lies back on the bunk. "This is better than Hollywood," he says.

71

"Have you been to *Holly*wood?"

"Been there? I worked there. Did you ever see *Silver Spurs?* With Buck Jones?"

We saw it, all three of us, and I saw it twice.

"I was in *Silver Spurs.*"

My mouth stays open so long my tongue gets dry. "Do you know Buck Jones?" I ask.

"Know him? Why Buck and me . . ." Texas Jack clears his throat. "A man gets mighty hungry working those freights all day. You think maybe we could rustle up some grub? And maybe a pot of java?"

I open a can of sardines while Goose slices some bread and Roman gets a pot of coffee started on top of the stove. Texas Jack pulls a black Barlow knife out of his jacket. He stabs and lays out five sardines across a slice of bread. In three gulps he eats everything. After five more slices of bread and another can of sardines he lies down on the deer hide and tells about his friendship not just with Buck Jones but with Ken Maynard and Tim McCoy and even Tom Mix. Tom Mix let him ride the famous Tony once, for about ten minutes.

The next day, Saturday, we work six hours shoveling all the coal into the bin. One of the things we talk about and decide on is that rather than go to a movie we'll have a party at the shack, in honor of Texas Jack. After we finish work Poppa pays us and treats us all to Eskimo Pies and soda pop. When Roman and Goose go home to take their baths Poppa slips me an extra dime.

While I sit in the tub in front of the coal stove, with Momma scraping at my head, I argue with her about the money. Certainly I should spend some of it, she says. I've worked for it. But spend all of it? Shouldn't I save part of it? Half, maybe? For a moment I'm shamed into considering the return of all of it to Poppa. I know how things are. I know that everyone works hard for the little money available and then everyone scrapes to somehow get together a dime every Saturday so I

72

can go to a movie. I'd give it all back to Poppa if we were still going to a movie. But we're having a party. A party for Texas Jack. When I don't agree or disagree with Momma, but remain silent, she remains silent, too, and scrubs my head harder.

We buy eggs and bacon and cupcakes and coffee and fruit and cigarettes. (We buy it all from Poppa, of course, so my conscience is soothed a little bit; at least the money all gets back to him.) Because Texas Jack just happened to mention that he loves ice cream we buy a quart of chocolate and a quart of vanilla.

He's asleep when we arrive at the cabin but he wakens and helps us unpack the food, calling us saints and buddies. His humility and gratitude stir in me the faint recognition of my own failings, my own inadequacies. I vow to be a better person, one whom a cowboy of virtue and integrity . . . a man like Texas Jack . . . can admire.

Goose, because he's been doing most of the cooking at his home (his father disappeared and his mother works as a maid in town), volunteers to do the cooking now. Roman settles the fire for him.

Everything has to be cooked and eaten fast so we can get to the ice cream before it melts. Texas Jack compliments Goose. He says the last meal he had that was even half this good he had in Butte, Montana, and it cost him two dollars.

When Texas Jack sits beside me on the bottom bunk I'm so grateful I want to drop into his hand the twenty-seven cents I have in my pocket. But he would refuse it, I'm sure, and then we'd both be embarrassed.

While a third pot of coffee is being prepared Texas Jack rolls and lights a cigarette and tells us about a lynching in Laredo. Then he tells a story about a battle with Mexican rustlers. He tells us next how he once saved Buck Jones' life, when a stagecoach carrying Buck rolled over a cliff.

Of all the names of the famous cowboys with whom Texas Jack has worked, Momma and Poppa would not recognize one. Jacob knows all about football and basketball and Reuben, in

73

his third year in college, is already a prize-winning writer . . . but compared to the life Texas Jack has led their lives are dull and trivial. They can't ride horses, they know nothing about guns, they rarely swear or play poker. They've never been in a round-up or a battle royal. Rachel? Rachel seems bland alongside the movie queens with whom Texas Jack has spent so many exciting days. And nights. Bebe Daniels? Why, he's dated Bebe Daniels. Four, five times. Lupe Velez? "Well, I'll tell you," Texas Jack says, accepting another cup of coffee from Goose. "Me and Lupe played in *Ace of Spades* together. Remember that one? Oh . . . that's the one they never let kids in to see."

We wait, hearts pounding.

"It was banned in lots of towns."

After another wait I manage to ask what it's about.

"Well, it was about this . . . this . . . do you boys know what a . . . no, I better not."

We beg him to tell us. He can't stop now. We're old enough. We know lots of girls.

"You do, huh?" Texas Jack asks, sitting up.

Sure we do.

"Why don't you bring them here, to the shanty?"

"Aw, come on," I say. "What's *Ace of Spades* about, Tex?"

"I'm serious, boys. A woman around the house . . ."

We plead. We all but get down on our knees. Goose promises to bring him home-made cookies the following day and I promise to steal him a pack of Lucky Strikes.

"Well," Texas Jack says, "it's about this . . ." He pauses and sucks some food out of a tooth. He rolls a cigarette. "It's about this whore. And I'll tell you boys, there ain't a man in this great country knows more about whores than me."

My throat is parched. A million ants are crawling around inside my lower abdomen. Roman's head is drooping over the edge of the top bunk, his flat face upside down. Goose sits absolutely still, his finger stopped halfway to his nose.

Texas Jack tells us, then, about *Ace of Spades*. When he fin-

74

ishes he says maybe he was wrong. Maybe it would be more fun to go to our girl friends' houses than to have the girls come to us. He asks if we've ever watched our girl friends.

"Watch?" Roman says. "Watch them what?"

Texas Jack shakes his head. "Ain't you ever watched a woman undress?" None of us have. "One of you got a sister?" All three of us hold up our hands. "That's fine. Now, who has a sister sleeps in a room we can sneak up close to?" I feel a bit uneasy. "Come on," Texas Jack says, "you ain't gonna let old Texas Jack down, are you? You wanta hear some good . . . I mean *really* good stories . . . well . . ."

"My sister sleeps in a room near a big tree," Goose says. "She's sixteen."

Texas Jack laughs. "I bet you sat out there in that tree many a night. Ain't you?"

"No," Goose says, but when he lowers his eyes Texas Jack, and Roman and I, laugh. "Once," Goose admits.

"What'd you see?" Texas Jack asks.

"Oh . . . everything."

"Everything? You mean her ringdangdoo, too?"

"Her what?"

Texas Jack and Roman roar. "Her what? . . . her what? . . ." I say, mimicking Goose's voice. "Oh boy, are you a dope."

Texas Jack turns on me. "What about you? Jew broads are hot stuff. Your sister undress in front of you?"

"No," I say, and Goose leaps to retaliate. We have the store roof, he says. It's easy to get on the roof and crawl up close to Rachel's window. The big guys are always talking about watching Rachel undress.

"Uh-huh," Texas Jack says, "holding out on me, huh, buddy?"

I would have told him eventually, I say.

"Yeah, but you didn't. And I thought we were buddies."

Almost in tears, I try to convince Tex that we *are* buddies, that my not telling him about Rachel means nothing. But he

75

just keeps shaking his head. He turns away from me to talk to Goose and Roman. I then make the offer I know he's waiting for. Tomorrow, Sunday night, Rachel will be home. Sunday night, I say, is the best night.

"What time?"

"She goes to bed early on Sunday nights. She gets up early to go to work Monday morning."

"What do you mean early on Sunday nights?"

"Well, about nine."

"O.K., everyone here tomorrow night at eight."

The rest of the night I try to listen to Texas Jack's stories but my mind keeps drifting. I think about Rachel. About the way she looked when she told me she couldn't take me to the movie. I think about the way her face glows when she sits beside Naty, the way she laughs when she beats Reuben and Jacob at parcheesi, the way she kisses Poppa's cheek and makes a face at the bite of his beard. I think of her and Momma combing and braiding each other's hair; the hair of one as long and raven black as the other's. I leap back to listen to Texas Jack but after a few sentences I'm thinking again of Rachel. How, in the summer that I hurt my head, she sat with me on the porch swing, cradling my head in her lap, singing to me, refusing to go to town with Naty or any other fellow, or even to go to work.

The next morning, Sunday, when I go downstairs, Momma tells me that Rachel stayed in town last night, too, as well as Friday night. It's the first time she's stayed two nights. "But thank God it was with Harriet Salomon," Momma says. "Someone else, I'd worry. But not Harriet." Naty has called and promised to bring her home in time for supper. "Ach," she says. "My sons should do so good as my daughter. A *mensch* she's got. A real *mensch*."

I stay in the kitchen all day and read the Sunday paper. And I write a long letter to Reuben. To keep from thinking about what time it might be I write a letter to my cousins in Phila-

76

delphia. Max comes to tell me that Goose and Roman are on the porch and want to see me. I ask him to tell them I'm busy and I'll see them later.

I keep toying with ideas I might use to wreck the plans for that night but each time I determine that one idea will work, and I will use it, I'm confronted by the terrible certainty that I will be excluded from the glorious friendship which Texas Jack will go on to offer to Roman and Goose alone. It is a conflict not between my friendship with Texas Jack and my devotion to Rachel but between my keeping Texas Jack's friendship and my losing it. I know that I will be embarrassed and probably humiliated if I lie on the roof with the others tonight and watch Rachel undress, but the need for Texas Jack's friendship is so powerful that I am willing to endure that pain.

About five-thirty Naty's old Chevy drives up to the gasoline pumps in front of the store. I've been upstairs, lying on my bed, trying to read *The Call of the Wild,* a book Reuben sent me for my birthday. I sit up and watch Rachel and Naty.

While they sit in the car, talking, Momma goes down the steps. I hear her say supper is almost ready so won't Naty come in and eat? Naty thanks her and says he has to hurry back to town. Rachel says she'll be right in. Momma tells Naty he's always welcome. A few minutes after Momma comes inside Rachel gets out of the car. Naty holds on to her hand. Rachel seems worried. Naty pats her hand. He is smiling. When she turns to come in the store I see Naty's face grow very serious and then, when she looks back, he grins, quickly, and he waves. The store door slams and Naty drives up the hill toward Summer.

I hear Rachel climbing the steps to her bedroom. I hear her bedroom door close. I intend to tiptoe past her door so she won't know I'm upstairs but at the door I stop. I want to warn her about tonight. But if I warn her, if I tell her to keep her window blinds down I'll have to say *why* I'm telling her. While I stand there, uncertain, I hear her crying inside her room. I try to open the door but it's locked.

77

When she asks who it is I tell her but she says I should not come in. She'll see me downstairs, at supper. I say I have to talk to her but she says she can't talk. Not now. I say it's important. "No!" she shouts. "Go downstairs!"

Rachel has never shouted at me before. Never in my entire life. I clutch at her anger. It justifies tonight.

Fortunately, I do not have to test my anger. She does not come down to supper. Momma goes to her room and returns shaking her head. Rachel's forehead is warm. But she won't eat. If only she'd eat. One bite of *tsimes* and her temperature would go down to normal. Momma shakes her head, muttering that she'll never understand the young.

I eat and rush outside before Rachel can change her mind and appear.

We climb onto the roof at eight-thirty. We're very quiet. We move carefully, so no one in the store below us can hear us and so Yenta, on the back porch, won't bark. We crawl on our hands and knees across the roof, to within five or six feet of Rachel's window.

Over and over I keep repeating to myself that Rachel, in getting angry at me for nothing, does not deserve my loyalty. Also, I must admit that as I think about the possibility of watching Rachel undress there has grown, in the vicinity of my groin, a surprisingly cozy patch of warmth.

Rachel walks back and forth between her bed and the dresser and the closet, hanging clothes, combing her hair, stretching, smearing cream on her face, and stretching, as if she has a pain in her back. She is wearing the red robe Naty gave her. When it opens and I see her thigh, I jerk. Texas Jack puts his hand on my shoulder. "Easy, old buddy," he whispers.

Goose moans and says, "Look . . . look."

Rachel has taken off her robe. She is standing in front of the mirror in her underwear. Her black hair, loose, hangs clear to her waist. I turn my face away. The gritty tarpaper shingles

78

scratch my cheek. No matter how hard I try to keep my face down it comes up. I let my eyes go to her window, hoping her light will be turned out. It isn't. She stands there, a tape measure about her abdomen. One hand flies to her face. I hear her moan. The tape measure falls to the floor. She sits on the stool in front of her dresser. Suddenly she cries out. She doubles over, clutching at her abdomen. She tries to stand, still groaning, and she grabs at the dresser for support. Her hand skids along the top of the dresser and she drops, screaming, to the floor.

I leap up and run to the window. It is not locked. I manage, somehow, to pry it open. I leap inside the room. I hear Yenta barking.

Rachel lies on the floor, groaning and crying, her knees tucked up into her chest, her hands tearing at her abdomen. Her eyes have rolled up into her head. There is froth at the corners of her mouth. Blood is pouring down her thighs.

I run downstairs, screaming for Poppa . . . for Momma. . . .

During the first few weeks after the funeral, at night, after everyone's asleep, I tiptoe down the hallway and into Rachel's room. From the edge of Rachel's bed I can look out across the roof of the store and see the hill where we built our shanty. Texas Jack is gone. He hopped a freight within ten minutes after he jumped from the roof that night. Naty is gone, too. He did not come to the funeral. He's not written or telephoned. Momma and Poppa assure us they understand. Coming here would only remind him of what he's lost.

It is better for them to believe that than to know the facts the doctor tells Reuben and Jacob.

Years later—after hundreds (or is it thousands?)—of sleepless nights, during which I lie in the darkness and think of Rachel's empty room, lie in the darkness and hear my own voice whisper in my ear, "You did not do it, you did not do it"—

79

years later I learn, and finally willingly and gratefully believe, it was not I who killed her. It was not I.

I wonder, now: Naty—how many sleepless nights have you lain in your private darkness listening to your own voice in your own ear? Your own voice whispering, "I killed her . . . I killed her . . . it was I."

About Jacob
Autumn, 1937

We're barely into autumn and it's cold. "It's this cold now," Poppa says, "it's gonna be twice as cold November."

Momma stays in bed every morning, staring through the window at the falling leaves. Sometimes her eyes are closed when I go into the room but I know she's not sleeping.

Early in the morning when Poppa stokes the fire in the coal stove, I see him interrupt his work to watch the dance of the flames.

Rachel is dead. This house, this life, will never be the same. Without Rachel their life can only be worse than it has been, than it is right now; oppressive, interminable, sour.

Since summer Momma has traveled to the cemetery four times. Each time after her return she has sat in her chair in front of the stove, seeing no one come or go through the kitchen, hearing nothing spoken. In her wanderings through the cupboards and drawers and closets the most trivial memento of Rachel's life brings a sudden burst of tears, a half hour of wailing questions to God about His cruelty, her own sins, the wretched loneliness of us all. Couldn't He reconsider? Couldn't

He, maybe, have made a mistake? Couldn't He bring her back?

To earn the money with which to play the numbers racket (and with which he promises . . . almost daily . . . to replenish the stock and restore our old life)—to earn this money Poppa starts to buy and sell junk.

Every day he drives off in his rattling, wheezing truck to roam around the countryside, to visit all the farms. Old cast-off automobiles and farm equipment deserted along the dirt roads or in the fields are stripped of all the brass and copper he can locate. He spends hours with farmers in their barns, tearing at the guts of some reaper or binder or tractor to get at brass and copper casings and gears and wires. He pays five cents a pound for brass and seven cents a pound for copper. On those days that he receives little brass and copper he fills the bed of the truck with iron, for which he pays one cent a pound.

After the truck bed's filled and the patched tires protest and threaten, Poppa drives home, to deposit each day's collection with that of the previous days. On Saturday mornings he loads the truck and drives to town, to G & G (Greenberg and Ginsberg) Junkyard. Roman and Goose and I go with him. We toss down the burlap bags filled with brass and copper. Poppa peers over the shoulders of either Greenberg or Ginsberg as they weigh the bags. Satisfied, he tells us to throw off the iron.

At the end of a week Poppa will have made a profit (if Greenberg or Ginsberg feel generous) of twenty or thirty dollars. With this he usually buys a few things for the store; a dozen quarts of milk or a couple cartons of cigarettes or a case of cans of sardines. And he'll still have enough to continue playing the numbers with Smiley Casey. "Soon," Poppa keeps saying, "I'll hit it big."

More important than anything else, so far as we're concerned, is the fact that such work keeps him out of the house, away from that door upstairs that opens into Rachel's room.

At night, when he comes home, smelling of oil and rust,

82

Momma fixes him a plate of eggs and . . . if we have it . . . a couple of slices of salami. Or she'll bake a carp or a pike or a bass if Roman's been lucky at the creek. Lucky and willing to trade a fish for a candy bar. Often Poppa brings home fruit and nuts he's gathered from a tree he's chanced on during his day in the country.

Next year we'll be able to have chicken more often, but right now we can't afford it. A weasel has raided the henhouse and reduced our flock of fifty layers to twenty-three. The carcasses of the twenty-seven hens, and two roosters, are worse than *traife*. Momma wouldn't permit them in the house.

"Give them away," Momma says.

"To who? To these *gonifs* around here? I'll bury them first." And he does.

Roman and Goose and all the other kids, as well as some of the big guys, find it more profitable to spend their days gathering junk and selling it to Poppa than standing idle, waiting for the County Relief truck. Pushing wheelbarrows, pulling wagons, carrying burlap bags, they bring Poppa everything they dredge out of the creek. The money they earn buys cigarettes and enough beer to get them drunk at least once a week.

"Drink," Poppa says, every time he drops a few coins in their hands. "Go on, drink. Maybe it drowns you."

There was a time when, on Saturdays, Poppa never did an hour's labor, a minute's labor. He sat in the house, at the kitchen table, studying his holy books. Those days, I've been told, were before I was born, or at least when I was too young to be impressionable. They're so far in the past that even Poppa seems to have forgotten them. One of the Jews in Summer might refer to those days but Poppa never does.

He works on Saturday mornings now. Every Saturday, after Roman and Goose and I load the week's collection of junk and then unload it at the junkyard (and after it's paid for), Poppa

83

joins Greenberg and Ginsberg in their office. Sometimes they sit there for an hour, drinking *schnapps* or coffee.

While they're drinking Roman and Goose and I crawl over and under and through the mountains of rusted auto chassis, the towers of tires, the caverns of rolled copper wire, the subways of iron pipe. Playing Follow-the-Leader, Goose and I follow Roman, performing acrobatics that would bring cheers from any circus audience. And frightened gasps from every mother. We challenge a tottering dump truck to fall on us. Twenty feet in the air we walk along a girder suspended on not much more than a feather. We swing over volcanoes of burning refuse and spit with utter contempt into the hungry flames.

Even if we didn't earn a dime apiece we'd beg for the chance, each Saturday morning, to ride to G & G with Poppa.

The only copper Poppa will buy is "clean" copper. "Clean" copper has had the rubber sheathing burned away.

At four or five places along the banks of the Connequenessing fires are kept alive throughout the day. Anyone bringing copper wire for cleaning must also feed the fire with their share of logs or tree trunks or railroad ties.

The odors of burning tar and rubber coat the skin. Even after I bathe, Yenta will sniff my hand and back away, her nose wrinkled in disgust.

In the afternoon the kids and those big guys who dig about in the creek bottoms, the old mine dumps, the deserted coal tipples, deliver their junk to the back of our store, where Poppa examines it all. He uses a magnet to separate the iron and a dozen different techniques to distinguish copper and the various grades of brass. He always empties every bag and box to personally check each load since, a few weeks before, he discovered the bag of what was supposed to be iron containing iron on the surface only. Under the surface were bricks.

For each ten dollars that Poppa pays out he receives, from G & G, fourteen. His weekly income is never less than twenty dol-

84

lars. He's earning more money now than he's earned in the store for the last two or three years.

"Pennies. For pennies he works. And such work."

"Momma," Jacob says, "it's money. It helps."

"A shame. Ginsberg . . . Greenberg . . . sure . . . *amorets*, they sell junk. But him, a *talmud khokhem*. Ah, I remember. . . ."

"No more *I remembers*, Momma. Things are different. You think I like working in a tire factory, with the temperature over a hundred twenty degrees? I'd rather go to college, like Reuben. But I can't. So? So I can't. If Poppa didn't buy junk there wouldn't be enough to even buy cigarettes for the store. At least he can pretend to keep the store going."

"Pretend. What's to get from pretend?"

"Well, what do you want? You want to rub his nose in his failure? You don't want that, Momma."

Momma hangs her head. No, she doesn't want that.

Jacob wraps his strong arms around her. "We spend every penny I make," he says. "Poppa's few extra pennies help keep Reuben in school. They're pennies from junk, but they're pennies."

I think that years ago Momma would have been more able to accept this crude decline in status. But now, recently, she hungrily grasps at any crumb of evidence that might prove Poppa's value, and so her own, has not diminished beyond recovery.

Her equanimity, her unyielding trust in eventual intervention by a kindly God, has been lost. She never used to react to Poppa's anger but now she shouts back, answering charge and attack with charge and attack. Once any thought but submission to his needs would have humiliated her. Now, after sneering at Poppa's business sense, she ridicules his promises, reminds him of his most recent failures. She shrugs, mumbles to herself, scowls for a moment or two and then, in her chair, she stares down at her hands in her lap.

85

"Junk. It comes to no good. I promise." Stretched out on two kitchen chairs in front of the coal stove, asleep, she'll jerk, sit up and stare at me or whoever's in the kitchen. "I know . . . it's no good . . . it comes to no good. These *huserei* . . . they'll bring him no good. . . ."

In a way, Momma's correct. It comes to no good. They bring him no good.

Someone sells Poppa a solid brass casing that he remembers, too late, he'd bought earlier in the week. It had been stored in the empty lot, in a crate, where he's been storing all his junk. He checks the lot. Sure enough, the casing he'd bought before is gone.

Now, every day, he examines the junk in detail. He's convinced he's being offered pieces he's paid for before.

He builds a wire fence around the lot and lets Yenta roam inside, to guard it. He reduces his payments to anyone who brings him junk to make up for the money he calculates he's lost.

Even Roman and Goose are angry. Just because one or two might be cheating him is no reason to punish everyone, is it?

What do they mean, *might* be cheating him? They *are* cheating him.

We argue about it. Though we've argued before, and even fought, this is the first time we stay away from each other for as long as a week.

The junk they collect now is sold to Ellsworth Cotton, who borrows a truck and takes his load, with Roman and Goose, to G & G Junkyard. Greenberg calls Poppa to find out why this *goyische* bum brings the junk. "You such big business now you hire a man? You buy a big truck?"

Poppa tells Greenberg the story. Greenberg says, "Ah-hah, Ginsberg says he smells a herring." G & G offers Ellsworth less than Ellsworth paid his customers. Ellsworth goes to the other two junkyards in town, both of which are owned by Jews.

86

Both, informed by Greenberg, offer Ellsworth less than what he was offered at G & G.

Ellsworth goes out of the junk-collecting business.

Poppa, criticizing Max's suggestion that we take prompt advantage by offering higher prices, says, "*We?* What do you mean, *we?* I own this business. Not *we*." Then he does what Max has suggested.

"Forget it," Jacob tells Max. "So what if he pretends it's his idea? You know it's yours. I know it's yours. So what's it hurt?"

Poppa gets more junk than ever before. Roman and Goose and I get two dimes apiece every Saturday. We're better friends than ever. And Poppa buys cakes and pies for the store. And candy bars. And canned spaghetti. "It's beginning," he tells us, grinning victoriously at Momma, who says, "Wait and see."

Someone . . . we think it's Ellsworth Cotton, though it could be anyone . . . someone reports Poppa for having received material stolen from the B. & L. E. Railroad.

On a Friday afternoon Brick Shiptick, the township police chief, and one of his deputies, drive up to our store. They place Poppa under arrest and order him to come with them to jail.

Poppa refuses. Brick tries to grab his arms. Poppa goes berserk. He lifts Brick, who weighs almost a third again as much as Poppa does, and he throws Brick through the air, into a large glass candy case.

Dazed, Brick sits there among the Baby Ruths and the Clark Bars and the Milky Ways, a delicate glass antenna protruding from his forehead.

While Momma stares, gaping like a fish out of water, and Poppa stands (his face almost black with fury), screaming curses, Brick's deputy brings his club down across Poppa's head. The club breaks. Poppa turns, eyes glazed, to curse the deputy. While Poppa stands there, reeling, the deputy slips a pair of handcuffs over his wrists.

87

I call Jacob at work. "They took Poppa! They took him to jail!"

"Who did? Why?"

"Brick Shiptick. They handcuffed him. He threw Brick into the candy case. They clubbed Poppa over the head. His head was bleeding. They took him to jail, Jacob, they took him to . . ."

"Calm down! Why'd they arrest him? What the hell's that noise?"

"It's Momma. She's screaming."

"Oh Christ! Why'd they take him?"

"Buying stolen railroad property."

"I'll be right home."

"What'll I do, Jacob?"

"You stay right there. With Momma."

It's a disgrace of such magnitude that Momma can't face us. She keeps her hands over her eyes. The thought of being confronted by the Jews in Summer sends her to bed, where she lies with her face to the wall, the covers pulled over her head.

Max, who's in his last year of high school and who now earns three dollars a week working evenings and weekends in the furniture store, stays home from work to help in our store. "In case someone forgets," he says, "and comes in to buy something."

Jacob goes to Summer to visit Poppa at the jail. That afternoon he hires an attorney, Aleck Schapiro, a classmate of Reuben's. Schapiro advises Poppa to plead guilty, to pay the fine. "It's not worth fighting. It'll take too long. It'll cost a lot of money and they'll *still* find you guilty."

Poppa can't believe that he's heard correctly. "Guilty? Of what? I'm guilty of nothing. Those scum . . . they're the ones are guilty. Arrest *them!*"

The trial's set for October 20. The lawyer obtains a writ to set Poppa free until the trial but Poppa refuses to leave the jail. "They arrest me. Fine. Let them feed me. It ain't my money."

Poppa lies on his bunk, ignoring Jacob's pleas.

"I don't know," Poppa says. "Maybe I'll stay right here. They let me play the numbers here, I'll stay. Till I die. It's peaceful."

"What's the worst he can get?" Max asks.

"If we're lucky, two or three months in jail."

"If we're not lucky?"

"A year in prison. A couple hundred, maybe a thousand dollars fine."

I've been standing there with them, listening. Poppa in jail, behind bars, in a bleak cell, for a year? A man who loves to roam the fields . . . who all through March watches the sky for the first sign of spring so he can smell the apple and cherry blossoms, so he can prepare the soil in his garden . . . a man who can lift a man and throw him through the air but who can also lift a newborn chick to tenderly wipe its wet down against his lips . . . who can steady his hand for five minutes while a butterfly, landed there in alarm, prepares to fly off. He's in a bleak cell now, behind bars. He might be there for a year.

Max, moved by an unusual tenderness, teases me, jokes with me, offers me an Eskimo Pie. Jacob, pacing back and forth through the store, thinks out loud. "If we could get Poppa to plead guilty . . . if we could find out who sold him the junk . . . or prove it's not stolen . . . if he'd only come home . . ." He turns to me. "Maybe," Jacob says, "if he sees you he'll change his mind. You want to visit Poppa?"

"Yes."

The township police use the county jail in Summer. It's a gray stone economy model of some ancient European fortress.

An odor of wet rust, or mouldy bread, spills out through the front door. We push through the odor and enter the visitors' room. Other prisoners are sitting there with their friends or their families. Jacob and I sit in a corner where there are three unoccupied chairs. The door opens and Poppa enters, blinking his eyes at the sudden light.

89

I should say blinking his *eye*. A gray turban of a bandage is wrapped around his head. There's a dark brown splotch on the turban above his right ear. His right eye is a puffy blue-black ball of flesh.

Inside his arms, I sob against his chest. He pats me gently on the back. "Hey . . . hey . . . don't cry. Hey . . . I like it here. Come . . . look at me." I look. His one good eye is squinted in a grin that shows one front tooth missing.

The Jews in Summer take up a collection. They want to hire a famous lawyer from Pittsburgh. Poppa won't accept their money and he won't talk to the famous lawyer. "I'm not guilty!" he shouts. "I should pay a thousand dollars to prove I'm not guilty? Bah! To hell with their famous lawyers!"

Momma accepts an occasional cup of tea from Max, an occasional slice of toast, but nothing more. Once, when I take her two soft-boiled eggs, she tastes a spoonful and shakes her head and lies again with her face pressed to the wall. "Such shame," she whispers.

Jacob spends part of every morning, before he goes to visit Poppa in jail, talking to Step and Cosco, or one of the kids, trying to find out who sold the stolen junk or if it was stolen. Everyone professes innocence and ignorance of the theft as well as the report to the police.

"Step knows," Jacob tells Max. "So does Cosco. Their loyalties aren't to us, that's all."

He finally goes to Ellsworth Cotton, who is sincerely surprised to see Jacob at his door. Seated in Ellsworth's living room, he's treated with almost unctuous courtesy. Ellsworth swears he knows nothing about this. He even seems angry at Brick Shiptick. "It's a damn shame," he says, "old Al had to go to jail."

There's one way, Ellsworth says, that he might be able to

90

help. How? Ellsworth's brother-in-law, Bud Hardt, the township commissioner. *He* might be able to do something.

"How? Do what?"

"Talk to Brick. Get him to drop the charges."

"Brick won't drop charges. Poppa's the only man who's ever gotten the best of him. He won't forget that."

"Bud has ways."

"What kind of ways?"

"Well . . . ways. I'll leave it at that. But they cost money."

"How much?"

"I'll find out."

That night Ellsworth tells Jacob that a hundred dollars would do the trick. "There's all kinds of legal fees," Ellsworth says.

For a moment Jacob is tempted. After all, the object is to get Poppa free. But a deal with people like Ellsworth Cotton and Bud Hardt would rob Poppa of his last bit of dignity.

"Shove those legal fees up your ass," Jacob says.

During the next two days I visit Poppa twice. Each time he plops me onto his lap. Normally, I'd be embarrassed. But I don't care at all here in the visitors' room, where the kids cheering their father or brother, or sister or mother, nudge each other and point at me.

"You see that man with one ear?" Poppa asks, indicating one of the prisoners. "He steals five hundred dollars. From a bank. That's his wife. She turns him in. Why? He doesn't buy her a nice coat. The man in the fancy-schmancy suit? A drunk. He drives his car through a red light. So a cop stops him. And the cop sticks his arm in the window, it's open. The man rolls up the window, the cop's arm inside. The man drives off, five blocks, dragging the cop. The woman, her hair looks like a mop? You get older, I'll tell you. She's a . . . a sort of businesswoman. The *schwarze?* He fights a man calls him a name. (Poppa whispers in my ear the word, *nigger.*) Never call a *schwarze* a (and he whispers *nigger* again in my ear). It's like

91

someone calls you a *kike*. So who they put in jail? The *schwarze*, of course. Nice justice, huh? Pretty justice, huh? You remember!"

"Poppa, come home."

"Now, now. Don't ask me I should come home. You know what?"

"What?"

"I'm learning checkers. Twenty years I watch the *goyim* in the store, they play checkers. I never learn. Now I learn. Cards, too. A man, he's a gambler, he's here. He teaches me tricks with cards. You'd never believe. Wait. I'll show them a thing or two." Poppa laughs and rubs his hands in anticipation.

Jacob is worried. He agrees with Poppa that those who sent him to jail are the guilty ones. But the fact remains, *he* is in jail. And Momma's wasting away, dying.

(Poppa says, "She'd exercise, give me a visit, she'd not waste." Jacob says it is hard for Momma, and Poppa should try to understand. "I understand," Poppa says. "Pride. So her pride, it's more important than her husband? Tell her I'm healthy. Ten hours' sleep. Thirty years I ain't slept ten hours. All of a sudden, I'm rested.")

"The important thing," Jacob tells us, "is to get him out of jail. And to manage to do it, somehow, without ruining him."

"Without ruining him?" Max says. "Hell, he's already ruined."

"Don't talk like that!" Jacob snaps. "Would you hold out like he is if *you* were in jail? Would you hold out just because you thought you were right?"

"He holds out because he's so damned stubborn, that's all."

Max knows better than to argue any further with Jacob when Jacob gets so angry. "No," he adds. "I guess I wouldn't hold out." Then Max says, "If we could get someone to say they *gave* that piece of junk to Poppa . . ."

Jacob, crying, "By God!" leaps to his feet. He goes to the phone and dials. "Jerome O'Hare, please."

Jerome O'Hare and Jacob have been close friends ever since grade school. Jerome's father owns the tire factory where Jacob works twelve hours a week (even though there's barely enough work to keep the plant open). Jerome is a foreman in the plant.

"Jerome, I'm asking a big favor. You know about my dad. You said if there was anything you could do, I should let you know. There is something."

At the trial Poppa's attorney calls Jerome O'Hare to the stand. He asks Jerome if he's ever given Poppa permission to haul junk from the tire plant. "Yes," Jerome says, "I have." The attorney then holds up the brass casing in question. Exhibit Number One. Could this casing have come from one of the hundreds of machines in the tire factory? "It could have, yes." Could he be positive? "No, I can't be positive. We have dozens of different kinds of machines. It would take a year to tear down all the machines to make sure. But yes, I can say it *could* have come . . ."

The attorney reminds the jury that the judge's instructions include a "beyond a reasonable doubt" clause. If there's the slightest doubt, and the railroad engineer admits there *could* be a doubt . . . if there's the slightest doubt . . . well, the ladies and gentlemen of the jury know their duty.

The jury acquits Poppa.

That night, at the kitchen table, Poppa drinks his dandelion wine. "This they didn't have," he says.

He's lost about twenty pounds. His face is pale. The bandage is gone and his eye has just a few faint blue shadows.

Momma comes downstairs. She says nothing to Poppa and he says nothing to her. With trembling hands she makes a pot of coffee. She sits in her chair in front of the coal stove, in which one of Poppa's fires rumbles.

Jacob and Max have brought the inevitable kosher salami and some bread and pickles from town. I make the sandwiches

93

and we sit around the table. No one says very much, but there is little doubt that we're feeling festive.

Yenta comes over to lick Poppa's hand.

Momma starts to get up when the coffee begins to percolate but she falls back, exhausted. Poppa beats Max and Jacob and me to the stove. He turns down the flame. "Ech! Their coffee . . . *pishachs!* This," and he leans over to smell the steam, "*this* is coffee." He holds a cup for Momma to see. "You want coffee?" She glances up. "Nu? You want coffee?"

She nods.

While he pours coffee into her cup he says, "Benny, get your momma a sandwich. She lost pounds. She been in jail?"

All, except Momma, laugh.

As limited as it is, it's more of an exchange than they've had in months.

Max, who's taken another night off from his job to help celebrate Poppa's acquittal and release, asks, "Is it good to be home, Poppa?"

Poppa smiles and nods at Max. I can't remember the last exchange between them that included a smile. "It's good," Poppa says. He swallows a large bite of sandwich and then shoves half a pickle in his mouth. He chews and swallows. "Better . . . I beat the bastards. That's a better feeling, I'll tell you."

Max starts to complain, to tell about Jacob's work, but Jacob, with a shake of his hand, warns him to say nothing.

For the next hour or so Poppa tells us all about the jail, about the other men in other cells, about the sheriff, about the food. I suspect it's the most dramatic event in his life since, as a youth, he left his home in Russia.

Late . . . about midnight . . . Poppa gets up and goes to Momma. He takes her empty cup. "You want more coffee?"

"No."

"You want anything?"

"No . . . no."

94

"I'm going to bed."

"Go . . . I'm coming up later."

On the landing, Poppa turns and waves goodnight.

"Goodnight," Max says.

"Goodnight, Poppa," Jacob says.

"I'm going to bed now, too," I say. I walk behind Poppa up the stairs, holding on to his hand.

And Jacob? Jacob permits Poppa to continue to insist and believe that this victory was due to no one but him, Poppa.

None of us . . . not Poppa, not Momma, not Max, not Benny . . . none of us thinks to thank Jacob. If he's hurt, if he's angry, if he resents the neglect, he never shows it. He even begins to put aside two dollars more every week than he has until now, to pay Schapiro, the attorney. It is Jacob who continues to pay the gas and the electricity and the mortgage, it is Jacob who continues to send Reuben five dollars every month (and more when he can) and it's Jacob who orders and pays for the headstone for Rachel's grave.

95

About Ellsworth
Winter, 1938

I drop four fist-sized lumps of coal into the stove. If anyone's walking on the road outside they'll see the red sparks exploding up through the darkness.

"Hi ya, Benny."

I thought I was alone. The voice startles me. When I spin around my finger brushes the stove. "Goddamn it, Step! You scared me. Where'd you come from?"

In the winter everyone—customers or family—everyone stomps their feet on the porch before they enter the store. (Poppa's shout, "Go get the snow off your feet!" is repeated three or four times a night. Each new arrival is usually greeted with a chorus—"Go get the snow off your feet!"—from the men sitting on the benches.)

Step's boots, I see, are free of snow. Since I didn't hear him stomping his feet I know he brushed off the snow with his hands. And that means he'd not wanted me or Poppa (who'd been in the store but is now in the kitchen) to know he was waiting.

"Where's your old man?"

"In the kitchen."

96

Step wrings his hands in the heat above the stove. "How'd you like to go to the mountains a couple of days, to Ellsworth's cabin? With me and Cosco and Ellsworth?"

This has to be one of Step's jokes.

"We're going Saturday. Early. About six in the morning."

Step is famous for his practical jokes. But this time he must be serious. He has no audience to watch him. And for Step an audience is as vital as a victim.

It was Step, with his natural talent for storytelling and his unnatural talent for blood-letting, who first excited me about the thrills to be won at Ellsworth's cabin in the mountains. There were stories about shooting bears and ripping off their skins and shooting deer and ripping off their skins and shooting rabbits and ripping off their skins. There were stories about tracking wild animals through the forests, about pack trips and about fish fries. There were stories about all kinds of contests: marksmanship, swimming, drinking, lifting. Sooner or later, in the most elaborate of details, there was the spilling of someone's blood by knife or bullet or club or foot or fist.

"Are you kidding? Do you really want me to go?"

"Sure we do. I'm not kidding." Step crosses himself.

During my life I've heard hundreds of names of Jews who've won fame in science and art. Momma and Poppa, and even Rachel and Reuben, have pointed to this or that famous actor or actress or writer or musician or scientist. I don't want to hear about actresses or musicians or scientists. I want to hear about men like Max Baer. I can hardly keep from jumping up and cheering when he becomes heavyweight champion. "A fighter," Momma says, disgusted, as if she'd just sniffed someone else's garbage. "He's a clown," Reuben says. I have to admit I'm just a wee bit uncomfortable at his playboy performances in the ring. But he's not an intellectual.

The world of the intellect doesn't interest me. It repels me (though I'd never dare admit it to anyone in the family, not even to Max, the least intellectual of us all). It's the life of action for me, the life of adventure. I mean to be the first Jewish

97

cowboy, the first Jewish explorer, the first Jewish big-game hunter, the first Jew in the French Foreign Legion. But I have no more chance for all this than I have to be a Catholic nun.

"Why me?" I ask Step. "Why not Goose or Roman?"

"Aw, they're kids. Babies. You're practically grown up."

Such flattery from Step or Cosco would usually swell my chest until it was in danger of bursting, but I go on pressing him. I have to know for sure he's not deceiving me. "You never invite Jacob. Or Max. And they're more your age."

"Max and Jacob wouldn't go. You know that. Max is in town all the time, at the store. And Jacob's always working, always tired. But look, if you don't want to go, say so. Roman and Goose . . ."

"I *want* to go."

The door behind the counter . . . the one sealing the hallway that leads to the kitchen . . . opens and Poppa comes out. Light from the kitchen streams along the hallway behind the glass showcases. Step says, "Think about it, let me know." He props his hands on his hips as Poppa comes from behind the counter. "Hi ya, Al," he says.

Poppa checks the fire and prods the coal with an iron poker. "Think about what?"

"Step says I can go with them this weekend. To Ellsworth's cabin."

"Yeah," Step says. "We thought old Benny'd like that."

"I would," I say. "I sure would." I know now that he's been serious all the time. But I still have to be cautious. Not with Step but with Poppa, who's unpredictable these days. The wrong word can bring a fierce scowl, a shake of his head, or advice that allows no contradiction. My shrug informs him, I hope, that neither his refusal nor his permission is important enough to argue about. Who needs to go to the cabin? But a reminder of my devotion could do me no harm. "If you need me in the store, Poppa, I wouldn't even want to go."

"What'll it cost?"

98

"Cost?" Step says, pained at the implications. "Cost? Hell, Al, we ain't trying to make money. You know us."

"I know you all right." Then, unable to even sustain contempt, Poppa sighs and sits on a bench and contemplates the coal bucket, thinking probably that after three thousand five hundred and eighty-seven trips with that coal bucket, or one just like it, he is about to have to make his three thousand five hundred and eighty-eighth. "Ask Momma."

Momma sits in front of the kitchen coal stove, mending a dress. Since Rachel died she spends most of each day in this same chair. Perhaps, for all I know, mending the same dress over and over. She only gives up the chair when Poppa goes to town on one of his periodic trips to search out credit for a few more cartons of stock. While he's away Momma settles herself on a bench behind the stove in the store. If Mrs. Chupek or Mrs. Slasca or Mrs. Trebuka come in, they'll sit together and talk in Polish or Russian about the dreary mysteries of America. I stand behind the counter, waiting for the customers.

"Poppa says I can go with Step and Cosco to Ellsworth's cabin. Can I, Momma?"

She knows Poppa's not given me permission. Not explicitly, anyway. I know she knows that, but I also know that today she's not likely to have the energy, or the will, to debate the fine points of the issue. She finds just enough energy to nod her head.

I kiss her cheek. The flesh, like the skin of a tomato left too long on a sunny window sill, slides beneath my lips.

Roman pulls our bobsled alone. Goose chases me around Roman and around the sled. The snow crunches under our feet.

There's not been a fresh snowfall for several days. The old snow, packed so tightly under the passage of feet and sleds and cars, is as dense and as slippery as ice.

The pitch of the road is steep, but Roman can easily pull the sled alone. Goose and I wrestle in the snow at the side of the

99

road. Because I wear a scarf none of the snow goes inside my jacket. But Goose, trying to prove he's as tough as Roman, wears no scarf. He pulls out his shirt and hops up and down to lose the snow I've stuffed inside.

I've not said anything yet about the trip to Ellsworth's cabin but, with the weekend beginning tomorrow, I feel safe. There's little chance it will be canceled now.

Goose, with his arms and legs stretched out, lies in the snow-drift, pretending he's mortally wounded. I grab the rope and help Roman pull the bobsled. "Step asked me to go to the cabin tomorrow. With him and Cosco and Ellsworth. All day tomorrow and tomorrow night and all day Sunday."

Goose bobs up out of the snowdrift and pushes me against Roman, who pushes me back against Goose, whose feet slide out from under him. He gets up and grabs my arm. "You're shitting me."

"I'm not."

"Your old man wouldn't let you go."

"He said it's O.K. So'd my mother."

"Why'd they ask *you?*"

I thump my chest. "Because they want a *man* with them."

Roman grabs one of my arms and Goose grabs the other and they heave me through the air into the snow. Every time I laugh Roman pushes another handful of snow in my mouth. Goose jumps up. "The sled! The sled!" he yells.

The bobsled's gliding down the hill. Its iron runners strike sparks through the blue-black moonlight whenever they cross a patch of cinders.

Several miners are sitting on the benches around the stove when I come home. Roman and Goose are still outside, riding the bobsled. In preparation for tomorrow I've decided to come in early. I'll need plenty of rest.

Poppa's talking to Smiley, setting up the special arrangements of numbers on which he'll gamble tomorrow.

I'm about to go into the kitchen when I see Step on the store

100

porch. He signals me so I go back through the store. Outside, I close the door and lean against it.

"Hey," Step says. "I forgot to tell you. Everyone's supposed to bring their share."

I'm relieved, because I was sure he was going to tell me the trip's been canceled. And yet, in a way, I'm more disappointed than I would have been if it had been canceled. Poppa won't contribute anything. I know that. He's been waiting for just this sort of trick. And it is a trick, I know. But I've bragged to Roman and Goose. I can't back out.

"How much?"

"Oh, as much as you can."

"O.K.," I say, and I turn to go in.

"When Reuben came up he brought potatoes. About twenty big ones. And bacon and bread and eggs."

I don't remember Reuben ever going to the cabin but I don't say that. I just say, "All right."

"Three or four loaves of bread. A pound, no . . . three pounds . . . bacon. That's all."

"I can't bring all that."

"You want to go, don't you?"

"Sure I want to go, but you know my dad won't . . ."

"Aw, come on, Benny, Reuben always did. He used to sneak the stuff out. Your old man never found out."

"Poppa had more then. It's different now."

I've sneaked things out before this . . . a pack of cigarettes now and then, a candy bar, a can of beans . . . but never in such quantity on the same night.

"We'll be leaving at five in the morning," Step says. "O.K.?"

"Yeah. O.K."

"Good boy. Listen, Benny, you won't be sorry. You'll have fun. I'll let you shoot my rifle. We'll get us a couple deer." He aims an imaginary rifle at an imaginary deer standing by the gasoline tanks. "Wham! Right between the eyes. After you knock him down you better let me stick him for you. You ain't experienced. He might just tear you open with his horns."

I start inside.

"Oh . . . and cigarettes, Ben. A couple packs."

Ellsworth Cotton has fought for attention, for notoriety, for as long as I can remember. As a veteran of World War I, as a member of Sundown's Volunteer Fire Department, as a self-delegated poll-watcher at all elections (routinely held in the basement of his home), he contrives to always be where everyone will have to look at him and even appeal to him for advice or hospitality. With a red-banded vaquero's hat (with red tassels shaking) on his head, he often rides a glistening chestnut mare through town. The hat was given to him when he was a child, by an aunt who'd visited Mexico City.

Unlike all other Sundown houses, which are covered by not much more than a mortgage, Ellsworth Cotton's house is covered with a new coat of white paint every other year. His lawn is always a tightly cropped mat of dark green. From the tops of any of the hills surrounding Sundown Ellsworth Cotton's house stands aloof from the peeling, soot-covered buildings that barely manage to keep themselves erect.

The house, and the cabin, he inherited from his father, along with three thousand dollars in cash and an established clientele for the liquor produced in the still in the two sheds behind the mountain cabin. The established clientele consists almost exclusively of township and city politicians, who also, during hunting season, rent his cabin.

The miners have no money to pay Ellsworth for his liquor. That suits him fine. In place of money he accepts their servility. They agree with everything he says when he argues with anyone, they laugh at his jokes, they accept his slurs about their courage and their intelligence (which would bring fractured skulls to anyone else daring to make such comments). When he derides Jews and Negroes and skinny women and Clooney, the idiot, everyone applauds his wit and insight.

Every autumn Ellsworth and his brother-in-law, Harold "Bud" Hardt, organize an old soldiers' reunion which attracts

102

the same five men. They drink to their memories of Château-Thierry, Verdun and Meuse-Argonne, battles in which none of them ever fought.

It is still dark when I go down the porch steps and cross the road to Ellsworth's house. I carry a burlap bag containing my extra socks and underwear and jeans. In the bottom of the bag, covered by the clothes, is the food and the cigarettes Step requested.

I was sure Poppa would be awake to see me off. He isn't. I'm glad. He might have asked how two pairs of socks and a sweater and underwear and a pair of jeans could make so much bulk.

They're all in the car, waiting. Cosco is in the back seat with me. We're off.

Everyone's loud and cheery. When we back out of the driveway and Ellsworth turns on the heater I know that all three men have been sampling Ellsworth's beer. The aroma is delicious.

We go north out of Sundown, the headlights breaking open the darkness, spilling onto the banks of snow. Step begins to talk about past hunting expeditions. Cosco tries to match every story. When the next batch of beer bottles is distributed I'm offered one and accept. Before I'm half through the bottle I get drowsy. My head falls against Cosco's wool-covered shoulder.

Ellsworth drives his 1933 Pontiac with such caution that both Cosco and Step tease him about being a little old lady.

"I've had this car five years," Ellsworth says, "and I'll have it another five because I treat it like it's the only piece of pussy for a hundred miles around."

Cosco is drinking his fifth bottle of beer. Step and Ellsworth are on their fourth. Cosco's taken off his plaid wool jacket but

103

he keeps on his red leather cap, the ear flaps tied up over his head.

When Goose and Roman and I sneak a drink from a bottle or talk about sex it is all boyish bravado. We are *playing* at being men. Step and Cosco and Ellsworth have laid hundreds of women, they've drunk enough beer to float a battleship, and during this ride I hear all the lurid details.

I hear about the night Step laid Betty Halyard, the night Cosco laid Rosie Chemnitzky, the day Ellsworth (while Dutch Cameron was at work) laid Edna Cameron. "That cross-eyed little turd, the baby, you think he's Dutch's? Ha! Take a good look at his snout. It's mine."

Goose and Roman and I dream of Betty and Rosie and Edna. But our dreams climax in our bedsheets. We awaken to the moist and dispiriting knowledge that those big-breasted women are not for us.

But tonight, after this weekend, who knows? Maybe Step will take me to Betty's house or Cosco will take me to Rosie's.

In less than an hour I've moved away from Roman and Goose, drawn across the border that divides manhood from boyhood, that divides reality from dream.

Ellsworth edges toward the side of the highway, careful to remain clear of the newest drifts planted that morning by the snowplow. "I gotta piss," Ellsworth says. "Benny, you wanta come hold it for me?"

Everyone . . . including me . . . laughs.

How liberated I feel. How mature. How gentile!

There are about fifty cabins in the village of Kettle's Pass. The inhabitants rely on the two sawmills for survival. In the winter, when the mills are closed, they depend on what they can shoot and trap in the woods.

Ellsworth's father was born in Kettle's Pass. At one time he owned one of the sawmills and half of the cabins. When the lumber workers were organized he sold everything but his own

104

cabin. Then he moved to Sundown. Ellsworth's wife, Josephine, was the daughter of a logger who'd been killed in a fight with Ellsworth's father. After the trial and his acquittal (Poppa, every chance he gets, reminds all who will listen that everyone knew that the jury had been bought off), Ellsworth's father supported Josephine. He brought her to his own home, treating her, most people said, like a daughter. Treating her, a few people said, like something more than a daughter.

The day after the funeral of Ellsworth's father Josephine threw herself in front of a train.

During the last ten miles we're restricted to two deep ruts in the snow. We could not change our direction if we wanted to. Twice in those ten miles cars coming toward us, caught in their own two ruts, slow down. The drivers exchange information with Ellsworth about the weather ahead and behind.

A half mile from the cabin the chains on a rear wheel break. Unwilling to repair the chain in the cold, Ellsworth does not stop. During the rest of the trip the chain strikes the underside of the rear fender with every revolution of the wheel. Step sings *Sweet Violets,* his rhythm fixed to that of the clanking chain.

Ellsworth decides against driving up the hill leading to the cabin. He parks the car so that on Sunday afternoon, when we leave, we'll have no trouble getting started.

While Ellsworth goes ahead to open the cabin and build a fire, Step and Cosco and I unload the clothes and weapons and rations. I sink in the snow to my knees but I work with a speed and a willingness that even draws reluctant approval from Ellsworth.

Then we sit in front of the fire to rest. Ellsworth opens a bottle of his whiskey. And the three of them are off again.

The cabin's interior is knotty pine. There are two bedrooms and two tiers of bunks in each room. The kitchen has a wood-burning cookstove and an icebox. The bathroom has a tank of water sitting over a wood-burning heater. Here, in Kettle's Pass as in Sundown, Ellsworth's house has a flush toilet.

"Benny," Cosco yells. "Rustle us up some grub."

"None of that Jew food," Ellsworth says, shaking his finger at me after he takes it out of his nostril.

"We oughta go catch us a couple rabbits," Step says.

"I shoulda brought my dogs," Cosco says.

There's a loud argument about whose dogs are superior.

"What'll I cook?" I ask.

"I brought ten venison steaks," Ellsworth says. "But they ain't for you. They ain't kosher. You bring any of them Jew crackers? You can have them and water. Kosher water." He bends over, laughing. So do Step and Cosco.

After they all recover Ellsworth tries again. "It's too bad that rabbi didn't cut it all off when he circumcised you, Benny. If he'd just left a little slit you'd sure come in handy on a night like this."

So they can't see the tears in my eyes I go into the kitchen.

By the time the steaks are ready Cosco and Step and Ellsworth are so drunk they can hardly walk across the room without knocking over a chair or dropping a glass.

When I take the platter of steaks to the table Cosco flops a hand against my arm. The platter falls, knocking over the bottle of liquor.

With a wild howl Step leaps to the table top and he drops to all fours. In a drunken imitation of a dog he laps up the liquor, interrupting himself to raise his head and bay at the ceiling.

Cosco reaches under Step from the front and Ellsworth reaches from the rear. They both grab Step's balls and jerk and squeeze. Step digs at the table with his front paws and rears his head back to bay again, to squeal and scratch and whine and pant. He's done this imitation of a bitch in heat before but never with such realism.

He flops over onto his back and spreads his arms and legs in what he and Ellsworth and Cosco pretend to believe is imitation frenzy. His body quivers and jerks and his flailing arms send the steaks in all directions over the floor.

The main room of the cabin is a rectangle of rough-sawn pine. At one edge is a fireplace Ellsworth's father built.

The furniture is a mixture of overstuffed chairs and sofas and wooden beer or nail kegs converted into stools and tables.

While the logs burn in the fireplace the heads of five beautifully antlered bucks and two does stare down from the walls in petrified fright at the rifles and shotguns stacked in the corner.

I wash the dishes after everyone eats. I don't mind; it keeps us away from each other.

They . . . Cosco and Step and Ellsworth . . . try to play poker but they're too drunk to distinguish hearts from diamonds. Ellsworth calls a card a king, Cosco says it's a queen.

Step brings the card to his eyelashes, squints and says, "It's a jack."

Ellsworth pounds the table and shouts, "Benny, you half-cocked Hebrew cock, you're sober. What is it? A king or a queen?"

I say, without looking, thinking it won't matter much either way, "It's a queen."

Cosco rises, apparently to celebrate his victory, but he falls to the floor. Step bends over him, tries to lift him and, when his own knees collapse, he falls on top of Cosco.

While they lie there, arms and legs entangled, Ellsworth, with a grunt and a wave of disgust, struggles across the room to the weapons. He pulls the canvas cover from a shotgun.

"I'll trade you my coonhound," Cosco says, from the floor, "for that shotgun and a hundred bucks."

Ellsworth sneers at him. "This gun's worth ten of your coonhounds."

Step, on his back, is waving both arms, conducting his own deafening rendition of *Home on the Range*. He stops singing.

107

"I'll trade you my wife for your coonhound and give you twenty bucks to boot."

"Who the hell'd want your wife? And anyway, you ain't got twenty bucks. You ain't got two bucks."

"I'll get it."

Ellsworth goes into one of the bedrooms. When he comes out he carries the shotgun, broken open, and a box of shells. After much concentration he manages to insert two shells. He staggers toward the door. Halfway there he trips over his own feet. The gun barrel catches between his legs. He falls to his rump. Both barrels explode.

Step and Cosco raise their heads. Cosco tries to sit up but his spine melts out from under him and he falls back, his head cracking the floor. "Shoot it again," Step mumbles. "It's still moving. . . ."

Cosco rolls over onto his stomach, cradles his head in his arm and starts snoring.

"What's that?" Ellsworth says.

"They're asleep. They're snoring."

"No, no . . . I mean *that*. It sounds like water."

I go into the kitchen. The faucet's not dripping. I go into the bathroom. The water tank is squirting water out of about thirty small holes made by the buckshot.

Ellsworth stands in the bathroom doorway, swaying from one side of the frame to the other. "Do something . . . stop it. . . ."

"What'll I do?"

"Turn it off."

The water's flowing across the bathroom floor and over the door jamb and into the front room. I find a valve at the side of the tank. When I turn it the valve comes off in my hand.

Ellsworth glares at the valve for a minute before he comprehends what has happened. "Newspapers . . . get some newspapers . . . get something, do something, goddamn it . . . soak up . . ."

I take all of the paper in the kindling box and spread it out

108

at the bathroom door. It's submerged immediately as the water continues to flow in thin silvery arcs from the holes in the tank.

I have to get Step and Cosco up and I'll have to do it alone, I know, because Ellsworth will be no help at all.

"Step and Cosco . . . they're going to get soaked."

"Leave the bastards. Stop the water."

I brush past Ellsworth, through the water that's now up over the soles of my shoes. I drag Cosco, by his feet, into the nearby bedroom. I lift his shoulders and then his hips until his body's on the bunk. It's a struggle because I no more than get his hips up than his shoulders roll off, or I get his head and shoulders up and his legs roll off. But finally I get all the parts of his body on the bed and they stay there. I repeat the process with Step, getting him out of the room just before the water glides over the floor where they've been lying.

Ellsworth is shouting for me to go outside and turn off the water but I push and tug and lift and manage to get both Step and Cosco covered with blankets.

The water has reached the fireplace. The flames die out with a hiss and a loud protesting spill of white smoke.

"Where's the water turn off?"

"Outside," Ellsworth says, "this side . . . no, that side . . . under the cabin."

I run outside without stopping to put on a jacket. The air is brittle and clear, without a hint of wind. I feel the moisture in my nostrils freeze before I take one step from the porch.

The snow crunches as I walk. Sometimes the crust is firm enough to bear my weight, sometimes I plunge through the surface to my hips.

It's about twenty feet from the porch to the meter but it must take me fifteen or twenty minutes to complete the trip. I find the valve but my fingers are so cold I can't bend them around the rim. I press my palms against it and using my body as leverage I manage to turn the valve. When it will turn no more I go back to the porch, my frozen clothes stiff as clanking armor.

109

Inside the cabin the entire floor is covered with an inch of water, the surface a thin sludge. It's already beginning to freeze.

Ellsworth, in what must have been his last real moment of complete rationality, has lifted all the weapons to safety, to the top of the table. He sits on the floor, in the water, before the smoking fireplace. His body trembles from his hair to his toes. But he continues to sit there, drinking from a bottle almost empty now.

"Ellsworth, we better sweep out the water. It's freezing on the floor."

He tries to focus his boozy eyes on my face but he gives up. "A jinx, that's what you are. You're a jinx. Nothing's ever happened . . . come here all my life . . . nothing happened . . . hundreds of men been here . . . thousands . . . nothing happened . . . you come . . . once . . . look! look! . . . Goddamn, I didn't wanta bring you . . . they talked me into . . . Goddamn Jew jinx . . . I told them . . . who wants your fucking food . . . we got food . . . trouble . . . always trouble . . . Hitler knows . . "

I want to get out of the cabin and let him freeze. I can go down to the highway and hitch-hike home and when someone comes to get him he'll be frozen right to the floor, his mouth and his mind a frozen block of filthy ice.

But I'd never get to the highway by myself. I'd get lost. The snow's too deep. It's too cold. I'd be the one that would end up being frozen. Maybe if I wait, and go down the hill to the other houses and get back . . . too late . . . I couldn't be blamed.

The pain in my wet, cold feet distracts me from my fantasies of vengeance. My clothes are not frozen but they're wet, soaking wet. I look down at my hands. They're turning blue.

Ellsworth leans against the wall, barely erect. The bottle, clutched in stiff, locked fingers, slides back and forth across his thigh and knee.

I won't argue with him. I'll ignore him. I have to change clothes. I have to sweep out the water, for my own survival as well as theirs.

I walk past Ellsworth and into the bedroom where I have my burlap bag filled with dry clothes. I peel off my socks and pants and my shirt and sweater. Shivering, my body covered with a purple rash of pimples, I sit on my bunk in order to dress. The first important thing is a sweater, a dry warm sweater. Wearing a sweater under long underwear is warmer than wearing it outside.

While my head's in the sweater and I'm fumbling for the arms, I feel the bunk jerk. An icy hand grabs me. I swing away from the hand as I pull the sweater over my head. Ellsworth is bent over. I butt him with my shoulder. He slips off the bunk, into the water on the floor. He sits there, bemused. He giggles. Then, with astonishing speed and agility, he stands, reaches out, and he tries to grab me again. I bring my fist down across his forearm. He howls. Dressed only in my sweater I leap over him and go into the front room.

Ellsworth is not a big man. In fact, he's not much taller or heavier than I am. I'm fourteen and weigh about one hundred thirty pounds and I'm in good condition. Ellsworth, thirty years older, huffs and puffs if he even walks fast. I know I'll have no trouble staying away from him and I even feel sure of myself if he were to catch me. But I don't want to fight him now; I want to get warm.

He moves toward me through the water and makes an awkward grab. I step aside. He almost falls. He drops the bottle and picks it up before he can lose any liquor.

My feet are numb. There is a crust of ice on the water that is so thick it snaps and scatters like pieces of glass.

After a few more futile lunges Ellsworth gives up. He drops into a chair, panting. His senses have been dulled by the vast amount of alcohol washed through them. His eyes droop, he mumbles into his chest.

111

At the table on which he's stacked the weapons I very quietly pick up a shotgun. I mask the click as I break the gun open. Moving my hand very slowly, so as not to catch the attention of his sleepy eyes, I pick up the box of shotgun shells.

Ellsworth's body stirs. His eyes open, labor to find me and succeed. He stares, his brain working, but it takes too long to comprehend my plan. By the time it does and he tries to rise from his chair, I have the shotgun loaded and pointed at his chest. I'm shaking so badly my teeth are chattering but I keep the gun aimed at him. "Y-you—stay wh—where you are!"

He lifts himself up and sways, undecided. I pull back the hammers. He blinks, bewildered, and falls back into the chair.

I take all the weapons . . . one other shotgun and four rifles . . . and the box of shells . . . into the empty bedroom.

"Get up."

He remains where he is. I'm nearly insane with cold and frustration. The hatred I feel for him almost overpowers me. I want so much to pull the trigger, to send the hundreds of buckshot pellets through his body. But some strange power restrains me, refuses to let the muscles perform in the way my brain pleads that they do.

"Get up, you lousy bastard!"

He doesn't move. An involuntary spasm of cold across my body jerks my trigger finger. The shot strikes the water in front of him, splashing it up over his face. He leaps from his chair, screaming words that are clear and coherent. "Don't shoot me . . . I was foolin'. Honest to God!"

Someone . . . Step or Cosco . . . mumbles from their bunk.

"Get in there," I say, waving the gun at the bedroom in which Step and Cosco are lying.

Ellsworth sloshes through the water into the room.

"The top bunk. Get up." He climbs the ladder, slides, falls, climbs again, slides again and finally with a helping shove from me, he makes it to the top bunk.

I pull the blankets over him. I ought to undress him, I ought to get him into dry clothes, but I can't stand being near him another minute.

I close the door to the bedroom and pile every movable piece of furniture against it. On the way to my room I have to set each foot down very carefully, to break the thin ice in such a way as to not cut my ankles.

The water has stopped flowing. If I don't get a broom soon and sweep out the water the floor will be covered with a solid slab of ice. But first . . . dry clothes. Warm clothes.

I pull on the long underwear and rub my feet with a towel to restore the circulation. I put on two pairs of socks and two pairs of pants and my jacket. And my shoes and galoshes.

I'm warm, finally. I lie back, trying hard to decide what to do. I listen to the wind begin to rise outside.

Someone is pounding. I leap up, the shotgun . . . that I'd forgotten about . . . falling toward the floor. I catch it and return it to the bunk.

My feet almost slide out from under me when they touch the floor. Ice . . . the floor is covered with ice.

The pounding comes from the other bedroom. I recognize Ellsworth's voice.

A lamp is still lit near the table. I can see my way to the door of the other bedroom. The furniture I'd piled there is fixed tight against the door in two or three inches of solid ice. So is the bottom of the door.

"Let me out," Ellsworth yells. "Hurry up."

I move the furniture that can be moved and I put my shoulder against the couch and the wooden benches but they won't budge. They might as well be nailed to the floor.

"Hurry up . . . let me out. . . ."

I hear him gag and choke and then I hear the unmistakable sounds of vomiting. Cosco shouts, "You goddamned pig . . . look at me, you goddamned pig. . . ."

113

It takes two hours for the fire I build to melt the ice. All the rest of the night and most of the next day Step and Cosco and Ellsworth lie in bed. They take turns at the toilet.

When we leave, Ellsworth is whiter than the snow we drive through. I sit up front with him. We don't exchange a single word during the entire trip home.

"Nu?" Poppa says. "It was worth it?"

"It was, oh . . . all right."

"No better than *all right?*"

"No."

I walk through the store behind the counter and into the kitchen. Momma sits at the stove. I don't think she's moved since I left.

Jacob sits at the table, eating a plate of fried potatoes. "Home is the hunter," he says.

"It was terrible," I say. I pour a cup of coffee and sit across the table from Jacob. "Did Reuben ever go to the cabin?"

"No. Why?"

"I thought so. I just wanted to make sure."

"He wouldn't stay in the same room with Ellsworth."

I don't just feel betrayed, I feel fouled, as if Ellsworth . . . and Step and Cosco, too . . . had vomited all over me.

How can I cleanse myself?

I go into the store. Poppa stands behind the counter, his chin in his hands. His eyes are closed. I put my arms around his vast middle. "Poppa."

"Yeah?"

"I got something to tell you."

"Don't tell me no secrets, please."

"I got to. And it's no secret."

"You don't got to."

"They lied. They wanted me because . . . I . . ."

"So what's new? Go eat something. Fry an egg."

"But Poppa, I got to tell . . ."

114

"Go eat or I give you a punch in *tuches*. You want a punch in *tuches?*"

"No."

"Then go eat."

I go into the kitchen and stand by the door, watching Momma, and then I go to her. I hug her and kiss her cheek. She does not respond.

I make an egg sandwich and sit beside her while I eat it. Once I break off a piece and put it to her lips. She takes it in her mouth and chews and swallows it. It must be the first thing she's eaten since the funeral. I take a bite and give her another bite. And again . . . and again. . . .

About Reuben

Summer, 1939

Ever since he returned to college after his Christmas vacation Reuben has been telling us, in his letters, that this summer he plans to come home and write a novel about the strike of the Sundown miners five years before.

It is summer and he's home and he's writing the novel.

Each morning I rush downstairs to see the stack of pages and guess how much the stack has risen since the day before. I can only guess, because he won't let me touch the pages to measure or count each day's addition.

Work in the coal mines is always slack in the summer but this summer it is practically nonexistent. Any time of the day there will be ten or twelve miners on our store porch, killing time. Reuben and two of the miners, Step and Cosco, went to grade school together. Sometimes, long after the heat has begun to dissolve and the breezes crossing the Connequenessing Creek grow cool, Reuben and Jacob and Cosco and Step go for walks along the highway. They cross the creek at Number One Mine and go through the woods to the hills above Sundown. I stay awake until they return. After Cosco and Step go home

Reuben and Jacob and Max often sit on the porch, almost directly under my window. They talk about college. Jacob plans to go in another year. Each such session with Reuben makes him more determined than ever. Max, who knows he will never go to college, has assured both Reuben and Jacob that in another year he'll be able to help enough, at home, so that they can make their plans with peace of mind.

They also talk about politics, about the depression, about the miners, about Momma and Poppa. Jacob has a half-time job in a tire factory and Max, who has just finished high school, is working for nothing in a furniture store in Summer, "just to learn the trade." In September I will be starting high school. Because I'm only four years away from college I consider myself Reuben's and Jacob's peer, but Momma and Poppa disagree. That is why I go to bed before midnight.

Reuben spends most of each day in the kitchen, on a schedule controlled by the alarm clock on the shelf of the gas stove. He gets up every morning at seven o'clock. While he eats his eggs and bread and coffee he reads the *Pittsburgh Post-Gazette*. At eight o'clock he starts typing. At noon he listens to the news on the radio and has a sandwich and coffee and then he types again until four o'clock. From four until we eat supper he reads the magazines and books I've gotten him from the library in town. After supper he is, as he says, "free to live."

When Momma's not working in the store or sitting on the store porch, she digs about in the flower and vegetable garden behind the house. Whenever Max or Jacob are near she complains to them that Reuben should not be writing the things she hears him read now and then to them or to Cosco and Step. It will only get him and everyone else in trouble. Take her word for it, she knows.

Jacob insists that Reuben should write whatever he pleases. Strikes and unions are subjects Reuben knows a great deal about, and they're important themes. Important, Momma says, Ha! Reuben—and Jacob too—should have lived the lives she

117

and Poppa have lived. Then they'd know what's important. Wait, Max says, until Reuben gets famous. Momma will be proud then. Momma asks who can be proud of a son who has a jail record.

Reuben is always trying to comfort Momma. He hugs her and says that when his book is published he'll buy her a house in Summer, right next to the synagogue. How would she like that? The temptation to dream on such a promise is too much to resist. She considers it and then shakes her head. "He'll never leave," she says. We know she means Poppa.

Once Reuben tells her that whenever she gets so concerned she should remember that the mother of Judas Maccabeus, fifteen hundred years ago, was probably frightened for her son's safety, too, but look how history has shown her son to be a hero and a patriot.

Momma says she doesn't need a hero for a son. "Heroes are dead," she says. "Be a dentist."

Poppa defends Reuben. Not because he believes what Reuben is saying in his book about miners—in fact, he thinks that Reuben, for all his education and prizes, knows very little about life and less about coal miners. Reuben is trying to make them look like angels while *he* knows, from experience, that they're worse than devils. He defends Reuben just to oppose Momma. Lately she's been committing the unpardonable sin of questioning the way in which Poppa operates the store. By proving she has faulty judgment in everything he will prove she has faulty judgment of his business sense.

Secretly, Reuben and Jacob and Max agree with Momma about the store. But they can't bring themselves to condemn Poppa. That would be a betrayal that could destroy him. Rather than risk his destruction they pretend to have faith in him and, if not in him, in the ambiguous promise of something he calls *p'shaert*, or fate. His trust of the miners, despite his hatred of them, is a failing which, as Reuben says, were it a failing of statesmen, could save the world.

Hearing this I wonder if Reuben, with his superior wisdom,

118

has a secret knowledge that the statesmen have doomed the world. Roman and Goose and I talk about it often at night and we wonder how, if the end comes, it will come. Roman says it will come by fire. Goose says it will come by ice. I ask Poppa about it and he says, "Good, let it come, whatever way." I ask Momma and she shivers and hugs me to her and kisses my forehead and says, "*Ach, meine bubele,* such a question. Don't ask."

When I'm in town with Momma and we visit one of the Jewish families and someone inquires about us, Momma replies, "My Reuben, he's writing a book. I know nothing from such things but big people in New York say it will make him famous. And Benny here, he worries about the end of the world. Maybe, who knows, maybe he'll be a *rebba.*"

My own contribution to Reuben's novel is no small matter. Every two or three days he gives me a list of books to get from the library. I walk the three miles with a great sense of importance. On the way home I leaf through the books. Some are about labor unions. Several are about strikes. There are thick books by men named Lenin and Trotsky and Marx. There are also books *about* Lenin and Trotsky and Marx, books in which there are such stirring pictures of soldiers on horses and men in street barricades that I often sit on the bank at the edge of the road and try to find the passage on the pages that might explain the pictures.

I try all kinds of tricks to steal secret readings of Reuben's book, hoping I'll find there the same sort of thrill as that stirred by the photographs. But he is very strict about letting no one touch his manuscript. Not even Jacob. His one concession is to let me measure the stack of pages every seventh day. At the end of the fourth week the stack measures one and one-quarter inches.

At night, long after my light goes out, I continue to listen to Reuben and Jacob and, occasionally, Max, when they sit on the porch. They talk about Germany and Hitler and Italy and

Mussolini and China and Chiang Kai-shek and Russia and Stalin. And they talk about books. Actually Reuben and Jacob talk. Max mostly listens.

Reuben often talks about the John Reed Club in Chicago, where he goes to college. Famous authors often come to the club's meetings. Jacob reads their books. Max does not read them but he listens to the discussions. His questions sometimes test the patience of Jacob and Reuben but they take great pains to explain things to him. Thanks to Max, I learn a great deal.

The day Reuben's stack of yellow sheets measures one and three-quarters inches the mailman delivers a notice to every family in Sundown.

TO THE RESIDENTS OF SUMMER TOWNSHIP:
Your Board of Commissioners, meeting in session this 27th day of July, 1939, has voted unanimous approval of the appointment of Ellsworth Cotton to the post of Constable. It shall be the duty of Constable Cotton to keep the peace and maintain order within the limits of Sundown. It is the responsibility of every citizen to obey Constable Cotton, who, in turn, can rely on the full support of the Summer Township Police Force.

At the end of the notice are the signatures of the seven Township Commissioners, one of whom . . . Harold "Bud" Hardt . . . is from Sundown. Harold "Bud" Hardt happens to be a brother-in-law of the new constable.

Every autumn Bud Hardt collects the apples and grapes from his orchard and his arbors and he makes wine and hard cider and sells it to his fellow commissioners when they, in turn, rent Ellsworth Cotton's hunting cabin in Forrest County. His profit could be much greater each year if he were able to protect his fruit from raids by kids and miners. (One autumn he hid several bear traps in the grape arbor. The bear traps were removed when Step's kid brother lost a leg.) Step has been waiting for a chance to repay Bud Hardt and he's let it be known that this just might be the season.

Within minutes after the mailman leaves there is a gathering of miners and their families on the store porch. They're sure the commissioners must be bluffing. After all, everyone knows Ellsworth is a coward.

There is more than the usual number of miners on the porch that evening, as well as several women. And children, who'd normally be asleep.

About seven o'clock Ellsworth's screen door slams. Very solemn, he moves across the yard and past the empty lot next to his house and down the dirt road to the store. A silver badge gleams on the crown of his straw hat and another gleams even brighter on the pocket of his blue chambray shirt. Around a waist as lean as any Texas gunfighter's is a wide black leather belt that stores about fifty rounds of ammunition. He must have spent the entire day polishing the brass casings. The butt of a .38 Police Special projects, dark and menacing, from its newly oiled holster. The holster's tied to his thigh with a string of buckskin.

Step and Cosco and Stash have placed themselves at the front of the crowd that includes Momma and Poppa and Reuben and Jacob and me. (Max has not yet come home from the furniture store.)

"I'll be goddamned," Step says. "It's old Evil Ellsworth."

"I bet you shoot off all twelve of your toes," Goose says, "before you ever get that gun out of its holster."

"Wyatt Burp," says Stash, his hands high over his head, "don't shoot. I got a hundred and twenty-three babies to feed."

"Ellsworth," Step says, "you better run before I turn the old lady's pet canary loose on you."

The slurs and the laughter seem to have no effect on Ellsworth. He hands out mimeographed sheets to anyone who'll

121

accept them and when he offers a handful to Poppa he says, "Better keep a supply of these in the store."

Poppa looks down at them, grins, but does not remove his hands from behind his back. He shakes his head. "Use them for toilet paper," Poppa says. Ellsworth slaps the papers on the porch and walks away.

NOTICE

There will be a curfew every night. After eight o'clock no children are permitted on the streets. After ten o'clock no adults are permitted on the streets except those people carrying special passes. These passes can be obtained from me. The carrying of firearms is prohibited except during the hunting season and then only by adults and only between the hours of seven A.M. and seven P.M. Anyone guilty of disobeying these laws will be subject to fine or imprisonment or both.

E. Cotton, Constable

Cosco lights a match on his thumbnail and sets the flame to the paper. Roman and Goose and I and all the other kids collect the notices and add them to the flames. Stash and Cosco join us in a war dance around the fire.

The next day everyone in Sundown eats supper early. By six o'clock the entire population of men, women, children and dogs is gathered at the store. By seven o'clock Poppa has sold out his supply of ice cream and soda pop. Runners are sent to Shorty's Beer Garden and by eight o'clock several of the miners are drunker than they usually are by ten or eleven.

While Reuben and Jacob stand with the miners on the porch the kids and I play caddy out on the road. There is a gang of nine- and ten-year-olds playing pump-pump-pullaway on the vacant lot next to Ellsworth's house.

Poppa has discussed the whole thing with Reuben and Jacob. Though he pretends to be unconcerned about what happens he can not conceal the fact that he's hoping for certain consequences. There has been a strong rumor that Ellsworth Cotton has been planning to open a store in the vacant

122

lot. Poppa argues that Ellsworth is one of their own kind; given the chance they'd be delighted to switch their business from Poppa to a *goy*. Max has suggested that maybe . . . just maybe . . . their hatred of Ellsworth could work to our benefit. Poppa, secretly, hopes so but openly he sneers at Max's youthful stupidity. "You'll learn," he says, "you'll learn."

Momma feels our store is doomed, regardless. She is sure Poppa is destined to lose this contest as he's lost all others. Ellsworth's setting up a store in competition will simply hasten our ruin. She says these things out of Poppa's hearing, of course. In his presence she wonders if we shouldn't remain outside the fight. Maybe, she says, if we soothe Ellsworth, we could persuade him not to open a store. That kind of servility outrages Poppa. "Just like you," he shouts, "just like you. Me, I don't kiss no one's ass. Let him open a store. An amateur, that's what he is. He'll close in three months."

Now, as the curfew approaches, Momma remains inside the store. She's given up trying to persuade Reuben and Jacob to force me to stay inside with her.

As usual Reuben has spent the day in the kitchen, typing and reading. On the porch now, he is strangely silent. He has the same expression that I often see when he is studying one of his books. Every so often he takes a notebook out of his pocket and he writes in it. Once I hear him say to Jacob, "Put this in a play and the critics would call it *agitprop*."

The atmosphere is festive, like the park on the Fourth of July during the union picnics. People are laughing and telling jokes and drinking beer and Goose is playing a harmonica and another kid, Johnny Trebuka, is playing an accordion. Roman, the same age as I am . . . fifteen . . . is drunk. This spectacle, I know, is as appalling to Momma as the possibility that I might be hurt. She knows that Reuben and Jacob and Poppa will be there to protect me, in case there's violence, but there's no one to protect me against the even greater danger of which Roman's behavior is an example. She is convinced . . . she was convinced, in fact, before I was born . . . that this disease

123

(and it is a disease!) will be lying in wait for me, to infect and destroy me, every time I play with a *goy*.

The day has been hot. Some of the men wear handkerchiefs inside the collars of their white shirts to absorb their sweat.

It has grown humid. There's a suggestion of rain in the air. A breeze stirs a twister of dust from the road and carries it toward the store. Yenta snarls at the twister and then stands, confused, as it disappears. Poppa calls Yenta to him and sits on a milk case, holding the dog at his side. He'd never been especially fond of Yenta—"Because she's a woman," Momma explains—but he's attentive to her tonight.

A half dozen other dogs, exhausted from the heat and hours of wrestling, lie in the dust, ignoring the flies feasting on a fresh pile of dung near the gas pumps.

A door slams at Ellsworth's house and Step says, "Here he comes."

Reuben is writing in his notebook.

Ellsworth Cotton appears, his Mexican sombrero on his head, pulled low over his eyes. From the bottom step he looks up at the crowd. "You all read my orders," he says. "You better obey the law and get these kids off the street."

"They are off the street," Cosco says.

"You know what I mean."

"What do you define as a kid?" Reuben asks.

"Anyone under twenty-one."

Many of the men on the porch are under twenty-one but have been working in the mines for five or six years. The thought that they're to be considered children even causes Momma, whom I can see through the window, to laugh. She quickly covers her mouth and is immediately apprehensive again.

Ellsworth shrugs, turns and walks away.

No one has expected the victory to be so easy. Stash passes a hat and enough money is collected for two cases of beer. Two men take a car to Shorty's Beer Garden and return in twenty minutes. Poppa distributes free pretzels. Everyone congratu-

124

lates everyone else. The kids continue their games in the vacant lot and the dogs, awake and excited, return to their wrestling.

It is almost as if the police cars have been waiting at the top of the hill. Two of them, sirens calling, come down the road and stop at Ellsworth Cotton's house.

Those two cars make up the entire Township Police force. There are two men in each car. (Additional help, when needed, is available from the City Police or the State Highway Patrol.)

When Ellsworth and the four cops come out of the house and walk toward the store Momma shouts for me to come inside but I run to a corner of the porch where I'm out of reach of both her hands and her voice.

The chief of the Township Police is the giant, Brick Shiptick. A Pole or perhaps a Czech, he lives in Lyndy. He's worked in the steel mills and he's been a professional wrestler. He's hated and feared as strongly in Lyndy as he is in Sundown or Eden or any of the other towns. His face is a caricature of the flat Slavic face. His jaw is squarer and his cheekbones are higher and his eyes are so pale blue as to be almost white. Whether he's smiling or frowning, rewarding a stoolpigeon or threatening an offender, his expression remains as dehumanized as a piece of armor plate. But some people say his wife and kids actually love him.

Brick Shiptick leads the group up the steps of the store with a slow, rolling gait. His black shirt is open at his single inch of throat. The wet spots under his arms reach almost to his belt.

He pauses on the second step below the porch. The others stand one step behind and below him.

"Evening," Brick says, as if, out for an evening stroll, he's happened onto a group of friends. He wipes his forehead and snaps the collected sweat at the ground. "Well," he says, "it seems just about everyone in Sundown's here. Good . . . that

125

means everyone gets the message at the same time. Constable Cotton, here, tells me you people refuse to disperse."

"No one's told us to disperse," Stash says. His voice is slurred, heavy with beer.

Brick turns his head and says, "Constable, you tell these people to disperse?"

"I told them, Brick."

"Ellsworth," Step says, "you're so full of shit it's coming out your ears."

Brick points a finger at Step. "You have any kids here?"

"Three," Step says. "And a kid brother lost his leg in a bear trap three years ago."

"Get them home," Brick says. "Now. It's past curfew."

"Up your ass, Brick."

Step and Cosco and Stash are the three most notorious fighters in Sundown. All are large men, almost as heavy as Brick. They're solid-muscled and quick with fists and feet. Each of them has fought the other more than once since childhood and though their fights brought people from miles around, there is still disagreement about which is the best of the three. Cosco and Stash line up alongside Step. Cosco says, "Brick, you better take that bastard out of here or we'll kick his ass up around his shoulders so he'll have to take off his shirt to shit."

"Cosco," Brick says, "you're under arrest for threatening an officer of the law. Get in the car. And I'm advising you other people: Get your kids home. The law says you're all supposed to be off the streets by ten o'clock. You better be off. Come on, Cosco."

Brick goes toward his car. The other cops, and Ellsworth, lag behind to make sure Cosco follows. He doesn't. One of the cops whispers to Brick, who stops. "Cosco," he says, "I said you're under arrest. You coming peacefully?"

From the alley that runs along the north side of the store about ten miners appear, with rifles and shotguns under their arms. Step, at the left of Cosco, says, "He ain't coming. Not peaceful. Neither's the rest of us. You better go get a couple

126

hundred state dicks, or state pricks, or whatever the hell they're called, to help you."

The other cops swallow hard and stare at each other and whisper support and advice to each other and wait, hopefully, for Brick to back down.

We've all heard stories about Brick having shot several men for resisting arrest. Standing there now, in the summer dusk, Brick and the cops bring the Saturday movies alive. Here are the good guys, on the porch; there are the bad guys, the corrupt vigilantes, on the steps.

Momma comes outside, shouting for me. Poppa pushes her back inside the store. I run down by the gas pumps so Momma can't get to me.

"You coming, Cosco?"

"Nope," Cosco says, grinning as more and more miners take their places in the circle that's formed about him. "Looks like you'll have to come get me, Brick. If you got the guts."

Roman and Goose and I and several other kids move in and mingle with the men, certain that our presence, too, contributes strength. Momma pounds on the window and screams for me to come inside. I work my way to Reuben. He's glancing from one man to another. I step in front of him and he puts his hands on my shoulders. I feel as if I'm in one of those photographs of the workers at the barricades. I stand straighter than I've ever stood, the way Momma keeps shaping my back when I walk through the kitchen. I feel that the inch added to my height this evening will never disappear; I'll be able to distinguish this specific inch from every inch I've grown until now and will grow in the future.

I'm pulled back and aside. Reuben moves past me, toward the front of the crowd. He stands in front of Brick Shiptick. "Brick, if you give me ten minutes to talk to these people, alone, I think I can get Cosco to go with you . . . peacefully."

Brick is a brave man, but he's also sensible. "Ten minutes," he says. He orders Ellsworth and the other cops to follow him to the cars.

Reuben turns to the grumbling crowd. "Wait," Reuben calls, holding up his hands. "Wait! Listen to me!" The crowd grows quiet. Reuben talks in a voice low enough so it won't carry to the cars. "Look . . . I hate the idea of a constable here in Sundown as much as you do. But this is no way to get rid of him and his so-called law."

"How do we do it, Reuben?" Cosco asks, his face hard.

"I'm not sure," Reuben says. "But this is how *not* to do it. With guns, fighting the cops."

"Reuben," Step asks, "you ain't afraid of the cops, are you?"

"Yes," Reuben says. "I am. Brick or any cop doesn't need a reason to kill anyone. It's stupid to get killed for no reason. So you kill him. How many women and kids here would get killed first? And then what? These cops are backed up by the State Police and, if they need it, the National Guard. And if we fight them here, with guns, we lose by every law on every book in every court in the land."

Reuben waits.

Over the years Cosco and Step and Stash, and other miners, have come to him and Jacob for the sort of help near-illiterate men always have to seek from learned men: the explanation of court directives, the clarification of parole papers, Revenue Service warnings, Welfare Service Directives, the replies to letters from other men's wives and lovers.

Step's wife, who's shaped like an hour glass laid on its side, calls out, "What do you suggest, Reuben?"

"Well . . . first I suggest we take up a collection and hire an attorney. I think we ought to take our case to the Township Commissioners. We ought to convince them to cancel Ellsworth Cotton's appointment. With a good attorney we could get more than we'll ever get using guns. Especially using guns on cops."

"That means I go to jail?" Cosco says.

"That means you go to jail. For one night. Maybe two. In the meantime we hire a lawyer."

"If I go to jail I don't want no lawyer from town. You be our lawyer and I'll go. You're smarter than any money-grubbing shyster I ever met."

The crowd shouts approval.

"Yeah," Poppa says, "then they won't have to take up a collection." It's meant as a slur but when everyone, including Reuben, laughs, so does Poppa.

"O.K.," Reuben says. "I'm your man. Cosco, as your attorney, I'll walk you to your car."

The streets and alleys are empty, as Constable Cotton has ordered. He must feel very much the feared gunman as he patrols the town. He doesn't know there's activity in the shadows.

Every ten or fifteen minutes there's a knock on our back door. By eleven o'clock eight miners are in our kitchen. Two of them, Step and Stash, have selected the other six.

Momma's been caught up in the excitement. She's made several pots of coffee and plates of peanut butter sandwiches and cheese sandwiches. She never once complains about the wet jackets and drops of mud on the linoleum. To impress Ellsworth that his laws are being obeyed, Poppa remains, alone, in the well-lit store.

After a brief and competitive exchange of boasts and threats about what will happen to Ellsworth Cotton, the men defer to Reuben.

"What do you think? . . . what's our plan? . . . let's go, Reuben. . . ."

"First," Reuben says, "I think we ought to do this by fair, above-board, democratic methods. But, just in case, we better have a plan in reserve. In case democracy doesn't work."

"What do you mean?"

"I mean we dig up information about every corrupt deal every single commissioner's ever been in or rumored to have been in or was imagined to have been in." Reuben grins at Jacob's expression of dismay and shock. "It's moral blackmail," Reuben says. "Call it 'a threat to tell the truth.'"

The miners at the table sit up. Blackmail? Moral or not, this sounds illicit and attractive.

Momma and Jacob and Max and I sit apart from the others, all of whom are gathered around the table. We're as impressed with Reuben's easy assumption of authority as the men are, but it's a bit jarring for Momma and Poppa, who are surprised and perhaps even pained at his immediate and total involvement with the miners and their needs. This is really a Reuben we've not seen before. We've heard about his debates at the university, we've read his stories, we've sensed a growing distaste with American politics, but here he is in action. Jacob is proud, watching Reuben's theories being expressed in action. Max is curious. It's all a matter of salesmanship. That's all. And Reuben's proving to be a master.

"Blackmail them how?" Stash asks.

"With truthful facts. But we'll blackmail them *only* if they don't give in."

There are meetings every night. Night after night. At each one the accomplishments of the preceding day are discussed as well as the proposals for the next.

Practically everyone in Sundown has a role. There are scouts, messengers and guards. Certain men . . . and women . . . are selected to investigate every inch of Summer Township. Those who have relatives or friends in other towns contact them, in person or by phone, and they, in turn, contact other friends and relatives. Every rumor or bit of gossip or shred of remembered fact anyone, young or old, has ever heard about is tracked down. Those who can not be trusted never learn why the information is being collected.

There are workshops in our kitchen during the day and here the scouts discuss the various tricks . . . tone of voice, ways to phrase questions, specific questions to ask . . . by which hesitant informers might be reassured. The guards, who drive the scouts to Eden and Lick Hill and Meridian and Lyndy, learn how to decoy, how to destroy information and even how to lie, should they be picked up by the police for questioning. The messengers learn how to memorize facts they don't have the time or the talent to put on paper. They carry the details to Reuben, who carefully stores them in an appropriate notebook. When a sympathetic notary public is located in Eden the guards spend many hours driving willing informers to have their stories notarized.

Every night, during these weeks of stealth and secrecy and labor, Ellsworth Cotton patrols the empty streets, swaggering, his revolver at his hip.

At the final meeting . . . the night before the trial . . . Poppa brings several bottles of wine from the cellar. Everyone toasts everyone else. "To victory," Reuben says, and he drinks. He pats a thick looseleaf notebook. "Just about every bit of graft and corruption every member of the Board of Commissioners has ever been involved in. I hope we don't have to use it."

Cosco rubs his hands together. "I hope we do."

People begin arriving at the store at three o'clock even though we're not supposed to be at the hall in Lyndy until seven o'clock.

Poppa's pick-up can only hold twelve but there are other pick-ups, as well as large dump trucks donated by Local 360 of the United Mine Workers. About fifty cars are loaned for the evening by sympathetic supporters in other towns.

From every radiator cap and fender light and radio antenna hang banners . . . paper, cloth and cardboard . . . with slogans printed and painted on them. COTTON IS ROTTEN . . . ELLSWORTH IS WORTHLESS . . . DOWN WITH TYRANTS (This one is mine.) REMEMBER ELECTION DAY (Max's.) . . . ELLSWORTH COTTEN STINKS! (Roman's.)

There is a cowbell or a whistle or a harmonica or an accordion in every car and truck. Roman, who's in our truck, has brought the battered bugle used by his father in World War I.

131

Since our truck—with Momma and Poppa and Reuben in the front seat and Jacob and me (and, tonight, Max), and six others in the back—leads the convoy, Roman sounds the charge. He's been practicing the call for days.

As we climb the hill leading to town I look back. There must be a hundred cars and trucks, every one containing almost twice its normal capacity. Bells are ringing, whistles are blowing, people are singing. The banners stretch out in the breeze. At the bottom of the hill I can see the store. It's empty, as is almost every house in Sundown.

Over the crest of the hill and across the line dividing Sundown from Summer, we pass brick and stone houses occupied by doctors and lawyers and businessmen. Families come out of their houses and stand on their porches. A few of the less restrained children skip along the curb, waving to us, asking what the parade is for. Everyone yells various things at the same time and the kids fall behind, no wiser.

Poppa leads us down Grady Street and up Main. Shoppers and clerks on their way home and farmers hurrying to finish their shopping scamper across the intersections, all of them succeeding somehow in not being run over.

Now and then a voice calls out, "Who the hell's Ellsworth Cotten?" and someone answers, "He thinks he's God!" Someone else calls out, "He aint God, damn if he is!"

In Lyndy the Poles and Czechs and Italians on our trucks exchange noisy greetings with the women and workers in front of the bars and the poolrooms and the gnarled, babushka-covered old ladies resting on the porch stoops. Friends and relatives from other towns join us as we unload in front of the grimy brick building that contains the hall in which the Township Commissioners meet once every month.

The hall has less than two hundred seats and there must be close to a thousand of us. Reuben, flanked by his lieutenants, Step and Stash and Cosco (Reuben in a suit and tie and the three miners in open-throated white shirts), are directed to a

132

long table facing the stage on which the commissioners and their secretary sit.

We file into the room until every chair and bench is packed and then we fill the aisles and jam the doorways and sit on the floor in front of the stage, five and six deep. The secretary . . . a woman named Natalie Lazynski, who had been a friend and classmate of Rachel's and who had once been in love, she said, with Reuben . . . is directed by the commissioners to inform Reuben that he'll have to empty the hall. She comes to the table where he is spreading out his papers. "The commissioners say you must empty the hall," she tells Reuben. She has a heavy accent. She adds, in a whisper, "Don't do it." Reuben nods. Then, for the benefit of the commissioners, Natalie returns to the commissioners and tells them Reuben says he has no right or power to tell these people what to do. The commissioners threaten to call the police or the fire department but it would take an hour for a commissioner to clear a path to a telephone. They finally decide that in order to accomplish their work on other problems they'll have to first dispense with whatever problem concerns this now eerily silent crowd that has them surrounded. An unprecedented and unanimous vote is cast to do away with all rules of order until after the Sundown case.

I'm separated from Momma and Poppa but I can see them. They're in the first row immediately behind the table at which Reuben sits. Momma's support of this entire project has been reluctant. Occasionally she's complained that it cost too much to supply coffee and sandwiches every evening. Poppa's denounced her. She ought to be ashamed. "For the first time," he said, "one of her sons is teaching the *fershtunkene* miners that there's an advantage to an education, there's a better way to settle arguments than with fists or guns. And what does she do? She sits like a monkey with a toothache, moaning, 'Oy . . . oy . . . oy.'" "And you," Momma said, "what's with you? You think suddenly these people, these miners, these *goyim,*

133

will change? Since time began they been any different? Ach," she said, shaking her head, "a man fifty years old, he thinks suddenly the *anti-Semiten*, they'll change. He'll never learn." And Poppa, torn between acknowledging and denying her claims, throws up his hands in disgust. "Go talk sense with a woman," he says.

But here they are, both of them, sitting erect in clean pressed clothes. Momma looks around, sees me and waves.

From the first word Reuben never once hesitates.

He stands erect and in a voice (Momma later describes it as "golden wine flowing from a golden cup") that appeals and then lectures and then denounces and then charms, Reuben talks . . . *sings* is a better word . . . about the American Constitution and the Declaration of Independence and Tom Paine's Rights of Man.

Reuben talks for about twenty minutes, reminding the commissioners that there exists, a few thousand miles to the east, a jack-booted Ellsworth Cotton with a black forelock and an insatiable appetite for tyranny. He makes brief but clear references to the actions and consequences of Galienus and Lysander and Nero and Robespierre and King George the Third. He talks about the origins of law and the responsibilities of elected officials and the inherent rights of men to rebel against evil leaders. In the entire hall not one person yawns or coughs or scratches himself.

When Reuben stops and sits down there is a period of perhaps twenty seconds when no one, not a single soul, moves. Then the people from Sundown explode.

The Chief Commissioner leans forward and exchanges a few brief words with Bud Hardt and the other commissioners. He pleads for silence and finally receives enough to be heard saying, "Thank you for your inspiring presentation. We'll elect a committee to investigate. . . ."

Every single person in the room, even Momma and Poppa, stands and shouts, "No!"

Reuben fights for quiet. Then he speaks again to the commissioners. "We won't accept your appointing a committee. We want action. Tonight. In case you aren't inclined to act tonight let me so incline you." He raises the thick notebook above his head. "This report," he says, "is entitled *Corruption in Local Government.* It consists of one hundred and sixty-seven documented, notarized . . . *notarized,* mind you . . . notarized cases of just about every kind of immorality and illegality a human being might engage in. Charges range from petty larceny to grand theft, from gambling to frequenting houses of prostitution to owning houses of prositution to illegal production and sale of alcoholic beverages to adultery to abortion to a rape of a fourteen-year-old child (a boy), to the manipulation of public funds to falsification of records for the purposes of tax evasion to poll-tampering at election time to the flaunting of postal regulations to . . . need I go on?"

It is as if someone has thrown a switch that activates a single electric outlet into which all seven commissioners are plugged. Each of the seven faces snaps alert, each of the seven bodies stiffens, each of the seven faces pales. One commissioner, oil squeezing out of his voice, suggests that the notebook be brought forward. But another commissioner, supported by a third and a fourth and a fifth, insists that the hands of a public servant ought not be soiled with such trash.

Five minutes later the commissioners decide that Ellsworth Cotten as an ex-constable is preferable to a review of alleged "Corruption in Local Government."

With one tremendous outburst the people of Sundown follow Reuben . . . on the shoulders of Step and Stash and Cosco . . . out of the brick building, onto the street and through Lyndy, singing.

For days there is no other topic. People come from outlying farms and towns to drive past our store in the hopes of catching a glimpse of Reuben. But Reuben is back to work again on his novel.

135

By the last week of August, two weeks before he's due to leave for college, the stack of yellow sheets measures a fraction under three inches. One week before he's to leave he finishes the novel. The very evening he finishes he receives an anonymous telephone call. A woman's voice, with a heavy accent, tells him that the police are planning a raid on our house. They will be searching for anything . . . magazines, newspapers, books, letters . . . that might be used as proof that Reuben is a Communist.

We work all night, under constant reminders by Momma and Poppa that hadn't they predicted this? Were we all happy now? Had Reuben had to go away to college to learn how to destroy his family?

By morning there's not a trace of Marx or Lenin or *The Anvil* or *The Left Front* or letters from fellow writers in the John Reed club.

Reuben wraps his novel in newspaper and then in oilcloth. He binds it with rope and suspends it, from a nail in the underside of the seat, in the toilet pit.

The entire Township Police force, led by Brick Shiptick, makes its raid. They find nothing but a family of yawning, red-eyed Jews. Brick leafs through a copy of *Moby Dick* and, deciding it must be an attack on cops, confiscates the book.

Later in the day Reuben goes to the toilet to retrieve his novel. He returns, his face white, his voice hoarse and weak. The rope has been cut. The novel is lost. He'd burned the carbons.

The following January Ellsworth opens his store. By June, Poppa has no more than five or six customers a day.

Momma stays in the kitchen most of the time. She sits in front of the radio listening to the news of Hitler's armies rushing through Poland, through Rotterdam, into France. Reuben is in the army. Jacob, who'd planned to go to college this September, will ask for a year's deferment and then will go into the army. If he's deferred he'll continue working in the factory.

Max is managing a furniture store in Summer and hopes that his ulcer will keep him exempt.

Each evening Poppa tells us the exact number of customers that have patronized Ellsworth Cotton that day. "Write Reuben," he tells me. "He should know what his college education gets us."

Momma stares at the mahogany box from which a flick of a switch, a twist of a dial, might bring the news that the war has ended.

About My Cousin
Summer, 1940

I lean out of the window until I can see beyond the roof of the store porch to the orange gasoline pumps. Balancing myself on the sill, I shout, "Rome! Hey, Rome!"

A boy appears below, coming from the porch. He strolls out to the pumps, shielding his eyes from the sun as he looks at me.

"I'll be down in ten minutes," I say. "We going to The Canyon?"

"Yeah, we're going to The Canyon," Roman says. "But hurry up. Me and Goose been waiting half an hour."

I pull myself back through the window and race out of my room. I build up enough momentum moving down the hall to conquer the stairway in three leaps. I'm not hungry and I'm anxious to get outside, but Momma will have breakfast for me and I'll eat it. She is easily offended these days, vulnerable to even the slightest suggestion of criticism. Though her brooding withdrawal began almost immediately after Rachel's death, the war and the departure of Reuben seem to have locked her in a despair from which she can not escape. I often catch her

138

staring at me, her eyes almost opaque behind their fear that eventually even I must go. I cannot distract her. I've tried. All I can do is assure her I love her.

Anyway, what does ten minutes more or less mean to us . . . to Roman and Goose and me . . . now? We have the entire summer ahead of us. Today—Monday—June 10—the first day of vacation—we plan to spend the entire day and perhaps even part of the night at The Canyon. I can certainly spare a few minutes now with Momma.

I nudge the door open and step down into the kitchen. Something is wrong. I sense it immediately. Why is Poppa sitting at the table? At this hour of the morning he is always in the store. He hardly ever just sits with Momma any more. Though she's his wife, and they've shared so much of their lives, and there are several languages with which they are both so much more at ease than with English, they rarely talk anymore in any language but English. It is almost as if they've agreed to impose the strictest boundaries on their relationship. But Poppa is sitting here now, and he's been here with her for some time, and they've been talking.

"Hi, Poppa."

Nothing is explained by the smile that appears, after much effort, on my father's lips.

At the stove Momma is absorbed—too absorbed—in breaking eggs.

"Benny, we got something to talk to you."

I wait. Has something happened to Reuben? In his last letter Reuben said that I could have all his German books. Was that a preparation? A will? Had Reuben had an intuitive sense of his death?

I try to convince myself that by concentrating on Poppa's face I can compel the news to be exclusively *good* news. What could it be? Am I going to Aunt Molly's in Philadelphia? It's been five years since . . .

"Your cousin, Herschel . . ."

"Herschel? Herschel who?"

139

"From Europe," Poppa says. "From Poland. You don't remember? A long time now we didn't talk about him."

The only cousins of importance to me at this moment are Morty and Ruthy, who live in Philadelphia.

"He'll be here tomorrow."

I'm not sure whether or not I've said "No" aloud, but I think it. I glance from Poppa to Momma. The expressions are blank and offer no clue. But I know that had I spoken they would be annoyed. At least Poppa would be.

What concerns me is the fact that a relative in the house now would only delay a possible vacation in Philadelphia. And there was a chance for a vacation this summer. Morty had written me. He'd promised that this summer *he* would teach me how to play tennis.

"He's fourteen years old," Momma says. "A year younger than you."

"Two years," I say.

"All the way from Poland," Poppa says, "he's been traveling. Hiding and traveling. All alone." He sighs and gazes into space, and I wonder if there at that vastness on which his vision is focused he sees something shocking, because his eyes close and he shudders and then he forces himself to return to this kitchen and to me. "A whole life," he says. "A whole life I've wasted, praying to a God can do things like this. This kind of God I . . ."

"Enough!" Momma says.

I hear what sounds like a sob from her, but I do not turn to confirm it. Lately there has been little provocation needed to bring long and brooding periods of silent tears. Sometimes she sits for hours at the stove or the window, not moving, not talking, not responding to my questions or complaints. She does not comb her hair, as she used to do when she was bored with sewing or cooking or cleaning or crocheting or writing letters to Aunt Molly. Her hair has lost its sheen; it often lies loose and uncombed and snarled. She does not wait for Friday night any more to light her candles and pray. She lights them any

140

evening, and spends not ten or fifteen minutes in prayer but an hour or more, so that often, to miss the ritual, I sneak out the moment she starts looking at the cupboard in which the special candles are stored.

At her insistence that Poppa not continue his attack upon the God to whom he devoted his life, Poppa pushes his coffee cup aside, sullenly, but he does stop his sacrilege. Momma brings the eggs to me and then she returns to the stove for my toast.

"It will be good to have a baby brother in the house?" she asks. She wants me to say *yes,* so I nod, but my thoughts say *No!* A baby brother! I'll have to drag him behind me all summer. A cousin is not a brother. A Herschel is not a Reuben or a Jacob, or even a Max. That a cousin, a stranger, should be considered a brother is bad enough, but that he should be permitted to ruin my vacation is intolerable. Here it is, the very first day of vacation, and there is every indication I'm going to be saddled with a baby who'll embarrass me in front of Roman and Goose and all the other kids, and who, from all I can guess, will stay all summer. Or even longer.

In a barely controlled, barely audible voice, I ask, "What about Aunt Molly? And Morty and Ruthy? You wrote them I could come in August. Morty promised to teach me to play tennis this summer."

Poppa's fist drops with such force alongside his plate that coffee spills out of his cup and onto the oilcloth covering the table. "Do you know what this war? . . ."

"*Chatzkel,* please."

It's the first time I've heard my mother use Poppa's Jewish name with such force. She usually murmurs the name, as if, originally, it had been a personal word of love. He ignores her. "Do you know what this war, it's about? *Do* you?"

Of course I know what this war's about. Haven't I gone to Summer each time the new draftees parade down Main Street? Didn't I cry, as everyone else in the crowd was crying, when Reuben boarded his bus and went off to the army? Don't I

141

read the letters from Reuben describing his marches and inspections and obstacle courses and combat problems? Don't I read the newspapers and the magazines and don't I go to town every Saturday and see every available war movie? Aren't all my talk and my games and the talk and games of all the other kids in Sundown about battles and weapons and victories and medals? Don't I beam each time Reuben comes home on furlough, tanned and smelling of wool and leather? Don't I, like Momma and Poppa, swallow the lump in my throat each time I steal a glance at the glass-fronted collection of names on the Lest We Forget memorial and see KAHN, REUBEN and, after Reuben's name, three blank spaces waiting for KAHN, JACOB and KAHN, MAX and, best of all, KAHN, BENJAMIN?

"Those letters, from Europe. You remember them?"

"No, I don't."

"Those letters," Poppa says, "two years ago. The ones you asked me about, with those stamps. They'll tell you good, what this war's about. What it is to be a Jew. You ask me, you become every day more *goy* than Jew."

Though I want to say *I don't ask you,* I know better. I have too many reasons to recall how fast his hands move, and how, sometimes, one of his words or glances can be even more painful than a blow. But my mother, of all people, replies. And in her defiance she regains some of her fire, some of her noble beauty. "Always it's him, or me, or someone else you blame for everything. Why blame him he's more *goy?* He's not *Bar-Mitzvahed* . . . no? Who quit praying six years ago? Who put away his *tallith*, his *tfillin*, he doesn't use them any more, he doesn't go to *schul?* Him? No. You! Who let him quit *cheder* he was twelve years old? Who keeps him out here three miles from a *schul*, from a rabbi? He's got only *goyim* around him, to listen to, to play with, so it's his fault he's more *goy* than Jew? What do you want from him, Chatzkel?"

"So. Now it comes. I'm to blame for everything. Me."

Momma clenches her hands at her mouth and shouts through her fingers, "What do you want?"

142

"I want a son he should know the truth! That's what I want. He should think a war it's all games, parades, bugles? Look at him. His cousin—his whole *mishpoche* is lost so he comes lives with us, *us*—strangers!—all he has in this stinking world. And what does this one say? *I want to play tennis.*"

"All right. You want he should say what you say? What I say? He should know what we know? God forbid he should be filled with such memories, such dreams every night like you got, like I got." I've never seen my mother confront him like this before. Not even before Rachel died. Reuben told me that before I was born and when I was a baby, when the store was a success and Poppa was not filled with such bitterness against the miners and his family and himself, there was always laughter in our house. Momma and Poppa used to dance and sing together and exchange jokes and even hold hands. It's almost impossible for me to believe they were ever anything but melancholy and bitter and desolate.

Momma's voice, which had been almost shrill, begins to waver. "This is not 1900. He don't stand on a ship watching the sky for the Statue of Liberty. On a ship packed like dead sardines. Has he ever starved—not just for a day but for weeks? For months?" Her voice is barely more than a whisper. "Has he slept in a room, kicking rats? Has he run from Cossacks? Has he seen . . . like you saw . . . like I saw . . . bayonets in his momma . . . a club over Poppa's head?" She sways back and forth, and her lips move several times before the words come out, "How can he know what it is, to be a Jew?"

Were thunder to burst from Poppa's mouth and lightning flash from his eyes I'd not be surprised. But, with only the momentum of his anger carrying him, his voice perched already on the edge of submission, he manages to say, "*I want to learn to play tennis:* that's what he says." Then, before my eyes, he seems to dissolve. He seems to be very old. His mustache was shaved off long ago but only now am I aware that his lips appear shrunken. What had once—last year? the year

143

before?—been dark bristles over his eyes have only now, this moment, turned gray, only now begun to wilt. I recall a hundred vivid scenes that display his energy, his astonishing strength . . . and here he is, slumped in his chair, small and old, old and vulnerable. What was once a solidly muscled, heavily calloused hand reaches out, touches my head, pushes my hair back from my forehead, cups my chin in soft fingers. The gesture, the touch, wrenches me back to a day, an hour, a moment when Rachel's fingers touch my face (and I think . . . I thought then . . . *her skin feels as if she's wearing velvet gloves*). "Ah," Poppa says. "A new generation. She's right, maybe. You don't know . . . you'll never know. Maybe . . . who can say? . . . it's for the best."

On our way to The Canyon Roman and Goose talk about everything we'll do this summer. There are the two shanties already built in the woods but they want to build one more, a tree house high in the giant oak near Devil's Dip. They want to dig a cave in the clay pits; a big one with rooms. They want to build a raft and find out if they can float down the Connequenessing Creek to the Monongahela River and on to Pittsburgh. The maps in my geography book show it can be done but Roman and Goose, long out of school and even longer in contempt of books, want to find the truth by themselves.

I walk with them but remain outside their rough, boisterous play. I'm content skipping rocks. It's the one accomplishment in which I am superior to Roman. Each time I throw now I count the skips but I can never better my April record of eleven.

Like Goose and Roman I wear what will practically be a uniform for the next three months: pants and sneakers, with swimming trunks dangling from a pocket. The weather has been warm enough for swimming only the past three weekends but all of us have copper-red bodies already.

"Hey," Roman asks. "You mad or something?"

144

"No."

"Well, you act it. First day of vacation, you act like it's first day of school tomorrow."

I shrug and examine the four flat stones in my hand, trying to decide which can break the record. Roman and Goose grab me and try to tickle me but I push them away. "Leave me alone." Roman trips Goose and runs and Goose, calling to me for support, chases Roman. Dodging and twisting and turning, they race along the banks of the Connequenessing.

I go on alone, grateful for the chance to skip my stones, and to think. I'm tired. Not tired so much, that isn't it. I just feel empty. I'm not sure why I feel this way. I wish it were the old days . . . with Rachel alive, and Reuben home. It has been so long since there has been anything like a festive Friday night dinner that I actually wonder if the ones I recall are not just fantasies. The kitchen is no longer sparkling clean, the store has many shelves that are empty and sometimes a whole day will go by without anyone in the entire building—the store and the house—except Momma and Poppa and me. Sundown has changed too. Many of the men have enlisted or been drafted. Saturday night is no wilder now than any night, and all the nights are strangely reminiscent of visits to a haunted house, where bats fly and hinges creak and dust lies on every surface.

I drop the stones I have and search for more stones, I hear Goose curse and then I hear Roman reply. Today, for once, their jokes and punches and exchanges of insults annoy me. Over the years the constant reminders that the *goyim* are dull-witted and uncouth and vicious and deceitful seemed to bounce off my skin, leaving me filled with resentment not for the kids like Roman and Goose but for those who made the repeated charges, Momma and Poppa and the Jews in Summer, the old Jews sitting in the *schul* or standing outside the kosher butcher shop. But now, today, walking here along the creek, I wonder if there might not be real truth in their

145

descriptions of the *goyim*. I find myself wishing that somehow, before my cousin's arrival tomorrow, their behavior might be quickly refined.

I hear my name called. Roman and Goose are waving for me to hurry. When I do not respond they wave in disgust and walk on, again pushing and punching each other.

Will they push and punch Herschel? Will they try to victimize him? Will he be the target of those ambiguous remarks that are honed so fine it's impossible to know whether they're facetious or serious? In the last year or so, especially since the war has started in Europe, it has seemed to me that the remarks have become more explicit. So explicit that three times in the last few months, I've been in fistfights. For a while, before that, not because I was afraid to fight but because I thought that victory in fights did nothing to ease the pain, I simply pretended not to hear the remarks about my nose and my hair and Poppa's trickery at the cash register and the comic ability of Jews to squirm their way out of combat in the army. When it was not possible to pretend I'd not heard the remarks I'd even joined the others and contributed my own share of innuendo. Late at night, in bed, my face burning, I was ashamed of myself and wished I'd fought.

Now, hearing the laughter of Goose and Roman, I wonder what I will do if they tease or challenge Herschel. I skip a stone across the water. It careens once and sinks. I scowl down at the water until its surface resettles itself. If they treat Herschel like that . . . just once . . . I'll kill them.

The Canyon was created a year before, in 1939, when the state constructed a highway between Summer and Lake Erie. One section of the highway, passing through the woods between Summer and Sundown, included a viaduct which spans the Devil's Dip, a valley at the bottom of which lies the Bessemer and Lake Erie Railroad tracks and the Connequenessing Creek.

During the construction of the highway thousands of tons of

146

dirt were dumped on both sides of the creek for a distance of a mile or more. The banks rise thirty and forty feet beneath the viaduct and often come to within a foot or two of touching the underside. Because of the railing and the steep banks no one in the automobiles can see the swimmers in the pool below.

The first time I swam there I said something about its being like the Grand Canyon and from then on it has always been referred to as *The Canyon.*

No matter what time of the day we're there The Canyon is always in dense shadow, either from the viaduct or from one of the banks. For a mile or more the water flows under arching willows, never warmed by the sun, and on the brightest days, when the water is the clearest, it is impossible to see the bottom. There is an air of danger about The Canyon, as if it has a reputation for disaster which, for some reason, we can acknowledge but cannot submit to. Of all the kids in Sundown only Goose and Roman and I remain unintimidated.

Normally, we would object to someone's proposing a walk of two additional miles just to go swimming. Had we objected, and never gone, no one would have blamed us. We could have said that the high, steep clay banks made the pool inaccessible. We could have given several reasons for shunning The Canyon, as everyone else in Sundown shuns it, but the fact that Roman and Goose and I were considered the bravest kids in Sundown forced us to prove our bravery. It took some time, and some planning, but we did it.

The climb down the banks to the pool was no problem at all. The climb up tested the last ounce of agility and endurance. In the rain, of course, the banks became smooth and glassy, and though a descent was like the wildest dip on a roller coaster, a climb of much beyond four or five feet was impossible. When we tried approaching The Canyon by swimming or wading to it from above or below, one or all three of us ended up bruised or badly scratched by the chunks of concrete, broken bottles or rusted cans that had been deposited in the water during the construction.

147

Roman and Goose and I had made several night raids on the storage depots of the construction company. We made off with enough lumber, tarpaper, nails and tools to build several shanties and rafts. We also took several buckets of tar and sheets of tin which we never expected to use but which, like the other materials, were simply there to be stolen. It was more fortunate for my mother and father than for me that we always carried off our raids successfully. Capture of Goose and Roman would only have verified all the charges about *goyim,* but capture of me would probably have brought charges of deceit and anti-Semitism upon the police.

So, three weeks before the vacation started, there we were, with all these materials. I suggested we use the tin and tar to make our own canoes so we could then move to and from The Canyon this summer quickly and easily, in sun or rain. Roman and Goose were enchanted. We spent several evenings and each of those three weekends, cutting and shaping and securing our canoes. On the last Sunday before vacation we had three successful canoes and that day we made three trips to and from The Canyon, where we swam in perfect seclusion, waving and shouting at the invisible cars above us. Not far from the regular swimming holes used by the rest of the kids from Sundown we found suitably secret little harbors under the willow branches in which to conceal the boats. Not just the canoes will be ours, exclusively, we agree, but so will The Canyon. We will be the envy of all the kids in Sundown.

The summer opening up before us promised to offer more fun than any summer that had ever been or ever would be.

But now there will be my cousin, Herschel.

I walk past the bunch of willows Roman uses to conceal his canoe and past those used by Goose. The canoes are gone.

I walk to where my own is tied. I leap from the bank to the thick branch of a willow, walk out to the middle and drop down into my boat. I sit very still, listening to the flies. A mos-

148

quito hovers above my arm and then settles on my wrist. I catch the insect between my fingers, am careful not to crush it, and I lie back. My hand drops into the water. I look up through the branches. The bright sunlight is a faint but constant twinkling through the branches and twigs and leaves.

My hand is still in the water, the fingers still pinched together, when I hear Roman's voice, and then Goose's. I open my eyes. The sun is behind a cloud. I've been asleep. I lift my hand. My fingers still hold the drowned mosquito.

I do not say a word when Roman and Goose pull back the branches. "Ah-hah," Roman says. "There you are."

Goose slaps the flat face of his paddle onto the water, sending a spray up over me. "What's the matter with you?" he asks.

"Nothing. What time is it?"

"About noon."

I pull myself up onto the branch and I stand there a moment, balancing myself. "Do you have to yell and curse and punch all the time?"

Roman and Goose, puzzled, burst out laughing. They purse their lips and slap daintily at each other. "Ooh," Roman says, "dear me. Goose, you said a dirty word."

Goose minces about in his boat like a little girl. "You sonofabitch, I did not. I never curse." He slaps Roman. "And I never punch. So there!"

They perform with such energy that they upend their canoes. They continue laughing as they swim about in the water and work their canoes back to the surface.

I promise to help in the store while Poppa drives his truck to Summer, where he's to meet Herschel at the bus station. But I'm not of much help to Momma. Occasionally I reach a box down from a high shelf or lift a heavy sack onto the counter, but most of the time I just lean against one of the porch posts, my eyes on the black macadam road down which, any minute now, Poppa will be bringing my cousin.

Despite their insistence that I go with them to The Canyon,

149

I finally convince Roman and Goose to go on alone. There are other invitations from other kids to go berry-picking or junk-collecting but I refuse them also.

Two miners who've worked overtime on the night shift and have not yet made it home sit on a bench at one end of the porch. I try to ignore them as they sit there, hunched over, the whites of their eyes glistening in their dusty black faces. Each of them holds a pint of vanilla ice cream they've bought from my mother. As they eat, grunting and burping, a white web of melted ice cream expands along their black hands and wrists.

During the night, while I lay in bed, trying to sleep, thinking—no matter how hard I tried not to—of the sounds of Rachel's heels in the hallway, the call of her voice as she kisses my cheek—thinking of Reuben marching along a country road in Georgia, of Jacob working ten- and twelve-hour shifts at the factory, of Max bemoaning, daily, the advantages he'll lose if he's drafted—while I lay there thinking of these things and all the while hearing Momma mumbling in her sleep and now and then crying out, and hearing Poppa snoring and coughing up his quota of asthmatic phlegm—while I lay there in bed these two men on the porch were burrowing like moles under the hillsides. Now they would sleep, while Momma and Poppa twisted the dials on the radio from one station to another and cringed at each mention of words like *Nazi* and *Hitler* and *Gestapo* and *SS*. Such words occupy not even the tiniest niche in the vocabularies of these men. What do they know about the tragedies of Herschel, my cousin? About the million Herschels? What do they care? They will continue pushing the ice cream into their faces and then, when presented with the bill on payday, will deny that they bought it or will delay the payment just as so many of them have denied and delayed for years. And when I'm gathered with them on the porch some night and Poppa's not near, they'll begin their sly winks and nudges and suggestions about Poppa's hidden treasure and Reuben's efforts to get out of the infantry. I wonder how I should prepare Herschel for such duplication and continuation of the tortures he's probably been led to believe he'll never know again.

"Here comes Cowboy Kahn."

Angry that it has been one of them who first sees the truck I try to convince myself it's not Poppa. But it is. The truck has emerged from the woods at the top of the hill and is rolling down the macadam road, just barely managing to keep its lead over the blue smoke chasing behind it. About now, I think, Poppa will be turning off the ignition. With gasoline rationed Poppa conserves it this way on every downgrade.

The truck, its motor idle, drifts past the gasoline pumps. It comes to a halt at the concrete steps.

I'm tempted to steal inside the store, to pretend to myself that I am needed there now. But my fingers lock me to the porch post.

Poppa opens the door of his truck and steps down from the running board. He is grinning. He seems buoyant; even, somehow, younger. I leap from the porch, race to the truck, stop and then walk forward.

Herschel has descended from the truck. He is intent on examining the tread of the truck's rear tire. His eyes dart to me and back immediately to the tire.

"He speaks Polish," Poppa says. "And Yiddish. You see, you little *tuches*, you. You went to *chadir*, you learned Yiddish, maybe you could talk, you and him." He hugs me to him and wiggles a finger at Herschel, beckoning him toward us.

He is short—shorter even than Goose—and very thin. At first I feel that he does not keep his head up because he's too weak. There are dark shadows not just under his eyes but above them. His sharp little beak of a nose and his pinched lips, below those recessed and haunted eyes, give him the appearance of a frightened mouse. He wears shorts and a shirt and jacket and open-toed sandals. On a tag pinned to his jacket are printed, in crayon, the words:

151

GOLDBOGEN, HERSCHEL
c/o C. Kahn
R. F. D. 2
Sundown, PENNSYLVANIA
U.S.A.

The screen door slams. Momma appears. She hesitates one brief moment and then, half laughing, half crying, she rushes down the steps, her arms open wide.

"Milk," I say, pointing at the bottle.

"Me-ilk."

"No." And I can't help giggling. "Not me-ilk. Milk. Say Mill. Mill."

We say the word together. Then, together, we review the five words we've been practicing from the first moment we first sat at the table. "Meat . . . salt . . . pepper." I point at each as I say the word. "Bread . . . sugar. . . "

During the lesson Momma and Poppa sit, silent, admiring their nephew. First from the front and then from the side. Then from the rear. Then it is time to start all over again from the front. Patting his head, forcing more milk upon him, more salami, more chicken, more bread, more cake. Squeezing his shoulder, hugging him, kissing his cheek. Clucking their tongues, sighing deeply, not sadly now but happily. It is as if, suddenly, all the drapes have been pushed aside, all the doors and windows opened, and what has been a dark room is now sunny and airy and filled with joy.

Momma and Poppa chatter with each other as they haven't for many months, and between themselves as well as with Herschel they speak Polish. But Herschel devotes almost all of his attention to me and my instruction. I enjoy emotions I'd never expected in myself. I too want to hug him, to touch him. I want to reassure him that all the terror is past. I want to start him immediately on his new life of happiness. A new life of fun. "Momma, can I take Herschel swimming?"

152

"He's been here three hours. Swimming already? No, no. . . ."

"He's been here four hours. Please, please? We'll be back early. Please?" I face Herschel. "Swim?" I ask. "Swim? You know." And I bend forward to demonstrate my crawl stroke.

"Ah . . . *plywac*." And he demonstrates his own stroke, nodding for emphasis.

"See? See, Momma? Please?"

"But rain's coming. The weatherman . . ."

"It won't rain. And if it does . . ."

Herschel bounces off his chair, beaming first at Momma and then at Poppa, talking to them in rapid Polish. It's evident to me that he's pleading with them. It's also obvious that he will get, from now on, anything he wants.

"Why not?" Poppa says. "Why not? The sooner he forgets" —and Poppa waves a hand toward the wall, toward Pittsburgh, toward the ocean, toward Europe—"all that, the better."

I rush to embrace Poppa. So does Herschel. He turns and hugs Momma, who is so overcome with a mixture of affection and relief and plans and promises that she babbles, between her laughs and her giggles and her hugs and her kisses, in Polish and in Yiddish and in Russian and even in English. She starts to say a word in German but stops. For one very brief moment we are all aware of the squeeze of tension, but then, with a hug and a Polish word, she tries to lift Herschel, who is, for once, someone smaller than she is. Poppa laughs so hard he leans back too far and his chair topples over and when we all run to make sure he's not hurt he lies where he's fallen, still laughing.

As we trot along the road leading to the Connequenessing Creek, I bombard Herschel with words which he, in turn, repeats over and over. Once, when I howl at his pronunciation, Herschel points at a stone. *"Kamien."*

"That's easy," I say. *"Kamien."*

153

He nods, approving. He plucks a blade of grass and displays it in his thin white palm. *"Trawa."*

"Trawa," I repeat. He nods again.

Pointing at my eye he says, with a grin, *"Bronzowe oko."*

I stumble over the pronunciation and Herschel jumps up and down, spilling tinkling laughter between his fingers, which he holds against his mouth.

Swinging an arm about his thin and bony shoulders, I receive, in return, an arm around my back. We trot across the field.

Since Herschel's not been exposed to much sun Momma has insisted he wear a shirt. To put him at ease I wear one too. I remove my shirt now and hang it from my belt. Herschel does the same. He wears an old pair of my sneakers instead of sandals and when he sees that I find it funny to hear them flap with each step he exaggerates his stride to make them flap louder. Ah, in three weeks . . . in one week . . . he'll be husky and tough and . . . and happy.

I step from the bank to the willow branch. With my finger to my lips I signal for Herschel to be silent. Lowering myself to my hands and knees, I move along the branch. I swing into the canoe. Then I help Herschel swing down. I hold the canoe stable until Herschel is seated.

Parting the branches, I peer up and down the creek. I bring the branches together and signal Herschel again to be quiet.

The sound of paddles can be heard before the sound of the voices. Roman is singing. "You are my sunshine, my only sunshine, you make me happy . . ."

"Hey, Rome." That is Goose's voice.

"What?"

"We ought to hide his boat."

"Nah."

"C'mon, let's hide his boat."

"Nah, I'm tired.'

"You're yellow, you mean."

154

The slap of the paddle on the water is followed by a burst of laughter. More splashing is followed by more laughter. Then silence. Minutes later Roman is singing again, only this time he is farther downstream. Then his voice, and Goose's too, are on the bank, far away.

I wink at Herschel, who sits rigid and wide-eyed. I smile. He relaxes. I untie the rope holding the boat to the willow, lift the paddle from under the seat and push away from the bank. The canoe moves out from under the branches and into the light. The sun is behind a cloud. A short ride, I promise myself, and then we'll go home.

As we move upstream the air grows heavier. Herschel slides off his seat until he's almost flat on his back. He drags his hands through the water. Once I guide the boat close to shore and point. Herschel sees the little wall-eyed frog clinging to the reed. He reaches out to grab it. The frog leaps. Herschel laughs, making no effort to fend off the water. "Ssh," I say, and he repeats it, "Ssh." We continue upstream. A water snake, head erect and out of the water, glides toward the opposite bank, leaving behind a zigzag of delicate ripples.

A minute more, I promise myself. After that there's another minute. A slight breeze rises, cool against my skin, but Herschel does not notice it. He sits in the boat, hands in the water. He seems so serene, almost asleep. There is a thin, delicate smile on his lips and I am elated at the fact that I have succeeded so early in demonstrating the kindness and calmness and fun in store for him here with me, with us, in Sundown.

The boat glides over a space of clear green water. Herschel glances down. In his excitement he almost overturns the boat. Below, to the side, a school of perch swim in easy, perfect formation. He dips his hand down and they break formation and scatter. And disappear. He groans and seems to feel he must apologize, but when he sees admiration on my face he relaxes.

I do stop paddling, though, and I point at the twisted steel rods also visible below us. As well as rusted fragments of steel barrels. With a stern face I point at the rods and the barrels

155

and wave an admonishing finger at Herschel. I shake my head and go through my swimming motions. Herschel nods and says, gravely, *"Nie plywac."*

"Right," I say, "I think. *Nie plywac."*

I stop paddling, trying to decide if the sound I hear is thunder. It is. I start to turn the canoe but Herschel, upset, waves frantically and shakes his head. *"Nie, nie, nie."*

"More?" I ask, pointing upstream.

"Ya, ya." He sets his mouth. "More." It comes out as *mawr.* I laugh and continue paddling.

"More," I say, over and over, and he repeats it over and over.

There are a few drops of rain. Then, abruptly, it is raining hard. Herschel spreads out his arms and lifts his face. He catches the rain in his open mouth. His pink tongue reaches for every drop. He squeals and hugs himself.

The boat rocks in the growing current and wind. The rain sweeps down. Faster. Harder. The creek banks are slimy-blue in the lightning flashes. We round the last bend; there lies The Canyon. I can barely see the concrete slabs and arches of the viaduct above us but I can hear, above the sounds of the storm, the occasional squeal of brakes and the sodden bleating of a horn.

"Plywac?" I ask.

He laughs and his head bobs up and down. I pull off my soaked trousers and sneakers and with an ease born of practice I arch up and over the rim of the canoe and into the water. I shoot far down and when I turn to go up I see Herschel's body coming toward me. We dart away from each other. A few seconds after I break the surface Herschel's head appears. Between his gasps of delight he rattles off several sentences in Polish and then remembers that I can not understand. He dives underwater. I dive after him.

We chase each other underwater and then, on the surface, we splash and chase each other, calling out in Polish and English through the rain. We tag and chase each other, and then,

156

fatigued, we rest, treading water, each permitting the other to float free. We lie on our backs, our faces up to the rain.

Lightning punches through the sky and Herschel, shouting, "Boom! Boom!" punches his tiny fists back at the lightning. Then he arches his body and his skinny white flanks and buttocks slide beneath the water.

I wait, my fist shaped like a pistol, forefinger extended. I intend to shout *bang!* when he appears. I try to predict the point at which he'll surface. When he does appear I start to say *bang!* but I stop. Herschel's head is bent back and he's howling. I think he's hurt but then I decide he can't be and I howl back at him. But he's not playing. He is mumbling to himself in Polish and seems very troubled.

"What's wrong?" I call.

He points down, talking rapidly, trying to explain something. I swim to him. Floating on his back he holds his left leg in the air. A thick string of flesh, torn from his calf, hangs free, remaining attached only at the heel. Blood is pouring down the suspended strip of flesh and into the water. I whirl to grab the canoe. It is gone.

I panic. I start swimming downstream, driven as much by the urge to recover the canoe as to find help. But then I stop. Be calm, I remind myself. Reuben's sentence, in his last letter to me, said that: "Stay calm. Always. No matter what. In a crisis a calm idiot's better company than an hysterical genius."

I wave for Herschel to follow me. I start swimming downstream. He swims, too, until the water becomes too shallow. We wade. I lead, feeling ahead with my toes for other debris.

I glance back. Herschel is sitting in the water, his knees up, his arms around his knees, his head in his arms. I go back. *Calm . . . calm . . . stay calm!*

At my touch Herschel struggles to lift his head. He mutters something and lets his head fall back on his arms.

I dash through the water to the bank. I must get to the viaduct. I must stop a car. I must . . . I must get help. But at the edge of the bank my feet slide from under me in the wet clay

157

and I glide back into the water. I leap up and charge the bank but I slide back. On my hands and knees I try to punch out holes for my feet, so I might work my way up the bank, but as soon as I have the hole dug the slimy gray clay moves in to fill it.

Herschel's no longer sitting. He's lying down, on his side. His chin is almost touching the water. I fight my way back to him, feeling but not caring about a quick sharp pain in my foot. I lift Herschel's body and try to run through the water. But the water's deep again and Herschel's body tumbles out of my arms. I clutch his hair and drag him back to the shallows. I prop him up and call to him and he opens his eyes. The rain is pouring down his face and the lightning flashes with no color across his gray face.

I scream and in my hysteria I find some power that propels me up the bank, far beyond the point I've gone before, ten or fifteen feet from the top. But then I'm on my back, sliding down the incline, shooting across the water. I leap up, crying out for help. I lean back and cup my hands around my mouth and scream, how many times I don't know. The only replies are the sounds of the rain and the wind and the horns on the viaduct above me.

I clutch Herschel to me. I try to hold him in my arms but he slips through, like a fish. I carefully lift him again and I sit there, my arms about his skinny body.

They bury Herschel on a Thursday. A rain that's not much more than a heavy mist has been shifting about in the air all day.

"Ashes to ashes," the rabbi sings. "Dust unto dust."

When they lower the coffin I turn away. Reuben, who's come home for the funeral, stands on one side of my mother, supporting her. Jacob is on the other side. Max, beside me, is crying. (He'd not even had a chance to talk to Herschel.) Momma, limp, barely conscious, gives out little whimpering sounds now and then. For a phrase or two, she ac-

158

companies the rabbi in his chant. Poppa, shoulders drooped, stands beside me. He can not seem to tear his eyes away from the mud on his shoes.

When we return to the cars several Jews from Butler guide Reuben and Jacob and Momma and Poppa around the mud puddles. Some of the Jews continue to pray; some are weeping.

I move ahead, like everyone else, but I'm dazed. I bump into what I think must be a tree. Looking up I recognize, after a second or two, that it's Poppa. He is staring down at the mud. He lifts one foot and drops it, splashing me and several others. He lifts the other foot, drops it, and considers the mud that's sliding down his trousers. Then, with one foot and then with the other, he stomps the mud, again and again. He raises his eyes to the sky as Mr. Salomon and Mr. Ginsberg and Mr. Sadler, from Summer, take hold of him and try to calm him. He tears free and races down the road. He stops under the green-black bough of a pine tree and lifts his fist and shakes it at the sky. "You sonofabitch," he screams.

He continues screaming until the rabbi and several other men succeed in getting him into a car.

I climb into a Buick that waits, black and glossy, under the dark dripping pines.

All the way home I sit in the car and peer through the window at the sky.

About Max
Spring, 1941

"You want a suit?"

A pair of gray trousers fly through the air, followed by a gray coat.

"Me? A suit for me?" I pull on the coat before Max can change his mind. It's loose about my shoulders (in fact, the shoulder pads fall over my biceps), but I have a suit. A *suit!*

The trousers are tapered so severely from the knees to the ankles that I have to take off my shoes to get the cuffs over my feet. I can push my fist and forearm into the space between my body and the fly of the trousers.

But . . . it's a suit. And it's mine.

"Honest, Max? Are you really giving it to me?"

"Yeah, it's too tight on me. Anyway, I'm tired of it. I'm getting a new one."

I tilt the small mirror Max uses when he shaves. To examine myself from ankle to neck I have to walk clear across the room and bend my knees.

"It's glen plaid," Max says.

I thought it was too good to be true. "Whose?" I ask.

Max looks puzzled. Then he chuckles. "Glen plaid . . . it's the name of a material. The pattern."

I sigh, relieved. "I thought you meant it really belongs to a guy named Glen Plaid."

A sharing of laughter, such as this, is rare between us. Max, too often a victim of the gentle but usually unrestrained contempt of Reuben or Jacob or Poppa (whose contempt is not usually gentle and never restrained), has often let the contempt sift through onto me. He and I have never been close, certainly not as close as the others of us have been with each other.

Max was twenty-one a month ago. He'll be able to vote in November. Is it that responsibility that's matured him, that's mellowed him? His arguments with Poppa have been less severe. He has offered to help finance Reuben's expenses when Reuben is through with his year of military service and returns to college. He even seems to have cultivated a sense of his own self: yesterday he informed me (though he's yet to inform Reuben or Jacob) that just because he's their younger brother, and someone who's always relied on their advice, they shouldn't take him for granted. They don't have his vote in their pocket. "I'm not interested in who's liberal and who's reactionary. I want to know who takes what stand on business." He performs as if I'm a politicking congressman anxious to be given the thousands of votes it is in his power to deliver.

I continue turning, bending, leaning, in a fruitless effort to see all of myself in the mirror at one time.

Max, not interested in my preening, goes downstairs. I follow behind him, wearing the suit so Momma might appreciate the evidence of the new comradeship of her two sons, but she's sitting on the back porch, in the swing, a blanket wrapped about her, asleep.

Max, at the kitchen table, selects those parts of the *Pittsburgh Sunday Press* he's not yet read.

"Wow! Who's this?"

I admire a photograph I just found in the jacket.

161

Max grabs the photograph and jams it into his pants pocket.

"A girl friend?" I ask. I'd seen the inscription. It had read: TO MAX, WITH LOVE AND KISSES. FROM MARY.

"Don't *nudge* me. You want the suit, wear it. You don't want it, take it off."

Max, I know, can be moved by a word to cancel the decision to which, a few minutes before, he'd been firmly committed. I say no more.

Before supper, as usual, Max drives to town. After he's gone I take one of his shirts and one of his ties. Just to try on. But I look so debonair I decide to keep them on. Then I decide that, since I've dressed, I might as well go into town.

To improve the drape of the jacket I have to keep my shoulders pulled back. To keep my trousers from falling I have to bulge out my stomach. After keeping these postures for an hour the muscles in my back are ready to tear loose from the bones.

Holding up my trousers, I walk home through the darkness, so preoccupied with my new elegance that I don't hear the usual night noises in the woods. Normally these mysterious sounds would still, at the age of seventeen, lift the hair at the back of my neck.

Max has less contact with the people in Sundown than Reuben or Jacob or I have. He has his own car, which he bought on credit several months before, and now he's hardly ever home. He leaves early every morning to go to Summer, to work, and he rarely returns before midnight. By then the store's closed and Momma and Poppa are in bed.

He works all day Saturday. On Sunday he sleeps until noon. Sometimes, just before he goes to town Sunday evening, he might sit on the porch for a minute or two with Goose and Roman and me. Usually he just waves as he goes past us on his way to his car.

"Max," Roman says, "he ain't ever here. I was him, I'd live in town."

162

Poppa shares that opinion. "Max, he lives here? Who can tell?"

It irritates Poppa to see Max actually making money as a salesman. Though he'd throw it back in Max's face (he says) were Max to offer him money, Max never does offer it. And so Poppa's pride is shored up by a strength he can be pretty certain will never be challenged.

"I ran into Nettie Schapiro."

It's Sunday and Max is eating breakfast, even though it's midafternoon. He's on his second bowl of cornflakes.

"You hear, Max?"

"Uhmhumm. You ran over Nettie Schapiro."

"I ran *into* Nettie Schapiro."

"*Gottsadahnke.* I'm happy for both of you."

"It seems to me a man, he wants to be a success of a salesman, he'd marry a nice Jewish girl."

Max wipes his face but does not rub away the suspicion. "What's that supposed to mean?"

Momma shrugs. "It means . . ."

"Nettie Schapiro told you she saw me with a *shiksa.*"

"It was none of her business. She said so. But . . ."

"Right. It was none of her business. But she still had to talk about it. So the next time Nettie Schapiro tells you . . ."

"A girl like that you want for a wife?"

"Momma, I don't want Angie for a wife. I don't intend to marry her. She's a friend. That's all. A friend."

"I knew. I told Nettie . . . believe me, he'll never marry a *shiksa.* Not a son of mine."

Max pushes his cereal bowl aside and he goes to the landing of the stairway that leads upstairs. As he stomps up the stairs I can hear him muttering, "Damn . . . damn . . . damn . . ."

At supper Momma shares her concern with Poppa, Jacob and me. "Max . . . this *shiksa* . . . I bet she tricks him. She catches him."

Poppa, who's been sucking marrow out of a large soupbone, looks up from his work, his cheeks moist and glistening. "Crap to crap," he says. "I ain't surprised."

"Go ahead," Momma says. "You gotta talk like that? Talk like that pushes him out of the house. Why you gotta talk like that? He's your son, your flesh. You treat him worse than Yenta."

Poppa considers the best route of approach to the remaining caves of succulent marrow. "A boy treats his poppa . . . from when he's old enough to talk . . . like *he's* the poppa . . . there's no respect. No pride. Nothin. I wanted I should *teach* him respect, but no! You knew!"

"Teach him, teach him, he says. With a stick he'd teach him. With a fist! By him everything's taught with a fist. *Love* you don't teach with a fist. Hate, yes. Love, no."

"Look," Jacob says. "Max is twenty-one. He's a man. He can do what he wants."

"He wants to marry a *shiksa!*" Momma proclaims, horrified.

"He wants to marry a *shiksa* he'll marry a *shiksa.*" Jacob replies. "What the hell can you or I or anyone else do about it?"

Momma gives a wistful glance at the thick soup she made for supper. I think she'd really like some but by now she's gotten so used to giving up her share, so *we* can have enough, that so much as a spoonful loads her shrunken stomach.

"I don't know," she says. "With Herschel! . . . He saw what they did to Herschel. I thought: now he'll see—Jews got to help each other. Got to save each other. Our only hope."

"Momma," Jacob says. "What happened with Herschel has nothing to do with Max. If you want to cry and pray about what happened to Herschel, if you want to hate the Germans . . . go ahead. But it doesn't have *any*thing to do with Max."

"Scum," Poppa says. "Let him marry. Scum to scum."

"Don't talk like that," Momma shouts. "He's your own flesh. You should be proud."

"I'll talk," Poppa says, setting his marrow bone aside and

164

wiping his hands on the towel that has now become a communal napkin. "Scum. I should be proud I got scum for a son?"

Momma closes her eyes and bends her head, refusing to acknowledge the existence of the sounds she's just heard.

"Momma," I say, "Max promised you. He said he won't marry a *shiksa*. He promised."

"Promises. His promises are nothing."

"I told you," Poppa says, at the entrance to the store. "Scum. You agree."

"I don't agree. He's a good boy! Max is a good son!"

"Scum!"

"Jacob, what do you think?" I ask.

"About what?"

"About Max and Angeline."

"Do you know her?"

"Sure I know her. She's in my class at high school. Her dad owns that Italian restaurant on South Main. By the viaduct."

"That spaghetti joint? What's it called?"

"Aquaviva's. That's it. I think if Max loves her . . ."

"Max doesn't love her. Max doesn't love anyone. He loves business. Selling. Buying. I pity the woman he marries. Do you realize that Max hasn't looked at a book . . . a single book . . . since high school? Three years ago?"

"Is that such a tragedy?"

"Well, no. It's just that . . . well, he doesn't have any interests except business. No thoughts about us, about Sundown, about the world."

"O.K., that's too bad. But what's that have to do with Angeline? With his right to marry whoever he wants to?"

Jacob leans back and screws up his face, a bit amused and pleased that I'm mature enough to be so concerned.

It must be difficult for Jacob. With Reuben away he must feel isolated. Max has never been interested in books or politics or sports and I have always . . . until very recently . . . been

165

a child, with whom it would have been foolish, and embarrassing, to discuss such questions as we're discussing now.

"It's not fair," Jacob says. "But I can't get too excited about what Max does. I never have been able to. Max has always been a sort of outsider. Not like Cosco or Step. More like . . . just another Jew. I've had a hard time seeing him as a brother. Reuben, too. He told me once that whenever he has to list the names of the members of the family on some form he almost always forgets to include Max. That's what I mean."

Jacob has touched on something . . . this exclusion of Max . . . that saddens me. I've thought about it recently, and the more I've thought about it the more compassionate I've felt toward Max. Max, the outsider. Max, the renegade. The black sheep.

Poppa does not build a fire in the stoves very often now. The kitchen is chilly when he comes downstairs in the morning but it gets warm so fast that energy and coal would be wasted if he spent much time over a fire.

Sometimes, after he has his coffee and bread and butter, Poppa will work in the back yard, turning over the soil in preparation for his annual garden.

When I wake up to get ready for school and walk along the path to the toilet, the scent of freshly turned soil mingles with the fragrance from the cherry and the apple blossoms. Now and then I can catch the scent of pine and sweet muir drifting down from the woods.

In the store, before Poppa turns on the lights, I stand near the window, looking across the road to the B. and L. E. tracks, across the tracks and across the Connequenessing to the green hill that contains the reservoir. The sun's not up yet. A blue haze shifts and settles and shifts again about the reservoir, up and down the hillside. A heavily antlered buck, two does and a fawn, grazing on the hillside, move in and out of the blue (lighter and lighter blue as I watch) mist. A passenger train exploding into sight does not disturb them. They all lift their

166

heads to inspect every car as the train rumbles past. Unimpressed, they return to their grazing.

During the day five or six customers will come into the store. They'll either request very little or they'll have no money to pay for what Poppa decides to give them.

In the icebox, where once three sides of beef would hang at one time, there is a small paper box half filled with wieners that are beginning to slime and stink. Six loaves of bread are almost lost in the immense showcase which used to store fifty loaves at a time and would have to be refilled before the day was half over.

Standing at the stove and looking across the room at the wall behind the counter, I can see the entire bank of shelves. They're empty. Under the counter Poppa has hidden six cans of pork and beans, along with four cans of salmon and a dozen cans of spaghetti in tomato sauce. If Mrs. Lemley or Mrs. Foggiato or old Caine Coom send their babies to plead for credit Poppa can safely point to the shelves and persuade the kids that as they can see he has nothing to sell.

There are a half dozen old men who have precious little else but memories to cling to and who, on mornings such as this, come to sit on the porch in the early hours so they can watch the children congregate for school. They shelter their aching old bones as they watch the kids play and they gum their tobacco and spit and ignore the kids' glares and protests and then, in the silence that follows the departure of the school bus, the old men remind each other that they have the whole day before them. If the morning winds are too cool the men hobble into the store and Poppa builds a token fire for them.

When Max, dressed in his newest suit, walks past them on his way to his car, on his way to town, they exchange sly, knowing grins. That one, I've heard one or another of them say at one or another time, is going to give trouble.

Saturday.

Goose works all day. Before he comes home I leave for

167

town, intending to miss him. I don't want him with me tonight. Tonight I'm interested in being alone with Julie.

Maybe I'll run into her on Main Street. Will she think I'm too much of a dandy? I'm wearing my new suit, with Max's white shirt and blue tie. Will she let me walk her home to Lyndy? I'm sure she'll not notice that a pin at the back of my waist keeps up the trousers and two handkerchiefs help fill out the shoulders of the jacket.

A casual search of Birdie's Pool Hall and Ox's Hot Dog Shop and Stepanides' Ice Cream Parlor reveals several friends from high school—Nick Dano, Paul Sopel, Sam Fako, Aloysius Nietrezeba, Mary Schneider, Betsy Griswold. But not Julie. If Goose were with me I'd go into the half dozen bars on Main Street where I'd find everyone who's come in from Sundown for the evening. Alone, I've no desire to see them. Julie's the only one I want to see tonight.

If Roman were home he'd probably tease me for wanting to spend the evening with Julie, but all the while he'd be teasing me he'd be keeping alert for her too. When we found Julie we would have found Helen, who's always with her. Then we would have paired off: Julie and me, Roman and Helen.

Roman's been in the army almost three months. He has four more weeks of basic training, then he'll be home. He'll be different. Bigger, bolder, with the authority of a seasoned traveler. Though his two letters have been brief their details indicated an investment in thrills that I not only could never afford but would never be offered here in Summer. (The letter describing Phoenix City . . . where for a dollar you could get laid by anything from a turkey hen to an eighty-year-old grandmother who'll whistle *Dixie* while she blows you . . . is what prodded Goose into volunteering.)

"There's Benny!"

I whirl around, thinking it's Julie. But it's Angie Aquaviva. And Max.

They've just come out of a movie. They have that pale,

puffy, bleary look that people have when they step out of a theater into the open air.

"We're going to Angie's restaurant," Max says. "You want to come?"

Something is happening. Within the space of forty-eight hours Max has (1) given me a suit, (2) talked to me without baiting me, (3) invited me to go with him and his girl friend to a restaurant. I have no idea who has converted him, or how they could have done it, but it promises a new serenity for all of us.

Angie has her right arm linked in Max's left. She catches my arm. "Come on," she says. "My mom'll treat you to spaghetti."

While we walk, Angie chats away, pretending not to notice the envious stares from other girls who don't have even one man on whom they might hook their arms.

Max leans forward to examine me. Without the slightest resentment he says, "You're wearing my shirt. And my tie."

Angie keeps talking while I say, "I'll take good care of them. I promise."

As Angie reviews the movie Max says, "You can have them. The tie *and* the shirt."

Is he sick? Is he just trying to impress Angie? Now it is I who lean forward to examine him. He's listening intently to Angie and he's saying yes, yes, he agrees.

"You went to the movie Saturday night?"
"Yes," I say.
"With them?"
"With *them?* With whom?"
"Max and his *shiksa.*"
"No."
"I hear different."
"You have very good hearing."

169

Momma drops into her chair. I'm sorry, immediately, that I had to be so snide. My heart goes out to her.

Poor Momma.

Reuben is in the army. Jacob will be going soon. Max soon after. In another year I'll be eighteen and I'll be going. *The war . . . the war . . .* over every word exchanged with every friend, over all plans, all thoughts . . . like those poisonous webs that appear on one leaf and then spread to one twig and then rush over a limb to envelop every branch on the tree . . . over all is *the war.* Momma, going to the window to admire the pink and white blossoms, sees, instead, in every fallen, wind-blown blossom, the head, the face, of Reuben, of Jacob, of Max, of me.

Max will leave her sooner, she's convinced, than when he goes into the army. He's promised but, as she says, "His promises are nothing." He'll marry the *shiksa.* She knows.

No matter how many times I try to reassure her, reminding her of his promise, Momma says, "Don't tell me. I know."

It's raining.

"Ben?"

"Yeah, this is Ben. This Max?"

"Yeah."

"You sound so different. I wasn't sure."

"It's me. Listen, Ben. I'm through work at nine tonight. I'm coming home to pick up my things. I'm moving out."

"Moving out? You can't."

"I have to. Don't argue. Just listen. I don't want to spend a lot of time there . . . explaining, arguing. I just want to pick up my things and go. Now . . . will you pack my clothes, whatever's clean, in some boxes? My suits and shirts, the stuff on top of the dresser, that stuff . . . put it in some cardboard boxes. Have it ready so I can drive up, pack it in the car and take off. That way it'll all be over in a hurry. It'll be easier for everyone that way."

"Max, what are you talking about? You can't just . . . just leave!"

"I'm twenty-one. I can do any goddamn thing I want to!"

"What about Momma and Poppa? This will kill Momma."

"Oh hell, it won't *kill* her. She'll survive. But *I* have to survive, too. If I live in that house another day I . . . I can't. I can't stay." He takes a deep breath. "Will you help? Will you do what I'm asking?"

"No. If you leave like this, do it yourself. It's dirty. And I'm not going to help you do your dirty work."

He hangs up.

I lean against the wall. I reach up and drop the phone in its cradle.

Momma is asleep upstairs. Poppa, in the store, is preparing his list of numbers which tomorrow will, again, start him on his way toward another million dollars. Jacob, at the YMCA in Summer, is probably playing basketball or handball. Or boxing. His deferment lasts for one more month. I've been studying, waiting for the rain to stop so I can go for a walk with Goose, who'll be leaving in three days for the army.

It's grown much cooler. The rain is splashing against the window. A bolt of lightning cracks open the sky, to spill more rain.

The phone rings.

"Ben, you better tell Momma I won't be home. Not for a long time. I'm moving to Pittsburgh. You can do what you want with my clothes . . . throw them out, wear them, do what you want."

"Max . . ."

"Now don't start bawling."

"I'm not going to bawl. I'm just asking you to consider other people's feelings. . . ."

We blunder through a long silence. When he replies it's with such a clipped, controlled voice, I wonder if, perhaps, he might not be going mad. "Consider other people's feelings? Why? No one in that house has ever considered mine."

171

"I don't understand . . ."

"You will. Believe me, you will." I don't, and I'm sure I won't. I wish I hadn't accepted the suit. It was a bribe, that's all it was. "Tell Jacob I'll be working at Stern's, in Pittsburgh."

We both wait. Then he says, "Try to understand me, Ben. Try to understand what *I* need."

The click of his receiver sends a pain through my ear and brain, and through my heart, as real as if it had been the fall of a trigger on the cap of a bullet in the chamber of a gun aimed at my temple.

When Jacob comes home I tell him everything Max said. Jacob starts for the phone, hesitates and returns. He uses a towel lying on the sinkboard to wipe the rain from his face. At the stove he lights a fire under the soot-covered coffeepot. He seems hypnotized by the flames. Then he shakes his head. "I bet he has her knocked up," Jacob says.

Momma does not weep and Poppa does not curse when Jacob tells them. Poppa does not say, "I told you," and he does not once mutter the word "Scum." He nods, just once, and then he lifts the loaf of crusty bread to his chest. He draws the knife across the loaf, stopping the blade just short of his flesh. He returns the bread to the table and he walks away, toward the store. He looks down and notices three red blotches on his slice of bread. He checks his hand and discovers he's nicked a finger. He sucks on his finger as he walks out of the kitchen into the store.

Momma asks me to build a small fire. I do.

She sits in her ancient chair. Her hands in her lap turn over and over: palms up, palms down . . . palms up, palms down. . . .

Ginsberg, the owner of the junkyard in Summer brings Momma home from the cemetery. She has seen and approved the headstone that Jacob bought for Rachel's grave. She's planted sweet-peas, her favorite flower, at the graves of both Herschel and Rachel.

We all sit at the kitchen table. *All* meaning, these days, Momma and Poppa and me.

"Max," Momma says.

It's the first time the name has been heard in the house since he left, five months before. Its sound at this time, right after Momma's return from the cemetery, is especially surprising, because since his departure she's considered him dead. She has said *kaddish* for him just as she has for Rachel and Herschel.

Shortly after Max had gone to Pittsburgh we heard that he married a girl named Mary (the Mary, I'm sure, in that photograph I'd found in his jacket). She's the rich daughter, I've been told, of one of the officers of the board of Jones and Laughlin, in Pittsburgh.

Poppa, no longer concerned with ritual, does not sit *shiva*, as he would have in another time, and he does not say *kaddish*, as he would have in another time. He does not indicate in any way his surprise or sorrow that this is the pass to which all things concerning Max might have come.

"Max," Momma says.

"What about Max?" I ask.

"There's a baby. I heard at the cemetery. Horwitz told me."

Poppa's head comes about, his mouth open.

Momma lights the three *yahrzeit* candles.

I write to Max, who's now living in California.

A reply comes back in four days. "Don't open," Momma says.

Momma lets the unopened letter lie on the table where Poppa puts all the mail. She cleans the crumbs and dirty dishes away from it. She adjusts it so that the composition it makes with the fresh flowers behind it looks more attractive.

Poppa makes several trips to the kitchen, to drink more water than he's drunk in years. Each time, on the way back to the store, he passes the table on which the letter lies. He al-

173

ways chances one quick glance at the envelope as if, since the last trip, something new might be visible.

I can stand it no longer. I grab the letter and rip it open. Poppa bends over the radio, pretending to be tampering with the knobs.

"A boy," I say. "Max has a baby boy."

Momma's hands clap together, once. They flow to cover her mouth, but not before there's a faint, sharp squeal. Poppa's fingers, on the knobs, do not move.

"Adam," I say.

Poppa walks to the stove and pours himself a cup of coffee. He sits at the table. When he raises the cup to his lips his hand trembles.

"Adam's a good name," Poppa says.

Momma straightens her body. She parts her lips twice, to speak, and then she thinks better of it. Finally she steels herself and asks, "He send a picture?"

About Goose
Winter, 1942

I feel poorly dressed and slightly underprivileged when Goose steps off the bus. He's taller than I am now, and heavier.

A year ago he lied about his age and enlisted in the army. Why he volunteered to fight with the British in Africa none of us in Sundown could ever know. But he had, and he'd been wounded, and here he was coming home on furlough one year after the United States entered the war.

We're both ill-at-ease at first. He's eighteen, as I am, but there's already something of an experienced adult about him. I'm sure that to him I seem young. I probably even seem unimpressed by his uniform, his ribbons, his barely perceptible limp that could, for someone who didn't know, pass for a swagger.

After he dumps his duffle bag in a locker and drops the key in his pocket, we walk out of the bus station. There's been no snow for over a week. The streets are bare, gray and cold and bare.

As we walk down Main Street, toward the business district, he seems to loosen up. "How the hell are you, Ben?" he grins his old lopsided grin. His teeth have been repaired. He's actu-

175

ally handsome. His once submissive manner is gone; lost, no doubt, on African sands. He used to be willing to play the goat for Roman and me, willing to play second and third fiddle. But he seems a leader now, not a follower.

"Damn," I say, grinning back, "you look like an Eagle Scout with all those ribbons."

For each ribbon, as he taps it, he has a comment. "This one's for smacking a whore in Louisville. This one's for shoving five turnips up the mess sergeant's ass at Fort Riley. This one's for hitting three home runs one time at bat with a WAC lieutenant." The old Goose would have giggled when I teased him and he would have wiped the discomfort from his face and changed the subject.

As we walk down Main Street people admire him openly. Around Summer a tan such as the one that he has isn't seen even in July.

I'm wearing a pair of pants which, due to war restrictions, have no cuffs. My jacket is one that Max just sent me from his new store in California. But I feel so pale and drab. And yet, as people continue to stare and nudge each other and point, some of his glamour brushes off on me. I walk a little straighter, in time with his marching steps, and I think that I'm even beginning to look stronger.

Goose turns into the first bar. There, facing our reflections in the mirror. I see for the first time that he has a scar running down his right cheek, jaggedly parallel to his nose.

"On me," I say, as the bartender waits.

"I accept."

We order two beers, watch the bartender draw them, skim them and slide them to us. We swallow, swallow again, set the glasses down, wipe our mouths and sigh, refreshed, revived.

"Well," I say, as we settle on our stools, "how's it feel?"

Goose pushes his overseas cap back on his forehead. "I never thought I'd make it."

"How long's it been, Goose?"

"Thirteen months. Almost fourteen."

"Christ, it seems like yesterday."

"It's changed a lot," Goose says.

"What? Summer?"

"Yeah. It's bigger. Busier. Crowded."

"There was no work when you left. Everyone's working now. Every factory in Lyndy has three shifts going."

"Reuben's in, huh?"

"Yeah. Jacob, too. Max was in but he's out." I think of the war memorial in the lot behind Ellsworth's store, with Reuben's and Jacob's and Max's names, and an empty space waiting for mine. "How's the leg?" I say.

"It's O.K. They took out the kneecap. I got a scar from my knee to my asshole. Another half inch and I'd'a had to join the WACs."

A farmer in faded gray denims, so drunk he has to pull himself stool by stool to get to us, finally reaches us. He makes one great effort to stand at attention, succeeds, salutes and drops to the floor. He lies there, his hand fixed to his forehead. Goose salutes back. "God bless you, soldier," the drunk farmer gargles.

"He already has," Goose says. He finishes his beer, stands, steps over the drunk and goes out the door.

There are several sailors and soldiers and a few marines at Sopel's bar. But mostly there are civilians. Men who work in the mills at Lyndy, at the mines around Sundown and farmers from fields fifteen and twenty miles away. And there are a half dozen beer-bloated women.

Goose has had three beers. I've had one. I don't know Goose's limit but I know mine, so I don't try to match him.

It doesn't take much imagination or sensitivity to know that Goose, rolling his beer about in his glass, is thinking about Roman. I am. I have been. Wishing he were here, thinking how great it would be if the three of us could walk back to Sundown and go up to the woods to our shanty . . . if it's still standing . . . and stay there overnight. To lie on the bunks

177

. . . or on the ground if the bunks have been hauled away by rats and squirrels . . . and reminisce.

"I saw him in New York," Goose says. "Just before I went to Africa. We got drunk, laid a couple women and sat up all night on the bank of the Hudson River . . . that's a river that runs through New York . . ."

"How was he?"

Goose cocks his head to gaze at the ceiling, as if the memory is pasted up there. "He was Roman, you know . . . he was Roman."

"They never found out who killed him?"

"Sure they did. Some whore."

"Christ, of all the guys who deserved, if he had to die, to die on a battlefield . . ."

Goose stiffens. His mouth twitches. He turns to me and it seems that his eyes have grown milky. "Ben . . ." He shakes himself. "That's . . . don't talk about . . . dying on a battle-field is . . ."

A sailor named Mike Bruno appears out of the crowd behind us. He lays a hand on my shoulder. "Benny . . . I wondered what the hell ever happened to you. How are you?"

Mike was in my class at high school. He's Julie's cousin. Sometimes, when I used to go to Julie's house in Lyndy, Mike would be there. He was never happy about Julie going with someone who wasn't Polish. That was bad enough. But to go with someone who wasn't Polish and who was a Jew . . . well, that caused problems. It caused problems because despite my being a Jew Mike liked me. We managed a casual friendship.

I wait now for the inevitable question. It comes in about six seconds. "You out? You been let out?"

I've learned that the best way to react to the question is to be prompt and direct. "I never got in."

"You 4-F?"

"He's been in and out," Goose says, speaking to Mike's reflection in the mirror.

178

"In and out of Julie, maybe," Mike says, with a malice he's never disclosed before. He waits for me to defend Julie's honor. I'd be willing to if I thought Julie's honor was really involved. I don't think it is. It's Mike's honor I'm being put in a position to have to defend. Or attack.

"I've been deferred, Mike. Sole support of my family. I've tried to get in twice. Let's go, Goose."

Mike's face grows threateningly sober. "I'll be a sonofabitch. What? You got five brothers?"

"I've got three brothers."

"Yeah, three." His loud belligerence has lured several men to our stools. "Three brothers," Mike tells them. "And he gets deferred. So I get sent to do his fighting. And *you* guys do. These fucking Jews . . . we fight to save these fucking Jews and then they stay home and make all the . . ."

It's the fastest and hardest and truest I've ever hit anyone.

Mike goes down, blood spurting from his nose. Two sailors and a Marine step free of the stunned crowd. The marine, quite businesslike, removes his bright blue jacket. He rubs his hands together, relishing the prospects before him.

There's a crash of glass and Goose steps in front of me, the jagged necks of two beer bottles in his hands. "You gyrene bastard, come on. You too, sailor boy." He leaps at them and they leap back, tripping over each other to get out of the way.

"Let's get out of here," Goose says.

Goose meets me at the factory. It's midnight.

Some of the men from Sundown who work on my shift shake Goose's hand. They make a few jokes about his ribbons, about the stories they've heard about his adventures and his decorations; they ask if he's ever run into their sons or brothers.

We walk home along the railroad tracks. The wind is cold enough for us to turn up the collars of our coats. The polished blue rails glisten in the moonlight. The cinders crackle under our feet.

179

It would be more comfortable to walk in the lanes between the sets of tracks, where there are no railroad ties, but we both choose to walk the ties, enduring the quick, short steps this requires. As we used to walk when we were kids.

The idle freight at our right lies in the darkness like some great sleeping animal ready at first call to leap into action. The swamp at our left breathes out its night sounds: an occasional croak of a water animal, a call of a chilled owl, the sleepy whisperings of birds clustering on their twigs.

"Remember how we played there?" Goose says.

"We knew every path, every goddamned . . ."

"Yeah, remember that big tree with the vines?"

"It was our hideout. The vines come down like the walls of a house. . . . I remember. . . ."

"Remember the poker games?"

"And the day we brought Peggy King and played strip poker?"

"We were lucky," I say; "we didn't knock her up."

"She got knocked up. But not by us. By her idiot brother."

"Remember old Hardy? The D.T.? How he used to try to keep us off the tracks?"

"That poor old bastard. He quit chasing us . . ."

". . . After that day he chased us through the swamp. I remember."

"You and Rome and me. He was chasing us. He'd never have caught us but Rome said to let him."

"He kept waving his club and yelling, 'You're under arrest, you're under arrest!'"

"We ran across that big branch that came down over the water."

"He followed us . . ."

". . . Got halfway across . . ."

". . . And Rome jumped on the branch."

We push and pound each other as we continue calling up the details. ". . . And the branch goes out from under Hardy."

"He stands there . . . I'll never forget his face . . . he stands there, his mouth open, and he sinks. He just *sinks*."

180

"Up to his knees. Up to his hips. Up to his waist. Up to his shoulders. He was sure he was gonna sink right under the water."

"Mud, not water. The water's only six inches deep. It's all mud."

"He doesn't know that's all the further he'll sink, but we know. We stand and watch. He screams."

"And Roman crawls out on the limb and bends over . . ."

". . . And dips his finger in the mud and he paints a mustache and glasses on old Hardy's face."

"Good old Roman."

We walk a bit in silence. "You know, Goose. Thinking back, that was pretty goddamned cruel."

"What was?"

"What we did to Hardy."

"We were kids. Kids is kids."

We walk the rest of the way to the store in silence. Going up the steps to the porch Goose says, "It *was* cruel."

Momma and Poppa have gone to bed. Goose and I sit on the porch. The dark cave of the store looms behind us.

Usually Poppa waits up for me at night. We sit on the porch if it's good weather, and we drink coffee. There's not much conversation, but Poppa likes our being together. Momma usually stays in the kitchen. She doesn't read the paper any more, she doesn't sew, she doesn't even listen to the radio. She just sits. Sometimes she fixes two chairs together in front of the stove and she stretches out on the chairs and sleeps. She's fallen once. It was summer, fortunately, so there was no fire in the stove. But she still has dark bruises on her arms and back.

Tonight both she and Poppa are in bed.

When they met Goose in the morning the first thing Momma said was, "You know I got three sons in the army."

"You want an ice cream?" was the first thing Poppa said. "Go ahead, take an ice cream. Ben, give Goose an ice cream."

We sit on the porch, drinking the beer Goose picked up at

181

Shorty's beer garden on our way home from the factory. I bought a bag of pretzels.

It's very quiet. There are no cars on the highway. Ten minutes before a freight had rattled and rumbled past, on its way to Pittsburgh, its cars loaded with coal. There will be another freight in fifteen or twenty minutes, coming from Pittsburgh, its coal cars empty.

"Goose, I'm glad you wrote me. I'm glad I could meet you."

"Yeah . . . well, you get homesick. Crazy, I got no one here and I still get homesick."

Two bottles are emptied. "What was it like, Goose?"

I should be embarrassed, and I am, at asking the question, but I really want to know. I must know, and there is no one else whom I can ask. Whom I would ask.

Goose gets off his milk crate and sits on the edge of the porch, his legs dangling free, the way he used to sit. It's been less than two years but it seems as if it's been twenty. Two years ago we were children. Today, tonight, we are men. Maybe I shouldn't think of it as *we*. Only Goose knows he's a man.

"I was never very brave," Goose says. "You know that. You and Roman, you guys were brave. I did things you did because you either made me do them or because I knew you two wouldn't let me go with you if I didn't do them. I used to take Charles Atlas exercises, in secret, thinking they'd make me brave like you two." He drinks noisily from his third bottle. "I ain't the hero type. Some guys are, they just are. Like Roman. Born that way, I guess. Well, when it happened . . . over there . . . in Africa . . . I was lucky. God really did bless me. Things happened so fast. I didn't know what was happening . . . I didn't know what I was doing . . . it was over all of a sudden and there I was, alive. The only one alive. I screamed when they picked me up. I kept screaming. They put me in five hospitals. Not just for my leg, either. I won three medals for doing something I still don't know what it

182

was. I read the paper they give you, with the medals, but it's just words. I was scared. I cried all the time, like a baby."

"You stood up to that sailor and marine . . ."

"That wasn't brave. I knew they'd fuck off. Even if they didn't, so what? So I'd get beat up. That's nothing."

"I don't know what you mean."

"I don't either. I'm just saying it ain't the same. That night after it was over and I saw heads and arms and feet and faces laying there in the sand I dug like a mole to cover myself. I wanted to dig, dig, dig to get deeper and deeper in the ground."

The freight comes then, rocketing out of the darkness, the engine singing to the hills. The caboose, one dim light glowing, passes. It's quiet again.

"You know I tried to get in," I say. "Twice."

"You don't have to tell me that, Ben. It doesn't matter."

"It does to me. I have to talk to someone about it."

"Not to me. Don't talk to me about it, because I don't care about it."

Perhaps I should be angry but I can't be. Even if it did matter to Goose, why should he listen to my complaints?

"They're going to discharge me," he says. "Combat fatigue. That's what they call it. Now that they've given me those medals and there's been those stories in the papers and everyone's proud of me . . . a Yank volunteering to fight for England and all that shit . . . they can't tell it the way it really was. They can't say I'm scared. You wanta hear something? I can't get a hard on any more. I try and try. I oughta be able to, all the doctors say I ought to, but I can't. I have nightmares. I'm awake almost all night and when I do sleep I have these nightmares. The other day, in Pittsburgh, I picked up this whore. I offered her a hundred bucks if she could get me a hard on. She tried everything. Finally gave up. I gave her twenty-five bucks anyway."

"Let's walk, Goose."

We go down the road, across the bridge by the railroad

183

roundhouse and over the Connequenessing Creek and up toward The Canyon.

I point to a series of ripples. "There's where you and Rome found me and my cousin that day."

"Yeah, I remember. That was the first time I ever watched anyone die. I saw dead people . . . you know, *after* they died . . . but I never *watched* anyone die. I have since. I sure have."

"I watched Rachel die."

"I remember."

"I have nightmares about *that*. Lots of times. Not as often as I used to, but I still do. You know, for a long time afterwards I really believed it was all my fault she died. I believed that if I hadn't let Texas Jack . . ."

"Texas Jack. I've forgotten all about that bastard."

". . . get up on the roof she'd still be alive. I know different now. I know it's not *my* fault she died."

"You ever hear from that guy she went with?"

"No. You know, he was the one who killed her."

"Honest to God? How?"

"He got her pregnant. He tried to fix her up himself. She got infected and died."

We're crossing Kearnsey's meadow now. The grass is high, sighing and whispering back at the wind. It's been a long time since I've walked here. Far off, at the end of the meadow, is the farm where Goose and Roman and I used to chase and be chased by Kearnsey's cows and bulls.

"Remember the day," Goose says, chuckling, "we had that battle in Kearnsey's barn?"

"You and Rome and me and Moldy Kearnsey . . . yeah . . . I remember."

"We started in the field behind the barn, throwing crab apples at each other."

"Then dried cowshit. We'd go chasing through the field, trying to find dry piles, and when we'd find some we'd sail them, like saucers. . . ."

184

"Then Rome started throwing the fresh stuff."

"And you run in and gathered up the horse balls because you could throw them like baseballs. . . ."

"And you started with the fresh stuff. . . ."

"Still steaming. I caught it while it was dropping. I still remember how they splattered when they hit."

We share a loud and jubilant ecstasy of recollection. A dog at Kearnsey's farm gets excited and starts barking and someone . . . it's probably old J.J. Kearnsey himself . . . that bearded, scarred old Indian-fighter, J.J. Kearnsey . . . someone yells for the dog to stop its racket. His voice carries clearly over the meadow. The dog stops barking. Goose and I walk on, humbled into silence by old J.J.'s voice, that old voice that was old when we were kids sitting there on the rim of the aromatic oat-bin and listening to him tell, for the tenth glorious time, how he pulled the arrow out of his arm and shot, just once, and knocked that Sioux brave deader'n Kelley's mule.

We stand on the bank of the Connequenessing. Here is . . . or was . . . one of the swimming holes to which we all used to walk every summer. It's been a long time since kids have swum here. The path that led from the top of the bank down to where the diving board had been secured between four posts is grown over. The board and three of the posts have vanished. A jagged stub of one post sticks up out of the mud.

Goose, clutching the long grass to keep from sliding into the water, goes down to the post. He balances himself on the stub. For a second I think he's going to dive in. But he steps down and kicks some mud in the water to disperse his reflection.

We're sitting on the porch when Poppa opens the door. There's a faint glow of sun in the east, through the trees on top of the hills.

"You ain't been to bed all night?"

"No. We've been talking."

185

"All night?"

Goose laughs and grips Poppa's thigh and shakes it. "Al, you fat old bastard, I missed you."

Poppa actually blushes. It's visible in the gray light. He rubs Goose's head. "You're a good boy." He goes back in the store.

"I don't think I'll go to work tonight," I say. "I'll take off sick. You think we'll lose the war if I take off sick?"

"Nah. You'll be raising a soldier's morale. Look at it that way."

"I'll sleep this afternoon and we can go to town tonight."

"I could use some sleep too."

Poppa returns, carrying two mugs of coffee. He hands one to Goose and one to me. It's black and steaming and strong. "You take milk?"

"Nah."

Poppa goes in and returns with his own cup. "So you sat up all night. You talked about the old days. *Old* days. Ha! Three, four years ago and it's *the old days.*"

Poppa leans against one of the scarred porch posts. How many times I've seen him in this very pose. A hundred, a thousand times. All the rest of my life I'm to recall, whenever I think of Poppa, I'm to recall him like this: standing against a pole, his hands in his pocket, his squat body bulging out of his trousers and shirt, his once wild hair thin and gray, his eyebrows . . . once a straight black ledge across his forehead . . . so sparse and pale now as to be invisible . . . his eyes squinting up the hill toward Summer, the hill down which, in a horse and buggy, he had come with a wife and a child an eternity ago. For what? For a lifetime of defeat. He moves his head to peer through the gold-gray dawn across the road, across the field, across the B. and L.E. tracks, to the distant hill where he used to walk every spring, every summer, to fill his bucket with blackberries or his basket with mushrooms. The gold-gray, gold-blue hill to which he's not traveled once these last five years, to which he will never (he knows . . . I know) travel again.

Goose reaches over and pats Poppa's rump. "You're gettin' bald, Al."

"Wait. You get old, you'll get bald."

"Not me. I'll never get old."

"You fooled me. I thought you was Goose. You're God?"

"No, I'm just saying I'll never get old."

"You know a trick, tell me."

"No trick. You just blow out your brains on your thirtieth birthday."

"Thirty," Poppa grunts. He shakes his head. "I used to think thirty was an old man. Then I think forty is old. Then I think fifty is old. Now I'm almost sixty and I know, I know it's old."

A freight goes past; the air and the porch tremble. It's getting cold. I wonder if it's going to snow. The sky looks like there's a snowstorm building up. I pull my coat tighter.

At the top of the hill the trees are bright, white gold. The sun leaps up above them.

"Ah," Goose says, "I keep hoping that sonofabitch might forget to come up some morning."

"It never forgets," Poppa says. He tosses the dregs of his coffee into the dust.

"I'll buy you a plate of spaghetti."

"I'll buy you one," I say.

"We'll toss."

We toss a quarter. Goose has to buy. We go to Aquaviva's, the single Italian restaurant in Summer. It's at the south end of Main Street, near the viaduct. Before the war it used to be a hangout for high-school kids, then, during the war, it became a hangout for servicemen. Tony doesn't like servicemen. Somehow or other a feud started between them. Some soldier teased Tony about Italian soldiers being cowards. He was insulted. He and his son threw the soldier out. Other soldiers teased him. There were more fights. It's a vendetta. Twice the place has been off-limits to servicemen. This has made Tony happy because now it's a quiet restaurant catering mainly to the few

187

Italian families in the area. There's no off-limits sign on the door tonight, but even so there are only two soldiers, with women, in the room.

The reason I come here so often is . . . well, there are two reasons. One: there are few servicemen. Two: Angeline, Tony's daughter.

Angie went to high school with me and was . . . is . . . in love with Max. She asks me about him every time she sees me. She always greets me with a hug and a smile.

"Hey, Benny," Angie says, her teeth flashing, "it's a long time."

I introduce her and Goose. "Now you be nice," she says to Goose. "Poppa says anything, you don't pay attention. O.K.?"

"O.K.," Goose says.

There are about fifteen people in the restaurant, including us. After Angie brings our food she checks the other customers, brings them up to date on their needs, and then she shouts at her mother, who's rolling meatballs, "I take some coffee with Benny?"

Her mother nods but does not interrupt her work.

Angie brings a cup of coffee for herself and she sits beside me. She lights a cigarette. "You hear from Max?"

"He's discharged."

"Discharged? Why?"

"I don't know. He didn't say."

"Aw, come on."

"I mean it. You know, we don't write each other very much. Mary, his wife, writes Momma and Poppa."

"They got any kids yet?"

"One."

Angie very softly, almost inaudibly, grunts, as if I'd accidentally poked her in the ribs. "Too bad," she says. Her eyes fill with tears. She shapes her hand around the coffee cup as if the cup contains the last source of warmth. "I been hoping. I give up now. You know, if he'd just wriggled a finger at me, just went like this"—and she winks—"I'd'a married him."

I'm not lying and she knows it, when I say to her, "I'd like having you for a sister-in-law."

"You," she says, "I'd go after you, you was six years older. I like them older."

"I'm your age, remember. I'm no baby."

"A girl likes older men. A man likes younger women. It's crazy." She wipes her eyes and tries to smile at Goose. "How much time you have?"

"Five days. Two already gone."

"Where you stationed?"

"Camp Kilmer now. New Jersey."

"I know where Camp Kilmer is. I got a brother-in-law there. Nick Spina. Ever run into a Nick Spina? Nah, I didn't think so. I got a cousin in Port Hueneme, in California, however the hell you say it. Hey," and she nudges me. "Maybe I get him to pay my way to California and I call Max when I get there. Whatta you think?"

"I think no."

"Boy, you Jews. You're real family men. You stick together. I like that. The family sticks together. Jews and Italians, we're both alike there. What are *you?*" she asks Goose.

"I don't know. My old man was born in Sundown and my old lady was born in Oil City. They met at a ball game."

"You Catholic?"

"No."

"What?"

"I don't go to any church."

"Yeah, but what are you? You must be something."

"My old man played baseball for the Second United Presbyterian Church. So I must be a Second United Presbyterian." He scratches his head, perplexed. "I wonder who's *First* United Presbyterian."

Angie checks her watch. "Hey, I get off in an hour. You doing anything?"

"We're gonna sit and talk," I say.

"You can talk at my place. You wanta come up? I got beer and I got coffee and stuff to eat."

189

I wait for Goose to say yes or no but he's staring very intently at his spoon.

"What about it, Goose?"

He shakes his head. "You go. I'll walk around town, see a couple guys."

"Boy, if it's that hard to decide," Angie says, "forget it. But I ain't exactly flattered."

"We'll meet you in an hour," Goose says.

During the next hour I drink one beer and make a good half dozen efforts, all in vain, to start a conversation. Goose drinks seven beers.

Finally I say, "Look, do you want to cancel out on Angie?"

"Nope."

When we meet Angie after work and walk down Main Street Goose takes her left arm and I take her right.

"It wasn't that we didn't want to be with you," I say. "We thought you might get bored with us. All we do is talk about old times."

"Me? Bored? I ain't ever."

Though Angie's close to her family and works in her father's restaurant, she has her own apartment.

"Don't get any ideas," she says, as we go up the stairway. "Just because I invited you to my place. It's . . . well, it's sorta for old times' sake. For me."

"We understand," Goose says.

For an hour or so it's beer and coffee and conversation. Goose drinks all the beer and Angie and I drink the coffee. She knows some of the people Goose and I occasionally talk about and when she doesn't know them she listens. She doesn't seem bored. In fact, she seems very interested in everything we have to say.

Before too long, after Goose has downed enough beers to bring a glaze to his eyes and a slur to his speech, he talks less and less and his chin drops on his chest. Angie and I talk almost exclusively about Max. I'm surprised. I'd not really known how serious she had been.

"How did you ever fall in love with Max?"

"He used to come down, when he worked at the furniture store. He always ate at our place. He started walking me home. All his Jewish friends . . . you know, Abe and Izzy and Irv and Hymie and Bookie . . . they all used to tease him, saying he was standing them up for a wop *shtup*. Don't look shocked, I knew what it means. They were sure we were going to bed together. We never did, I swear to God. Not once. Oh, we necked. Hot and heavy sometimes. In confession I use to confess I was having evil dreams about a Jew. Boy, how many Hail Marys I've done for your brother. There were times . . . if he'd'a asked me I'd'a jumped right into bed with him. But he never asked. He said he knew he wouldn't marry me, ever, and it just wasn't right, the way he saw it, to go with a girl just to go to bed with her. What if he got me pregnant, he said once. He'd not marry me. So that would be wrong. So why do it? He's the only guy I ever went with didn't take it for granted I was gonna end up in bed with him. Boy, that guy . . . I'm telling you . . . they broke the mold after they made him."

Goose begins to snore. He shakes himself and tries to stand up and falls back in his chair. "How about my sackin' out for an hour or two?"

Angie says sure. She goes in the other room and opens up her bed. Goose goes to the bathroom and finally, after much stumbling and bumping, falls into her bed. Angie pulls the blankets over him and closes the door.

She keeps on praising Max as she puts on another pot of coffee, telling me about Max and other men. She's still a virgin, she says, and she thinks she will be until the day she gets married.

When we first arrived at the apartment her words were delicate, almost proper. As the evening wore on they become less delicate. "Go to bed" became "lay" and then "lay" became "screw." Now, with Goose gone, the harshness, the almost sullen coarseness, falls away from her voice and a soft tenderness creeps in. She's not loud now, nor brusque, as she always is at the restaurant. Even the movements of her body seem to change from a hard, almost mannish brusqueness to soft, gentle, kittenish rhythms.

She reaches up once, absently it seems, to untwine my curls. Her hand falls on my cheek. I take her hand and then her arm. Then we're kissing. Each of us is washed by the other's flood of hunger. We tear off our clothes and make love greedily, noisily, like two animals rutting in the forest. She falls asleep in my arms. I doze and open my eyes to see Goose standing there, leaning against a wall. He waves and walks out.

By the time I dress and get downstairs he's disappeared. I can't find him. The streets are empty. It's begun to snow.

I go back to Angie's.

"Don't worry," she says. "He went home. You'll see him tomorrow."

I leave at dawn, wondering if Goose will be sitting on our porch watching another sun come up.

He isn't. He hasn't been home all night.

The army lists him AWOL, then charges him with desertion.

I've not seen or heard from him since. Neither has anyone else.

192

About Us
Autumn, 1943

Reuben's letter arrives one month, to the day, after my birthday; six weeks after my appeal to him to write me and tell me about us.

It is more than a letter. It is a collection of memories, notes and reflections. Twenty pages. Some of the passages are written with pencil, some with pen; some have been scrawled with haste, some contain that precise script of his that I've always envied and have never been able to duplicate, though I tried at least a hundred times in my tenth year.

Italy
September 20, 1943

Dear Ben:

Ever since I received your letter I've been hoping we'd be pulled back to a rest camp long enough for me to devote the time and attention to the reply that letter deserves. We haven't been and there are no indications we will be. I've been haunted by the fear that I'll be killed before I get the chance to reply. So I'm sending you these pages torn from the yellow tablet that has served me not too faithfully as a journal. They're really just notes for the long letter to come.

Your letter was strange. Disturbing in a way.

Whenever I've thought of you . . . and it's been often . . . your face and voice and attitudes have been those of four years ago, when I saw you last. Now you tell me that because of the intervention of some of the Jews in Summer you've been deferred so you can take care of Momma and Poppa. To be deferred you have to be draft age; the draft age is eighteen. I added and subtracted and finally realized that by God you're nineteen. I shouldn't have been surprised. If I'm nineteen years older than I was when you were born, you must be, too.

You ask if I've written anything about the war. I haven't. My mentioning a journal might suggest to you that I intend to write about it some day. I will, if I survive. Efforts to keep a journal might indicate some degree of optimism. Don't be fooled.

I've written two stories since that novel four years ago. They're in that wooden trunk in the attic. Look them up and send them to me, will you. They were damned good, if I remember correctly. I need the reassurance they'll bring. That novel, if you remember, ended up in a place I'd guess, in retrospect, it belonged. I wrote it that summer we fought and whipped Ellsworth Cotton and the Township Commissioners. If I ever do write again I think the story of that summer deserves first crack. Incidentally, I realize only now that I haven't seen you since then.

"Tell me about us. About Momma and Poppa when I was a baby. Before I was born. Tell me about the house, about the store, about Sundown. About you and Max and Jacob. About Rachel. I remember certain things, but they're hazy. They're things I heard everyone talk about when I was very young, five or six. Since then there's been little talk. Each year there have been fewer left to do the talking. Now there's no one to talk and no one to talk to."

Why has the need to know these things struck you with such intensity now? Since you don't enlighten me I'm free to guess.

194

You find yourself, at nineteen . . . deferred, with Momma and Poppa to care for; with all your friends from Sundown in the war . . . you find yourself in painful conflict. You say, with great passion, that you can't wait to get into the war. But you can't bring yourself, I know, to desert Momma and Poppa. And yet the thought of staying there, with them, in that old house, in Sundown, is frightening. Threatening. Am I right? You'd feel better if you could find it easy to stay. But it's difficult. And it's disagreeable. The present, with Momma and Poppa, is bad enough; the future can only be worse. From what you've heard the last fifteen years you know that the past was different. Momma and Poppa . . . in the past . . . were strong and proud and beautiful. What I think you're really asking me now is to disclose that past in terms which might explain the present. If you can somehow love them for what they were you might possibly understand them for what they are now. And maybe even love them. That would prove you humane. Assured of humanity, a man can endure almost any indignity. And it must be a terrible indignity to be ashamed of your mother and father, to be anxious for them, by their dying, to liberate you.

I'm cruel, perhaps; and, perhaps, wrong. If so, all I can ask is forgiveness. And knowing you, I know you'll give it.

I hope these notes help.

My love to you, and to
Momma and Poppa.
Reuben

(Ben: These are very random, very incomplete,
very disorganized, very personal notes.)

Italy
August 14th

Families disintegrate. Like Marx's capitalism the family contains the seeds of its own destruction. But the disintegration of our family has been unique. Sons and daughters have not gotten married and left their parents to begin their own families

195

which in turn will also disintegrate. Momma and Poppa do not sit in comfortable old age, enjoying their grandchildren.

Whatever hopes and promises are contained within our home when you are born are to be obliterated before you're five years old.

Poppa is considered a learned man by the Jews in town, in Summer. During the evening, before he goes to bed, and in the store during the slack hours, he studies the Torah.

He is addicted to study. He happens also to have a thriving business. If the store did not do well and he had to live off the Jewish community in town, or on public welfare, the Jews would scorn him as a beggar, as an *amorets*, an ignoramus. But Poppa, a scholar as well as a business success, enjoys the envy and respect he receives from the Jews in Summer.

As certain as God's existence is the belief that Poppa, a *talmud khokhem*, has inherited along with his drive for scholarship an automatic comprehension of God's will and an unyielding subscription to it. Being my father's son I inherit this knowledge and dedication just as naturally as I inherit my brown eyes and my black curly hair. So it has been since the days of Abraham.

To this fanatic and naïve trust that has deceived us into regarding ourselves as the Chosen People I say . . . too late to save myself but I say it anyway . . . *Bullshit!*

There is no God and so there can be no Chosen People.

At the age of eighteen or nineteen or twenty . . . or whenever it was that I came to the conclusion that there is no God . . . I experienced one of those terrifying sinking sensations you feel when, relaxing yourself to sit on a chair you discover, too late, the chair has been pulled from under you. You collapse. Onto your back and your head. For one brief fleeting moment you know, without a doubt, that nothing . . . nothing! . . . will ever be secure again.

For me the moment was neither fleeting nor brief. I thank Momma and Poppa and their mother and father for finding

196

myself now with a most painfully fanatic belief in absolutely nothing.

Italy

August 15th

Study and learning promises the future life, the *Olam Habo.* Momma's parents, dreaming of a son-in-law who, being a *talmud khokhem*, would reward their daughter with a share of his eternal happiness, sang every night to Momma, when she was a child, a lullaby I now hear Momma sing every night to Rachel:

Under Rachel's *khupah*
Stands a dream-pure man.
The man will act as groom
With prayers and blushes.
But what is the best prize?
Rachela's bridegroom will learn;
Torah will be loved.
But good and pious
Shall Rachella endure.

Rachel is good all right, and pious. But she doesn't live to have a bridegroom.

To all of us, right up to the time I go into the army, you are always The Baby.

Like the rest of us you've been born at home, not in a hospital. It's raining the day you're born. I'm delivering papers. (The distance from Sundown to Summer, where I pick up my papers, is three miles. During school I pick them up after class and walk home to Sundown. During the summer I walk to town and then, with a hundred pounds of newspapers on my back, I return. All in all, whether it's hot sun or ankle-deep mud or hip-deep snow, the job takes about three hours. For $1.12 a day.)

197

The day you're born I walk into Momma's bedroom. She pulls back the blanket. "Reuben," she says. "You like the baby?"

I say, "Momma, don't let him be a paperboy."

Today, nineteen years later, I can think of several other things I'd tell Momma not to let you be.

Italy
August 15th

For the Sabbath every square inch of every wall and object in the house . . . animate and inanimate . . . is scrubbed.

I'm ten, maybe eleven. You won't be born for another eight or nine years. Jacob's about nine. Rachel is in between Jacob and me, about ten. Though Rachel doesn't go to *cheder*, as Jacob and I do, she knows as well as we do the significance of the Sabbath.

There are two tables in the kitchen, one for preparing dairy meals and one for meat meals. We have two separate sets of dishes, of cutlery, of pots and pans. In the attic, in two large wooden barrels, are two more sets of dishes and pots and cutlery, for Passover.

If, by chance, dishes are contaminated . . . such as the dishes for meat accidentally being used for dairy food . . . they are scalded. If a knife or fork is contaminated it is thrust into dirt. The dirt of a flower pot or the dirt in the back yard.

I've been trying to place various events in their proper sequence and I've been trying to figure out how old you were when Rachel died and how much you knew then, how able you were then (and are now) to realize what Rachel's death did to Momma and Poppa.

It seems to me that with Rachel's death Momma's and Poppa's faith begins to dissolve. That day it is brought home to them with a clarity they can no longer deny, or evade, that the rituals of orthodox Judaism that they've transplanted to this world are meaningless and useless. It is as if a different

198

God reigns here, an alien God, a God who scorns and mocks the Jew.

And yet they'd known this, they'd really known it, long before Rachel's death. Ours was not the ghetto world to which they'd been born, in which they'd been raised in Russia and Poland. Even as we walked from Sundown to Summer to go to *cheder*, they tried not to see that the processes of assimilation were taking their toll. Though they would not let their minds form the thoughts or their mouths speak the words the truths were here: Jacob and I, and maybe even Rachel, must secretly be eating ham or bacon whenever we go to Summer, or whenever we visit one of the homes of the *goyim* there in Sundown.

Food: It's always well-cooked. Soft and tender. Or chopped. Meat, whether it's chicken or beef, is always fat. Lean meat is scorned.

Vegetables are rarely cooked. Radishes, cucumbers, onions. Beets are pickled, or boiled. Tomatoes are pickled or stewed. Peas, beans, lentils and barley are always boiled in soups.

All food is accented with red and green peppers, red and green tomatoes. And horseradish, always horseradish. Starches are noodles and potatoes. And bread. All shapes, all sizes of bread. Always warm, always steaming, always fragrant, never enough. Black rye with sweet butter . . . three or four loaves in one night.

Except for Sabbath and holidays and special occasions there is no set schedule for meals. We all eat whenever we're hungry.

Poppa gets the best food. After all, a man needs good food to keep up his strength. Momma eats constantly, nibbling and tasting everything she cooks. She rarely sits down to eat. Feeding others is so important she neglects herself.

When she's not cleaning or cooking or helping in the store there is the never-ending work of patching and mending torn clothes, making over garments Poppa has cast off or I've outgrown. When a dress can no longer serve as a dress it's converted into an apron. When the apron's beyond service it becomes patches or washrags.

In the summer the back yard is dug up and a garden planted. In the autumn there's the bustle of canning and preserving and pickling. In winter there are geese and chickens to set. (I can still smell the scorched feathers as Momma swings the carcass of a plucked chicken across the gas flame to burn off the pinfeathers.)

Italy
August 16th

Sundown, when I'm a child, is different from what it will be when you grow up here. When you are ten or twelve there will be more Poles and Russians. Now there are mainly Irish and Welsh. Except for a few families the central and eastern Europeans have settled in Lyndy, at the southern edge of Summer, around the mills and the factories.

And there is an attitude that exists now, an attitude that will not prevail when you are growing up. The miners and their wives and their kids are rough and tough, but our being Jews does not seem to incite much suspicion or hatred. Perhaps because the few Poles and Russians act as a bridge. Momma and Poppa talk to them in their own languages. The others . . . the Irish and the Welsh . . . abuse us, when they do abuse us, as much because we're European as because we're Jews. But as times change, so do the people. Motives become more refined. (You, in your generation, have fought more kids for calling you a *sheeny* or a *kike* than Jacob or I ever had to.) During the depression, when the miners have to find someone other than themselves to attack, they turn, of course, on us. Despite their hatred, when they come begging for food Poppa gives it to them, and gives it on credit. Momma denounces Poppa. "They don't pay, they don't even say *thanks*. You're a fool." It's naïve to demand, or even expect, gratitude. No one thanks someone to whom they're indebted, whether the debt is money or love.

Before the depression, when I myself am a child, there is a

200

really intoxicating spirit of small-c communism in Sundown. For example, in autumn the kids go into the woods to pick apples. Then, on two or three consecutive weekends all the families gather at the store. The road in front of the store will one day be macadam, but now it is dirt. Bonfires are built in the middle of the road and huge cauldrons are hung above the flames. Everyone peels apples and gathers wood for the fires and takes turns stirring the apple butter. When it's finished each person who's worked takes equal shares. In late summer every family gathers cabbages from their gardens. We meet in the store, where, for hours, we slice and shred the cabbage. We fill the great vats that Poppa keeps in a back storeroom and we add the brine. Over the next few weeks everyone takes turns stirring the contents. When Poppa considers the sauerkraut ready, it is divided equally among the families.

August 18th

Except for the company stores at the coal mines ours is the only store for miles. Customers come from Sundown and Eden and Lick Hill and from farms as far away as Slippery Rock and Grove City. The miners don't trust the company stores, where prices are very high, the clerks are hired crooks and all debts are deducted from the paychecks. Unable to extend their credit from month to month at the company stores, the miners come to our store. Once they come and Poppa gives them credit he has no choice but to let them keep coming. If he refuses them additional credit they'll walk to town, to Summer, to buy what they need. And he'll lose what's owed him. His reasoning isn't faulty but it is tragically suicidal. We all know . . . and in his heart so does Poppa . . . that it is wiser to lose a small amount than, eventually, a large amount. But Poppa interprets his self-destructive attitude as intuitive business sense. And none of us even consider questioning his right to determine policy. In the end it is this refusal to speak out that ruins us all. The miners can no more be blamed for their brutal destruction of us than we can be blamed for our just as brutal destruction of ourselves. When we finally take steps to stop our sacrifices just to save Poppa's mountainous ego, it is too late.

Jacob sees it all as a trap in which the bait is Poppa's own good will. That's always been the basic difference between Jacob and me. I've never attributed good will, as a motive, to any man. Not even to Poppa.

Eventually Poppa is practically subsidizing every family in Sundown. His once fair-sized savings begin to disappear.

August 19th

When Poppa walks to Summer to the synagogue, he wears good worsted suits he's bought in Pittsburgh.

He always comes home from Pittsburgh with cartons of food he's bought in the Jewish markets there. Little wooden barrels of *schmaltz* herring, long sticks of kosher salami, kosher wieners, pastrami, corned beef, *halvah*, kosher pickles.

Momma wears starched white blouses with crocheted collars and ankle-length gray linen skirts. She has one pair of small, very delicate golden hoops she never removes from her ears. She never wears any other jewelry. She hires girls from Sundown, *shiksas*, to sweep and scrub the floors and to wash and iron the laundry. Because she hires others and manages to treat them with dignity (even though she holds them in contempt . . . "You grow up, you keep on like this, and you'll marry a *shiksa*, believe me") there is, in the minds of the miners, something of *the great lady* about Momma.

She is barely five feet tall, but because of her bearing and the grand sweep of her movements she manages to create an impression of great height. When she comes from the kitchen into the store the miners sitting on the benches around the coal stove leave off their dirty stories. Even Poppa softens and guards his voice.

Poppa, with his thick black curls and his long black mustachios, and his enormous self-esteem, is courteous or even deferential to Momma. But not to anyone else. In these days there is no reason for Poppa to admit that he could fail in any

202

task he might attempt. Later, in your time, after the unending series of disasters, Poppa's self-esteem begins to wane. To minimize his own failings it becomes necessary to exaggerate failings in others. In an astonishingly brief time he holds everyone, including himself, in great contempt. His, and our, decline begins.

But I get ahead of myself. You're interested in the past.

August 24th

Momma always wears her hair pulled back and piled in a tight and intricately woven chignon. She washes her hair every Thursday morning so she won't have to do it on the Sabbath. When she removes the last pin it is like the wall of a dam bursting. Her hair tumbles and rolls like black water. If it's summer she sits on the porch in the sunlight to dry her hair after washing it. While she sits she crochets tablecloths, working into the pattern figures of flowers blooming at the side of the porch. If it's winter she sits in front of the coal stove, turning and shifting to expose the still damp portions of hair, while she writes long letters, in Yiddish, to her sister, Molly, in Philadelphia, or to her brother Wolf in Johnstown, or to Poppa's sister Zivia in Pittsburgh.

In the evening Rachel combs Momma's hair. Max and Jacob and I sit at the kitchen table, listening to programs like Town Meeting of the Air or Spencer Keane, Tracer of Lost Persons, or Lowell Thomas or H. V. Kaltenborn. Or we talk about politics or books. Or we play parcheesi or Monopoly. There is always that one moment when we all stop simultaneously, to admire Rachel as she glides about the figure of Momma, combing and brushing and setting and pinning her hair. After you are born Momma always holds you in her lap while Rachel works. Now and then Rachel stops, leans forward, pulls Momma's hair aside and kisses your mouth and then pulls Momma's hair across your face again. Poppa, standing in the kitchen doorway so he can hear any customer come into the store, laughs and says, "Ach, my two wild roses."

203

The shelves and counters in the store and the kegs behind the counters are filled with any item anyone can want to buy. There are wool jackets and gloves and socks and shirts and underwear on the shelves. There are shotguns and rifles and boxes of ammunition. There are barrels of carbide and kegs of nails and sacks of beans and rice under the counter. The icebox, which covers a third of one large wall, is filled with sides of beef and slabs of bacon and hams and cold cuts and wheels of cheese. (Sitting in the store now you'd never believe that in those days Rachel and I often had to help Momma and Poppa take care of the customers. Sometimes we had to hire four or five kids to help Jacob and Max deliver the orders.)

You are crawling and stumbling in and out of the kitchen, dragging at the end of a string a car that leaps and bucks and twists and turns.

"Where's the baby?" Momma says, suddenly aware that she's not seen you for the last five minutes.

"Here," Rachel says. You're at her feet, like a loving puppy, and she, no matter how frantically she runs, moves with great care so as not to kick or step on you. Too often, after she makes sure Momma's not watching, she plops a Hershey Kiss into your mouth.

Most kids find an excuse to get out of their homes in the evenings, to stay away for as long as they can on weekends. Rachel and Jacob and Max and I are always anxious to finish whatever is keeping us away from home so we can return and be together in the kitchen, around the big table. Sometimes no one talks, sometimes everyone talks at once, sometimes one of us will fry onions and salami and make sandwiches and the feast will go on and on until we are all nodding and numb with fatigue. But we're reluctant to leave each other. I'll read an article in a magazine or a story or a poem and even Momma and Poppa will become impassioned in their critiques. Max and Jacob and Rachel go to incredible lengths to dispute each other and sometimes shout and threaten each other, but always, at the last moment, Momma or Poppa or I smooth all the tempers and we have a pot of soup, or coffee and cake.

Friends of mine or Rachel's from Summer, who visit us, constantly beg us to let them return. Their parents always ask them why they never invite us to their houses but always want to come to ours. They keep coming, mesmerized not just by the exotic rituals of my mother and father but by the love that is palpable in every gesture, every word, every joke, every scrap of food.

(As I write this now I look back with astonishment, with disbelief. Not one of us knew then . . . could possibly have known . . . that our house was a virtual Eden.)

By the time you are old enough to follow the footsteps of Jacob and me the footsteps will be erased. Poppa will be degraded to the status of an *amorets*.

But wait. I'm trying, as much as I can, to keep some sort of order to these notes.

Before that . . . before you follow my footsteps, I set down my footsteps for you to follow.

Jacob and I have been going to *cheder*.

I learn faster and better than poor Jacob.

By the time I am ten there is no doubt I will be a *talmud khokhem*. I am even possibly a genius. I can recite a hundred prayers and a third of the Pentateuch. No matter what Jewish house I go into I receive almost the respect Poppa receives.

At night I hear Momma singing, as she helps me get ready for bed, the song she'd heard sung to her brothers by *her* mother.

> Torah studies by light
> And sound sleep by eve
> And you'll be a *koehn*
> That I with pride love.

and:

205

My Reuben shall study all day
All day shall baby study
Sweet money shall Reuben bring
Loud songs shall we sing.

In the cradle I was observed every minute. By Momma, Poppa, aunts and uncles. Any sign of precocious intellectuality . . . a deep chuckle, a touch of the finger to the temple, a sudden expression or gesture that brings to mind some respected adult . . . any such sign is a *khokhmeh*, a guarantee of inevitable genius. "Look," someone would say, "look, look. A genius, surely."

Momma teaches me to replace my grunts and gurgles with religious blessings. I sit in Poppa's lap while he studies. I learn very early that there is some mysterious respect due those little black points on the paper. Poppa, chanting as he reads, rocks back and forth as he prays.

As Poppa reads I can turn the pages, but only if I treat each page very gently. "Like a baby's *tuches*," Poppa says. "Gentle, make gentle." Once, when I want to crawl onto Poppa's lap and he ignores me I knock the book to the floor. I don't do it again. The pain of Poppa's spanking lingers to this very moment.

Every Saturday Poppa holds his weekly Hearing for Jacob and me.

Jacob does not do as well in the Hearing as I do. Momma and Poppa criticize him.

"Another mistake! That's three! What do you want for your life? A tailor? A shoemaker? A butcher? An *amorets*?"

I weep, though Jacob does not, when Poppa whips him with his belt.

"I shake the stars," Poppa shouts, "to make money for your *cheder*. Do you appreciate it? No! But don't worry. You'll be a *talmud khokhem* if I got to boil your brains."

206

August 24th

Rachel's sixteen when you're born. Her purity, her trust of even the most wretched miner, twists my heart. Poppa, embracing her, whispers, "Rachela . . . Rachela . . . my poor Rachela." Who can know or say why he calls her that? Is it possible that he, of all people, was the only one of all of us to prophesy the tragedy her innocence would bring us?

It is inevitable that she should die young. It would be the worst obscenity to have that face and body dulled or deformed by age.

We spoil her dreadfully and yet she never grows selfish, never demanding.

We love her and she adores you. Momma says God has come to the earth in the disguise of Rachel to care for you, our baby.

You fall one day from a grapevine the kids use to swing out over a cliff. Tony Slaska carries you home. Your eyes are closed, your head hangs as if the bones in your neck have been pulverized. You're covered with blood. You're icy cold. Surely you must be dead. We all run, clearing a place for your body on the tabletop. Someone gets wet towels, someone tries to phone a doctor, someone else tries to find someone with a car to rush you to the hospital.

Rachel remains outside the panic. She leans against the wall by the window, her eyes lifted, her lips forming silent words. The crisp October light falls harshly on the windowpane but softly on her face. She murmurs aloud, once, "Benny," and you move. She comes to the table and she lifts you in her arms and your arms go about her neck.

Italy
August 26th

Before the depression, Momma and Poppa are devout. As devout as any religious fanatic I've ever known. The strict codes that they obey are firmly imposed on us.

207

Jacob and I are eventually *Bar-Mitzvahed*. Rachel is confirmed. We respect the codes not because we are devout believers but because we will get our heads thumped if we don't.

There is one ceremony around Yom Kippur where a chicken is waved above the heads of the children. The chicken absorbs all the evil. None will be left for the new year. The prayers that evening are perhaps the most serious of all prayers. It is an intimidating experience . . . standing there in a room lit only by the flame of a flickering candle, with Poppa . . . bearded and erect and fierce . . . peering down at his book while he waves the live chicken around and around his head. Being older, and wiser, and more restrained, I repress the impulse to giggle. Jacob, younger and far less wise, peeps up from under his *yarmulke* and his head rotates in rhythm to the repeated circling of the cackling chicken. As feathers flutter down through the faint light and Poppa prays and the chicken cackles Jacob begins to giggle. Without stopping his prayers Poppa lowers the arc of his swing. The chicken strikes Jacob across the mouth. Both Jacob and the chicken scream. Poppa returns to his solemnity while a chastened Jacob races to retrieve his *yarmulke*, which has sailed across the room. "Cover your pagan head!" Poppa roars and immediately his voice grows rich and solemn again in prayer as the chicken glides— wings outstretched—around and around.

The windows are always spotless. The floor is always polished. Twice a year Momma and Poppa and the rest of us climb ladders and wipe the walls with a smelly, rubbery, commercial wallpaper cleaner. Before we begin the walls are flat planes of homogenous gray. After we finish the walls are pink, with red roses and trellis and climbing green vines and bell-capped minstrels playing mandolins.

Dishes. *Fleishaca* for meat, *milchaca* for dairy. I would no sooner put meat in a *milchaca* dish than I would admit an interest in some *shiksa*. As I grow older, as Momma and Poppa grow less and less devout and I dare to admit an interest in a

208

red-haired Irish *shiksa,* there is a resignation to our desertion that grows, eventually, into conscious neglect. Dishes which once, when I was going to *cheder,* had never contained anything but cheese or butter are not only used very often for serving beef but might not even be washed before or after.

If I were to plot a curve of the dissolution of their faith it would coincide with the curve of the growth of our cynicism . . . Jacob's and Rachel's and Max's and mine. The faith that had nourished and sustained them when we were children not only does not sustain us; we rebuke it. That it is, at the same time, rebuked by the *goyim* means nothing. This is as it has been for centuries, as it will be forever. But for *us* to rebuke it, to scorn it, proves Momma and Poppa failures not just as parents but, more important, as Jews.

It is as if we spit upon the Talmud.

The future life, the *Olam Habo* . . . gone forever.

When Rachel dies there also dies the last possibility of a reprieve. Surely, had she lived, she would have chosen as a husband a *talmud khokhem.*

Italy
August 28th

In the attic are two barrels very carefully packed with all the pots and pans and dishes that will be used during Passover. The first night both cupboards in the kitchen are sealed. The walls and floors are scrubbed again. Every gram of evidence of any previous way of life is purged from sight. Then, when Momma and Poppa are satisfied that there will be no contamination, Poppa and Jacob and I haul down the barrels. The Passover feasts begin.

During the year the store is closed before dusk on Friday nights. After that no one turns on a light or even burns a match until dusk Saturday night. Should a burner go out on the stove or a bulb need replacing, one of the kids from Sundown, one of the *goyim,* is called in to do the dirty deed.

All day Friday Momma has cooked and baked enough food so that there need be no work until Saturday night. Just before dusk on Friday she lights the candles and she prays, rolling her hands through and over the flames, calling up again (from their week-old graves) the spirits of every dead sister and brother and parent and grandparent she's ever known and loved and lost. The rest of us . . . even Poppa . . . sit in silence at the table, waiting. Finally, exhausted, drained of tears, Momma turns and we eat. There is steaming chicken soup and chopped liver and potato *kugel* and kosher tomatoes and pickles. There is chicken or roast or, occasionally, goose. There's *challah* and apple pie and fruit. Poppa serves, even to you, the baby, his dandelion or elderberry or clover-blossom wine.

After supper we talk. Sometimes there are Jews from Summer. There are arguments about Europe today and Europe yesterday, about America today and America tomorrow. There are reminiscences about Poland and Russia, about departures and arrivals, about births and deaths. Stories about pogroms, about flights across continents and oceans. There are stories about lice and mice and rats and bats, about beatings and berry-picking picnics. Details about sad and funny marriage ceremonies, uniting tragic and comic characters, are remembered, disputed, forgotten and told again.

Saturday mornings Momma and Poppa are up before dawn. They walk the three miles to town, to the synagogue, where they sit on the hard benches. They have dinner with one of the Jewish families in town.

Poppa ignores all the criticism for keeping such a good Jewish family so far away from the synagogue and other Jews. Momma never once joins the critics; she sits in silence and appears to be thinking of other things. (These last few years all those complaints, piled one on top of the other for forty years, begin to fester. They're seeping out now, a constant ooze of pus.)

In *schul* Poppa sings the liturgy with a powerful baritone. No other Jew can hope to match the power and beauty of his voice. The cantor, knowing this, uses Poppa. Back and forth they toss their prayers. Standing before the golden arc, the cantor turns and sings to Poppa. Poppa, weaving back and forth, sings back, his shawl up over his shoulders and up over his head, almost covering his dark, pious face. The young Jews who've been lazing in the sun outside hurry back in, drawn as if by trumpets. They stand, silent, humble, reverent.

From beside Poppa I look up to the balcony where the women sit. I see Momma in the first row. Her own dark face is flushed. A mist seems to lie across her large dark doe-eyes. One hand rests on the railing. A finger lifts to give me a delicate signal that she too is witness once again to Poppa's glory.

During the week, in the early morning, every morning, Poppa comes downstairs to the kitchen. Momma follows soon after.

Poppa wraps his phylacteries about his arm and head and he faces the wall—across which are strung hundreds of drying, aromatic mushrooms—and he *dovens*, with the smell of the woods in his nostrils.

Momma sits at the table, listening, her own lips shaping each syllable of every word. She knows by heart every prayer for every occasion.

August 30th

With Rachel's death their devotion dies too. Poppa no longer *dovens*. They go to the synagogue less and less often. They do not even lament the horrifying probabilities that Jacob and I might be eating ham or bacon at the home of our friends in Summer.

The only ritual that continues is the Friday night feast but . . . after the lighting of the candles and the even more hysterical weeping memories . . . the food becomes less and less tasty. The talk grows more forced. Eventually there is only

211

the lighting of the candles and the prayers that exhaust Momma and send her to bed (Poppa no longer sits in the kitchen now, and often he keeps the store open). We make sandwiches for ourselves.

The last Friday night before I leave for the army I sit at that table. It's impossible. The linoleum floor is dull and spotted and worn raw. The sink is full of a collection of unwashed pots and pans. At the top of the walls the paper is beginning to peel, chipped plaster shows through. The globe is gone from around the bulb, which hangs on a long fly-specked wire. Momma, wearing a thin and not too clean dress, stands by the coal stove, almost dazed. In the store, which has been empty of customers for hours, Poppa leans on the counter, staring at the flames in the coal stove, encircled by shelves and counters and glass cases, all of them nearly empty.

September 5th

When I am eighteen, Jacob is fifteen.

Jacob is the conscience of the family. He always has been and, to his misfortune, always will be. When customers move and leave me to pay their paper bills, Jacob worries more than I do. When Momma is sick it's Jacob who calls the doctor, arranges for her hospital care, makes sure she follows the doctor's orders. When Poppa's in jail it's Jacob, nineteen or twenty then, who works nights in a tire factory so he can keep the store alive.

During the time that Poppa's in jail, Max, delegated by Jacob to keep the store operating, decides to organize Poppa's impossible bookkeeping. When Poppa comes home from jail he's furious.

Max says he only wants Poppa to be sure he knows what everyone owes him.

"I know, to the penny, who owes me what."

Jacob, on his way to work, stops to mediate the argument. Max says Poppa's owed more than we can ever get.

212

"What do you mean, *we?* Who's *we? I* own this store. *I* run this business. Not *we!* Not *we!*"

Max insists Poppa only guesses at the amounts of the debts. It's a terrible way to run a business. Poppa's furious. A child, a baby, is telling him . . . *him!* . . . with years of experience, how to run a business.

Jacob intervenes. He puts down his lunch bucket and picks up the notebook Max has so carefully organized. "Poppa, how much do the Caseys owe you?"

Poppa thinks. "One hundred eighty-six dollars, fifty cents," he says.

"Right," Jacob says. "Pettibone?"

Poppa thinks for a moment and says, "Ninety-four dollars, seven cents."

"That's right. How about McClellan?"

Poppa thinks. "Two hundred fifty dollars," he says. "And thirteen cents."

"That's right," Jacob says, and he tosses Max's notebook into the stove. He shrugs at Max. Max, saying nothing, walks away. He knows, and accepts, what Jacob tells him the next day. Poppa was wrong on every figure, sometimes by as much as fifty dollars. Jacob knew that of the two Max was more able to accept defeat.

I realize now that Poppa knew, intuitively, that that was what Jacob knew and felt.

Italy
September 8th

Max is an enigma. He's not the conscience that Jacob is, nor the intellectual which I presume to be. He's practical, realistic, openly and admittedly ambitious.

(I used to resent him. Recently I've begun to wonder if he's not the wisest of us all. His needs are all material, all very tangibly satisfied.) Momma can not understand Max and Poppa can not abide him. After all, he senses in Max the very potential for success that has been destroyed in himself.

213

Max, about seventeen, is standing in the store, in front of the coal stove. Six or seven miners sit on the benches. It's snowing outside. The stove is glowing pink. There is an odor of steaming wool as the miners' clothes begin to dry in the heat.

It is early in the depression; 1932 or 1933. We are one of about five families in Sundown that are not on relief.

Max, his back to the stove, has been studying the nearly empty shelves. Suddenly he says to Poppa that he has an idea. Business is bad, he says, because Poppa does not have the products for sale that the miners need. Remodel the store, Max says; make it smaller. Specialize in things the miners need and cannot get anywhere else . . . not even in town. "And don't sell any of it on credit," Max says.

Poppa, of course, starts shouting.

Max says he is only trying to help. Poppa says he doesn't need help, not from a wise-guy smart-aleck who takes money from the drawer.

Max is furious now. As a child he *had* taken pennies but since then he's more than returned, in hours worked, everything he's taken. He says something, Poppa says something, Max says something else and Poppa, roaring like an animal, leaps over the counter. He lifts Max in the air and throws him. Max strikes the stove, which collapses and showers him with hot stovepipe and ashes.

The scars on Max's neck and forehead are from that night. Can you wonder that Max is dedicated to being the success in business that Poppa could never be?

Benny, until this moment I've never understood, Max. I do now.

Italy
September 14th

Benny:

I could go on for days and days and pages and pages. There are things I would like to have said, things I'm glad I haven't said. I must stop now or not even these notes will get to you.

214

I hope I've given you something of what you've requested; something of . . . apparently . . . what you've needed.

The one incident I've not touched on that I wish I could is the death of Herschel. For his death to have come the way it did, at the time it did . . . well, it was perhaps the cruelest blow. Voltaire says that *chance* is a word void of sense; nothing can exist without a cause. What could be the cause for Herschel's death except God's own despicable lust for torture? If God is a vengeful God who has to torture, I, for one, can not adore Him.

The day I received the letter from Max telling me about the death and the funeral I felt a betrayal of such dimension that my mind couldn't accept it. I've had to feed it into my mind piece by piece, over a period of months . . . of years . . . or else I would simply have put a .45 to my head and blown out my brains that very day. I've wanted to believe in a God, I've needed to, for so long . . . but how could I? *Why* should I?

If *I* felt betrayed, try to imagine how Momma and Poppa (who, ever since they had learned how to talk, had adored and trusted Him) . . . try to imagine how betrayed *they* must have felt first at the death of Rachel and then at the death of Herschel.

If Rachel's death was the beginning of the end, Herschel's death was proof that the end was inevitable and at hand.

In your letter you sound so anxious to fight against the Nazis. Don't be. There will be others to fight . . . plenty of others . . . called by different names, perhaps . . . but there will be others as foul as the Nazis.

And don't make the grandiose mistake of assuming . . . as you appear to be doing . . . that the United States and her allies are on a holy crusade to save the Jews. They are not. The United States . . . Roosevelt, Congress, the people . . . couldn't care less about the fate of the Jews. It is the merest coincidence that the country cremating millions of Jews happens to be our enemy. If Hirohito, in his insanity, had not forced the United States to enter the war Roosevelt and Congress and American businessmen and farmers and workers would have loved to do profitable business with Hitler.

Why am I here, then? I'm here because I'm a Jew. And that's degrading because I detest nationalism, I detest patriotism, whether it's Russian or German or American. Or Jewish.

What will be changed when the Germans are defeated? Nothing much. Perhaps, as an incidental consequence, Jews won't be used as fuel logs in German furnaces, but, in a few years, the same German bankers, the same German industrialists, the same German generals will be back in business. As our allies.

Though theologies and economic systems fade and societies rise and fall, man goes on. My grief comes not from being a Jew but from being a man.

I've almost come to regret each evening that I've made it through another day. I'm saddened that I . . . we . . . leave such a legacy to you and your generation. Unfortunately, you're fated to leave as degenerate a legacy to the generation that follows you.

And yet . . . despite all my despair, what do I find?

I find that I end this letter with a statement of love. For you, for Momma, for Poppa. A surprising and somehow reassuring little discovery, a subversive little testament, perhaps, to my . . . our . . . grace and salvation.

Reuben

Two days after I receive this letter a telegram arrives, notifying us that Reuben has been killed in action in Italy.

About Momma
Autumn, 1944

The Summer bus stops at the city line, so I meet Momma at the top of the hill, at the last bus stop. She doesn't mind riding the bus but she does not like walking down the hill, through the woods, at night. When she and Poppa used to go to town every weekend to the synagogue, they would always be driven back to Sundown by someone from the home in which they'd stayed . . . usually Mendel Leventhal or Abe Levine or Sol Mintz. Momma would always invite them in for coffee and cake and Poppa would open a bottle of dandelion or clover-blossom wine.

Passing through the store to the kitchen, they'd comment on the new ice cream freezer or the modern light fixtures or they'd squeeze the vegetables and praise Poppa's talents for selecting produce or they'd grunt at the price of some can or bottle on the shelf and ask, loud enough so the miners could hear, how we could make a living, our prices were so low. Then they would sit with us in the kitchen and over the coffee and cake and wine there would be a loud and animated debate about life. Life in Sundown, in Summer, in Pittsburgh, in Poland, in Russia, in Germany.

Today neither Poppa nor the store can stand the test of such attention.

This weekend has been the first in almost a year that Momma has gone to the synagogue. As we walk down the hill she chatters about Ginsberg's new truck, the Mintzes' new meat market. With gas and building materials rationed, Ginsberg has been forced to build his own tow truck from various ancient deposits in his junkyard. Sol Mintz has had to tear down three deserted farmhouses to obtain enough lumber and pipe and wire to expand his market. Momma laughs. "The only new thing in the market," she says, "is the meat. And the meat I ain't so sure about either. I only thank God it ain't a kosher market."

As we walk she continues chattering about the new young rabbi and his pretty wife, Reba; about the most recent marriages, the most recent births, the most recent deaths. The Selznick boy was killed in the Philippines and the Hirschbergs have received word their son is missing in action. But this news, as Momma relates it, does not move her to tearful apprehension for her own sons, as it would have done only yesterday. The trip to the synagogue and the weekend with old friends has revived her spirits. As she holds on to my hand to keep from slipping on the loose gravel, to keep from tripping over something in the darkness, I promise myself that somehow or other I must see to it that she goes to Summer every weekend.

Then a blade of sound . . . of roaring motor and screeching brakes . . . cleaves the darkness, which falls apart and reassembles. In the new darkness, the new silence, I discover that Momma's hand is no longer in mine.

I call out, "Momma." No reply. "Momma."

I crawl on my hands and knees, from one ditch, one bank, to the other. Nothing. I move up and down the road, from bank to bank. A cold object I'm sure is a wrist becomes a beer bottle. I continue crawling, screening the gravel and asphalt with my fingers. I call out but hear no reply. Not a sigh, not a groan. Not even the wind rustling the grass.

A light flickers through the trees. A car appears at the top of the hill. The lights lower, falling ahead of me, throwing my shadow down the road to the next bend. The road is empty. Has Momma been plucked from the earth?

The car stops. "Benny, for Chrissake, what are you doing? You sick?"

"Mr. Trebuka, help me find Momma."

The doctor tells Poppa and me that the fractures in Momma's legs are serious but even more serious . . .

Yes?

Well, there are fractured ribs. Possibly, probably, a fractured vertebra. And almost certainly very serious damage to the liver and spleen.

What, I ask, does the doctor suggest?

The doctor suggests that if Momma were his mother he'd send her to Pittsburgh. Here, at Summer Memorial Hospital, the staff facilities are limited. "The army gets everything, you know. The best doctors, the best equipment, the latest drugs. But," and he shrugs, *"c'est la guerre."*

Momma will have to be taken immediately, by ambulance, to Pittsburgh. There is a specialist there, at Haven of the Good Shepherd. A Dr. Herman Apperson, who's too old for the army. He's Momma's only hope.

I send two telegrams to California, one to Max in Los Angeles and one to Jacob, in care of his Port of Embarkation in San Francisco. Both telegrams are the same.

MOMMA IN HAVEN OF GOOD SHEPHERD HOSPITAL
IN PITTSBURGH. CRITICALLY INJURED.
PLEASE COME IF POSSIBLE.

I receive a telegram from Max the next day.

AM VERY SAD BUT MY COMING WOULD BENEFIT
NO ONE. IT WOULD BE TOO PAINFUL FOR
EVERYONE. MARY AND I SEND OUR LOVE
AND OUR HOPES.

The day after Max's telegram a reply comes from Jacob.

WILL ARRIVE TWO TO FOUR DAYS.

Poppa sits in the store, in front of the coal stove. It's late October. This is the second or third fire in the stove since last winter. The firelight through the door's grating sends little yellow claws scampering across Poppa's face. In the last hour two miners and a miner's wife have come into the store on the pretense of buying bread or milk. They know there is no longer a loaf of bread on the shelves or a quart of milk in the refrigerator. Each of them asks if they can do anything. Yes, I tell them. They can leave us alone.

I'm unable to get Poppa into the kitchen to eat. A glass of wine I set before him an hour ago is still untouched.

"Poppa, please eat."

"I'm not hungry."

"But you have to eat."

"I don't want to eat."

For lack of anything else to do I pick up his glass and drink down the wine in one gulp.

"You'd think," Poppa says, "the army, someone's mother gets hurt, they'd let him come home."

"He'll come. He said two to four days. It's been two days since we got his telegram." Poppa knows I notified Max and Mary, too, but I remind him, since he's not mentioned them at all. "Max and Mary can't make it. They send their love." I wait for some reaction, but there is none.

At one time Poppa, like Momma, would have said, at any reference to Max, "Max is dead." Tonight it seems that the energy required to mobilize even moderate passions about

220

Max is depleted. My brother's name draws less response than did the glass of wine when I'd placed it in front of Poppa.

Poppa sighs. "Such a life she's had. Such a filthy life. A life a pig shouldn't have."

Anger spreads up through my chest and across my face. I feel its flush in my cheeks. The words *And whose fault is that?* leap to my lips, but I stop them. Poppa wants to hear me say, as I've said many times recently, *It's no one's fault.* I can't say that, either. I go to the window.

There is a voluptuous harvest moon in the sky. My stomach twists as I think of such a moon a few years before, when Roman and Goose and I, with three girls from Lyndy, sat in a car on a hilltop overlooking Gornick's farm. Roman is dead, Goose has been decorated for bravery in Africa and has disappeared. I've seen Julie, who was my girl that night, several times since then. She will be leaving to join the WACs in two weeks.

"I try to fool myself," Poppa says. "I should know better. From the old country, from Momma and Poppa, from their life, I should know better. But what do I do? Rachel . . . *olov hashalom* . . . she dies . . . she gets sick, she dies. An omen, that's what it is, such a perfect angel dies. But everyone gets sick, I say. Then Herschel dies. Another omen. Straight from the mouth of God. An accident: that's what I say. Anyone can drown, can bleed to death. But I know . . . I know . . . that day Herschel dies it comes to an end, my world."

His reflection in the window brings up a fist to shake at God, but instead the fist presses his chest. Unused, Poppa's hand falls back into his lap.

Outside on the porch there is one solitary milk crate. The porch has never seemed so deserted; the store, the town has never seemed so neglected. At this hour a few years ago there would be kids chasing each other under the streetlight or playing pump-pump-pullaway or hunch-me-go-punch-me or, if there were snow, there would be a gang of kids in the vacant

221

lot, stomping a giant circle in the drifts for a game of fox-and-geese. But the last game has been played in that lot. It is vacant no more. Ellsworth Cotton's gray cube of concrete blocks is there: well-lit, fully stocked, with a sign over the cash register that says: IN GOD WE TRUST . . . ALL OTHERS PAY CASH.

While I stand at the window Mrs. McClellan comes out of Ellsworth's store, a sack of groceries in her arms. She throws a brief glance at our store and then scurries out of sight into the shadows. She is one of those few who seem ill-at-ease about patronizing Ellsworth, perhaps because she owes us a few hundred dollars more than most of the others do.

In the darkness at the other side of the road, beyond the railroad tracks, the Connequenessing is swelling itself with water and debris from the recent rainstorm. Uprooted trees and now and then a bloated corpse of a horse or a cow drift toward the Monongahela River. On the hills sloping down toward the Connequenessing the oaks and maples and birches are beginning to drop their leaves. At this very moment the early evening frost is scorching the green leaves that remain. Tomorrow the reds and the oranges will be even more intense than they were today. In two or three weeks the hillsides that ripple with fire colors now will be converted into mounds of mud the color of soggy ashes. Soon, very soon, the trees will be black scratches in the snow.

"I wonder who hit her," I say.

"What's it matter?" Poppa says. "What would you do, you knew? You'd shoot him? You'd sue him? For what? I used to think: they curse me, I'll curse them worse; they punch me twice, I'll punch them four times. It's no good. It doesn't matter. Me . . . I give up. They win."

The scent of ether and lysol and medicines in the corridor of the hospital is reassuring. Diseases are being cured here, injuries are being healed. The nurses . . . all of them . . . are nuns. Quiet, calm, efficient. Their piety, their self-assurance is contagious. I know without doubt that they will help Momma live.

Outside the room Sister Rose Marie grips my elbow. "Ah, your poor mother eats nothing at all," she says. "If she eats we can, with God's help, save the poor woman." There are a few maternal pats on my shoulder. "See what you can do with her. That's a good lad."

I wonder if I've been directed to the wrong room. The bed is empty. No, not empty, but the patient in the bed is a pale, emaciated child. The eyelids roll open and the large dark orbs search me out and find my own eyes. It is Momma.

"Benjamin . . . come close." I lean over the bed, trying not to touch her with my body for fear I'll crush her. Her lips, once so soft and cool, are hot and dry, rough as sand. "Benjamin . . . hurry . . . I want home . . . they poison me . . . I know . . . I hear them talk . . . they whisper but I hear . . . they hate the Jew . . . I know them . . . they push their *traife* food in my mouth . . . I spit it out . . . take me home . . . I can walk . . . I'll show . . . help me up. . . ."

"Momma, you're sick. You have to stay here."

"They poison the Jew. I know. They hate the Jew. I hear them. Whispers, always whispers."

"That's the way they talk, Momma. Please, you have to stay. You have to eat. Jacob's coming . . . you want to be strong for Jacob, don't you?"

"You think you're smart, with your stories. You don't fool me. Jacob don't come."

"He is coming. I promise. He sent me a telegram."

"I won't eat. The food's *traife*. . . ."

"Momma, there's a specialist here, the best doctor . . ."

"A Catholic, like them."

"Momma, he's a Jew."

The bottle suspended above her head, dripping liquid into her veins through a tube, jiggles now as she stiffens her body and tries to turn her head to see me better. "Apperson?" she asks. "Apperson a Jew?"

223

"It's Abelson, not Apperson."

"His first name . . . what's his first name?"

"Hyman. Hyman Abelson."

Despite herself, she can not retain the suspicion in her eyes. "You're certain?"

"I'm certain, Momma."

She relaxes, with a sigh. "You'll stay, I eat? They poison me, you'll stop them?"

"I'll stop them. I promise with all my heart."

I inform Sister Rose Marie of the story I've told. She is outraged. "I'll be no party to such deceit," she says, storming into Momma's room. She brushes Momma's hair back from her forehead. "Your son tells me you'll have a bit of food."

"The doctor . . . what's his name?"

"Now what did your good son tell you it is?"

"He tells me it's Abelson. Hyman Abelson. Is it true?"

Sister Rose Marie gasps. "You don't believe your own son? I've never heard such a thing."

"He's a good boy," Momma says. Her hand creeps out from under the blankets and fumbles for mine. I close my fingers about hers. "My only son home. The war takes all my sons, all but my baby . . . *mein teir, mein hertz.*"

Sister Rose Marie murmurs, "I'll send a tray in." With a soft rustle of cloth she glides from the room.

"Benjamin?"

"Yes, Momma?"

"You'll stay here?"

"I'll stay right here."

"They hate me. You don't believe but it's true. They're taught in school they should hate the Jew."

"Momma, they don't hate you."

"You don't know. None of you know. You got it so easy in this country you're fooled. You eat their *huserei* in their house . . . I know, I know. Don't tell me different. You walk at night on the road with them, the *shiksas*. You'll learn. They wait a chance to beat you, to spit on you, take the food from your mouth. All my life I see it." Tears pop out of her eyes and roll down her cheeks. I wipe her face with a corner of the sheet. "In Germany . . . Poland . . . Russia . . . we knew. It was out . . . not hid . . . everyone knew it, could see it. Curse the Jew . . . beat the Jew . . . steal from the Jew . . . kill the Jew. But here . . . you don't see it you think it ain't here. It's here. Believe me, you'll learn." Her voice fades and she seems to sleep. But she jerks awake. She glances wildly about the room, sees me and asks, her voice shrill, "Max, he'll be here?" The sound seems to awaken her to the fact that for a moment she's been hysterical. She settles back. "Don't ask him. Don't tell him. I forget him. You heard, I don't once say his name."

Poppa prods me awake. "The phone," he says.

I stumble out of bed and down the stairs to the kitchen. It is too cold to disturb the air around the string hanging from the light bulb. I sit in the darkness. "Hello."

"Benny, that you?"

At first I'm sure it's the foreman. He probably wants me to work an extra shift tomorrow. Or is it Dr. Apperson?

"It's Jacob. I'm in Pittsburgh, at the hospital."

My legs begin to quiver and then my upper body. I almost drop the phone. I can't think of a word to say. Suddenly I am crying. I'm embarrassed, but more than that I'm astonished. I'd been, secretly, quite proud of myself and the grown-up way with which I'd been managing things. Yet here I am, crying like a baby.

"Go ahead, kid. Let it go."

"I'm . . . I'm O.K. . . . I just . . . I'm just tired. How are you?"

"I'm fine. It's been a wild three days but I made it."

"Have you seen Momma?"

"She was asleep when I got here. I missed you by about ten minutes. How the hell did it happen? I tried to ask Poppa but

225

he ran off as soon as he knew it was me. It wasn't him, was it? Did Poppa do it?"

"God, no, Jacob. I'm as worried about him now as I am about Momma."

"Why? What's wrong with him?"

"He . . . he just scares me. All day, all night, he just sits and stares. He keeps shaking his head. It's as if he's blaming himself for everything."

"Look, he's never blamed himself for anything. It's always been someone else's fault. Momma's . . . Max's . . . Reuben's . . . the miners' . . . never his. If he's doing it now he has a lot of time to make up."

There's a fuzzy sound of fatigue coating the bitterness in Jacob's voice. He must be tired. It's been a long trip.

"Don't worry about Poppa, Ben. He's tough. Tell me what did happen."

I tell him everything, including the fact that the driver never stopped.

I can almost see Jacob, standing in the telephone booth at the edge of the lobby. He's looking across the lobby at the information desk. What is he thinking now?

It's been almost two years since he's been home. I was in my last year of high school, hoping that I too (as Reuben and Jacob and Max had) would be leaving soon for the army. I did not fear for Jacob as I did for Reuben and Max. Jacob was tough in the way I imagined soldiers had to be to survive.

Young and healthy, I was anxious to get away from Sundown, from home, from Momma and Poppa. Steeped in the lore of the persecution of Jews, I was being offered an opportunity for revenge that very few Jews had ever been offered. After centuries of torture the torturers were about to be repaid. Here was the enemy . . . the Germans . . . the Nazis. Like the word *Cossacks* the words *Germans* and *Nazis*, at the sound, excited memories of atrocities performed before my birth, before Momma was born, before her mother's mother had been born.

I wanted to enlist. I wanted to be there, face to face with the Nazis. I didn't want to be in the navy or the air force or the artillery or the quartermaster . . . I wanted to be in the infantry, where I could see and smell the enemy, where I could touch him, could grab him, could pound and stab him, where I could see the blood pouring out of his wounds.

But the Jews in Summer intervened. They thought I should stay home to take care of Momma and Poppa. I was not drafted.

I know that Momma's sadness at the departure of her other sons would be nothing compared to her sadness at the departure of me, her baby. I didn't care. But yes . . . I did care. I yearned to go but I also wished I might stay, to do just as the Jews in Summer had urged me to do: help Momma and Poppa, support them, comfort them. I don't know which tormented me more: the *need* to leave them or the fear and regret that I would *have* to leave them.

Before the accident the decision would not have been mine to make. It would have been the draft board's. I could always have defended my departure by insisting that it was the law. There was nothing I could do about it.

But now if Momma survives she'll be an invalid. She'll need more help than ever. I'll be wanting more than ever to leave and I'll be hating more than ever to desert her.

" . . . Benny, are you there? Operator, were we cut off? Benny . . ."

"Yes, I'm here."

"Is she badly hurt?"

I tell him what the doctor told me.

"And you have no idea who did it."

"I have an idea, yes."

"Who?"

"I'm only guessing, Jacob, but . . . well, I think it was Cosco. He hasn't been around. Usually I see him two, three times a day. His car's always parked outside his house. He's gotten ration stamps somewhere, so he doesn't worry about gas. He's about the only one in Sundown who drives to Summer. His car always used to be parked in front of his house. It hasn't been. I've tried to get inside his garage but it's always locked. With a new lock. It's never been locked before."

I can hear the muffled paging of a Dr. Burch in the background. Jacob asks, "Ben . . . what would you do if you found out for sure that it was Cosco?"

"I don't know. Poppa asked me the same thing. He said it wouldn't do any good, even if we knew. All we could do is put him in jail. If we could prove it."

I can hear Jacob's breathing in the phone. "Are you coming tomorrow?" he asks.

"Yes, in the evening. I'm working day shift now."

"I'll stay in Pittsburgh tonight. I'll see you here tomorrow night. And Ben . . ."

"Yes?"

"Take it easy."

"I will." We wait, each reluctant to break off contact with the other. "I'm glad you're here," I say.

I sit there in the darkness after I hang up the phone. How will it be now, with Jacob home? With the two of us . . . and Poppa . . . sitting here at the table? Not long ago . . . But no reminiscences now. It's too cold.

Upstairs, in the doorway of Poppa's room, I hear his heavy breathing.

"Jacob's coming home with me tomorrow night. He says to give you his love." His breathing is heavier. "Poppa, did you hear me?"

"I hear."

I go to my room and sit on the bed. My eyes burn from the lack of sleep. I'm trembling. Pulling on a sweater and a pair of pants, I go downstairs. Maybe, if I make some coffee and have a sandwich, I'll be able to sleep better.

I fumble in the darkness for the string that hangs from the light bulb. It's as if the room has never been illuminated for me since Jacob left for the army.

228

The once distinct wallpaper pattern . . . the roses, the trellis . . . have faded to a barely discernible splatter of gray spots on a gray background. Shreds of paper hang from the ceiling trim. Webs of dust billow in the corners. On the walls, at the level of the chair-backs, the laths, brown and splintered, show through the cracked plaster.

Layers of newspapers stick to the table's surface, glued there by an aged accumulation of eggs and grease. Curious, I examine the pages. Some are three and four weeks old.

Every flat surface in the kitchen is covered with dishes, pots and pans. The sink is packed with refuse. Deposits of coffee, chunks of soggy bread, potato peelings, eggshells spill out of every bowl and cup and pan. Jackets and shirts and trousers are draped across the arms and backs of chairs.

For twenty years I've been living in this room. Has this sweet aroma of rot been present forever?

I rub my eyes and half expect, half hope, the disorder will be cleared when I look again. But it's there. The linoleum floor that was always . . . once upon a time . . . so gleaming and so smooth is cracked and chipped, covered with dust and hair balls and papers, with spots of a hundred different sizes and a thousand different textures and colors.

When . . . what day . . . had this happened?

I see Momma on her hands and knees polishing the floor and the furniture. I see her wiping vigorously at the windows with vinegar-soaked newspapers. I see her brown-dove hands touching the blossoms and flowers in the yard. I see the flowers in bottles and glasses and vases on the table, the windowsill, the sinkboard. I see the starched white tablecloth covered with platters of steaming chicken and bowls of potato *kugel* and fresh green beans and warm bread and boiled beets and sliced pickles, with thin-stemmed wine glasses and heavy water goblets to the upper right of her gold-rimmed china.

I see all this, but it's not here.

I go upstairs to my room. Has it been weeks or months since the bedding was laundered? It's been months. I know by the telltale spots left by the crushed bedbugs that have not been active since summer.

The first time . . . that first time I was bitten . . . I was not aware that the bite had been from a bedbug. The third time I was bitten . . . on the neck . . . I was asleep. I reached up to feel the painful area and caught a bug between my thumb and forefinger. I could feel the tiny legs racing.

I got out of bed and pulled the light cord. Some kind of flying insect, I thought, new to Sundown. I laid it on the floor and when it tried to scurry under the bed instead of flying out the window, I picked up a shoe and squashed it.

Bitten more and more often each successive night, I awakened once to find several of the bugs crawling across my pillow. I picked them all up and threw them out the window.

Before long I was being awakened by bites ten or twelve times a night. On one especially hot Friday night I leaped up, lit the light and discovered hundreds of the red-brown bodies . . . some as large as the head of a match, some as small as the head of a pin . . . crawling across the blankets and across the edge of the mattress. I threw back the mattress. Every single spring and every single depression around every single button on the mattress was filled with a fine creamy down that simmered with white eggs and red-brown bugs of all sizes.

I rushed downstairs to the kitchen and found Reuben's large dictionary. I turned to the three pages of colored illustrations. There it was: *cimex lectularius*. In parentheses: *bedbug*.

The definition for bedbug:

A wingless, bloodsucking hemipterous insect (cimex lectularius), primarily a parasite of human beings, sometimes infesting houses and especially beds.

Where had they come from? What could I do to get rid of them? There was no one to go to for advice. Reuben was in the army, so was Jacob. Max, discharged, was living in Los An-

230

geles. I couldn't even ask Goose or Roman, since they, too, were gone.

I went back to bed and finally fell asleep but I awakened to find the slick, crisp little things creeping in and out of my mouth, across my tongue, into my ears. I spat them out, grabbed them from my face and hurled them through the darkness against the wall. The next morning I noticed, for the first time, the red welts on Momma's legs. That was enough.

I washed and changed clothes and went to Summer, to a hardware store operated by an old man who'd been a friend of Poppa's. He'd once helped Poppa get rid of rats.

"Kerosene," he said. He loaned me a gallon can and a spray gun.

I walked back to Sundown and collected every piece of bed-clothes. Momma watched as I boiled pot after pot of water and prepared the aged washing machine for one of its final endurance tests.

Momma used to change the linen on every bed in the house at least once a week, sometimes twice a week. It had been months since these bed clothes had been changed. While the old washing machine thumped and throbbed and tried to walk across the floor Momma stared, just barely interested, as I mopped up the water that leaked out of the tub and onto the linoleum.

After I boiled more water and rinsed the clothes and ran them piece by piece through the hazardous wringers, I hung them, as well as I could manage, on the clothesline. Then I went upstairs and pulled back the mattresses. I sprayed every spring, every button. I sprayed every crevice and crack in the plaster of every wall. By the time I finished it was dark, time for me to go to work.

The following morning, when I came home from work, barely able to crawl up the steps, I saw that the clothes had been rehung, efficiently, on the clothesline.

Poppa had hauled my mattress downstairs and had swept it and pounded it with a carpet-beater. It was being aired in the

231

sunlight. I helped Poppa carry it back upstairs. While I washed, Momma made up the bed with fresh linen.

She'd dusted my room and had begun cleaning the rest of the house. She'd bathed and changed from her old, sour-smelling dress to a clean one. Poppa, who'd shaved and also changed clothes, was in the process of filling boxes with trash and garbage from the kitchen and the back yard and the back porch.

I slept until Momma awakened me for supper. The kitchen was filled with the aromas of boiling soup and baking bread. Jelly and peanut butter jars on the windowsills and sinkboard were filled with flowers. The floor had been scrubbed. There was a white cloth on the table.

When I went into the store to tell Poppa supper was ready, he grinned at me and waved his arm. The shelves had been dusted and washed and the few cans neatly restacked. The empty glass cases had been cleaned.

We didn't talk about what had happened. Each of us felt the same, I'm sure. To try to explain or defend our neglect would end up being embarrassing. Better to go on as if there's been no diversion from the old days, from our old way of living.

The three of us sat there, exhausted, clean, friendly, exultant. Making noises of satisfaction as we ate and drank. Now and then we talked of the garden, my job, the latest gossip from Summer.

For several nights Momma stayed up past one o'clock, ironing clothes that she and Poppa had washed during the day. She began to cook again. Not just fried potatoes but all of my favorites . . . baked fish, chopped liver, *gefilte* fish, chocolate cake, *challah, strudel.*

Poppa, clean and newly shaved every morning, began to read his prayers again, in the morning and at night. He did not wrap his arm and forehead with his phylacteries, but I knew that he would soon. It seemed to me that both Momma and Poppa were resettling themselves, going back to the kind of life which had been theirs in their youth.

It was then that Reuben's letter arrived, a letter in which, in

232

answer to my pleas, he described in detail what it had been like in this house when he had been a child. It had been much as it had been these days.

Poppa had been sitting at the table with me every night, before I went to work. The three of us talked about restocking the store. We planned to start out slowly, with bread and milk and basic canned goods. We'd advance to meats and vegetables. Then candies and cakes. Then clothes again: work shirts, Levis, underwear. In three months Ellsworth Cotton would be on his knees, begging us for relief.

Momma hummed as we talked. She darned my socks, patched my work clothes and even began to knit Poppa a sweater for the winter. She seemed untouched by the grim predictions of news reporters on the radio. Her faith seemed not only to have been renewed, it seemed firmer than ever. Despite all the terrifying predictions she was certain that things would turn out well. Wait, we'd see. Everyone would come home. The world would be at peace. Reuben and Jacob would be sitting, like the old days, here in the kitchen, drinking coffee, eating sandwiches, arguing about books, about politics. As strong as her faith was, it was not yet strong enough to permit her to mention Max.

I did not read them Reuben's letter. After all it was a reply to a very personal plea from me. (They knew about it. The envelope was too bulky to be missed. I told them it was simply more copies of the army newspaper, *Stars and Stripes*, which Reuben had sent to me before.)

Reuben was correct. Knowing more about the past, I was ready to accept the present. I lay in bed and reread the entire letter several times. This weekend I would write him a long reply. The news I had would reassure him. He sounded so cynical, so depressed, so desperately in need of the very letter I would write.

His letter arrived on a Monday. Wednesday the telegram arrived from the War Department, notifying us that Reuben had been killed.

Within weeks the few bedbugs that had survived were

233

spawning new armies. The flowers died in their vases. They began to stink. No one . . . neither Momma nor Poppa nor I . . . threw them out. The dishes and pots and pans collected again on the stove, on the table, in the sink. The dress that Momma wore began to smell sour.

Since it is autumn Jacob will at least be spared the bedbugs. But what of the spotted bedclothes? The filthy kitchen?

I go upstairs and remove the linen from my bed and I put buckets of water on the stove. The washing machine no longer works, so I wash the towels and sheets and pillowcases by hand. I build a fire in the stove and drape the wet clothes on the chairs arranged around the heat. I work all night. By dawn I've managed to bring some sort of order into the kitchen. The rest of the house . . . the bedrooms upstairs, the closets filled with dirty clothes, the porch and yard covered with weeds . . . all that will have to wait. At least we'll be able to sit here, in the kitchen.

Poppa comes down at dawn, red-eyed, stoop-shouldered, his loose shoes thumping. He takes no notice of the work I've done. He goes into the store and sits in front of the stove. I don't think he hears me build a fire for him. The heat seems to comfort him no more than the fresh coffee I offer him. I sit at his side, my arm around his shoulders, and I hold the cup to his lips and wait until he swallows.

"Hi, Momma, it's me, Jacob."
She opens her eyes and looks at Jacob's face.
"A dream . . . God tortures me with dreams."
"It's no dream . . . it's me, Jacob."
"All my life I've been a good Jew. Why do you torture me?"
"Momma, I'm here. The army let me come home."
Her hand touches Jacob's face. *"Ah, mein schoener Yakov."*

We have shoved and pulled Poppa into the kitchen and we have propped him in a chair beside the coal stove. He says nothing as Jacob and I talk. "I saw Max in Los Angeles," Jacob says. "He told me he would have been a hypocrite if he'd come."

"Oh, for Christ's sake. Momma's in the hospital. She could die. And he's not concerned? Not at all?"

"Sure he's concerned. But what the hell, he was disowned when he got married. His wife wasn't allowed in the house. Momma said *kaddish* for him, the way she did when Rachel died. Ever since, so far as Momma and Poppa have been concerned, neither he nor Mary really exist. Is he supposed to forget that? Is he supposed to forgive them?"

Poppa seems completely unaware, or concerned, that Jacob has sounded so bitter about his treatment of Max. I wonder if he's even heard a word that Jacob has said. He's staring beyond Jacob, at the cookstove where Momma has prepared a thousand suppers. His face is white wax. He shaved off his mustache years ago but now, as he does so often, he wipes his upper lip, as if the mustachios were still there, in need of a trim. The gesture wrenches my heart. It is as if he's recalling his own youth, recalling the bright hopes that had spurred him on through adolescence and young manhood, as if he is recalling, too, the daily bluntings of each of those hopes, the constant challenges, the constant defeats.

"In a way," Jacob says, "he's better off than any of us."

I try to change the subject. I ask him about the army. But he won't be distracted.

"Strange," Jacob says, "very strange. Reuben and I . . . and everyone else . . . we all felt Max was the one who had no brains. He never read books, he didn't want to go to college, he couldn't have cared less about politics. And look at him. He has a beautiful home, a lovely loving wife, two beautiful kids, a successful business. He's calm, relaxed, independent. He's happier with his *shiksa* than I'll ever be with a nice Jewish girl. And you ought to see his store."

"Why did you come?" Poppa asks.

For about three seconds Jacob's face is dark with anger. He shakes his head. "I wish I knew."

235

Poppa tries to rise. The hand that once, with a single blow, could smash out the lid of a wooden barrel, can barely pick its way through the air. He totters above his chair. With a cry Jacob springs across the room and catches Poppa in his arms. He lays his cheek against Poppa's head.

Jacob has insisted I come with him and remain near him. He stands in front of me.

A shaft of light leans down from the kitchen window, to touch the road. We wait in the dark shadows at the side of the garage.

The whistles at the mine rang out about an hour ago, so Cosco should be coming up the road any minute.

I'm not sure why we're here, or what Jacob intends to do. The night I talked to him on the phone, when he first arrived in Pittsburgh, he'd promised we'd talk about Cosco and the accident. But we've not talked. Tonight, in the bus, on the way home from Pittsburgh, he barely spoke at all. He stared out the window at the fields, tried in vain to doze, and several times mumbled to himself and replied, "Nothing, nothing," when I asked him what he said. He's been especially attentive to Poppa, not talking to him (Poppa has nothing to say to either of us) but trying to feed him, wrapping him with a coat to keep him warm, buying him magazines, which remain unopened.

"When you were a child," he says now, as we wait in the darkness by the garage, just outside the border of the light coming from Cosco's house, "did you ever wish you'd never been born a Jew?"

I say yes, I had. I tell Jacob how I used to wish I'd been tall and blue-eyed, with a short straight nose and hair that was blond and straight. Jacob's fingers, clamped suddenly around my wrist, stop my voice. I hear the crunch of boots.

Cosco appears in the shaft of light.

"Cosco."

236

Cosco leaps back, lifting his metal lunch bucket to defend himself. He sees Jacob and he laughs. "Christ, you scared me, Jacob." He sticks out his hand and he laughs. "How the hell have you been, Jake?"

He comes forward and Jacob's fist catches him on the point of the chin. Cosco falls, and while he lies on the ground Jacob kicks his head. He kicks and stomps, whispering, his voice choked, "You bastards . . . you rotten fucking bastards . . ."

The thud . . . thud . . . thud of Jacob's boot fixes itself to the beat of my heart . . . thud . . . thud . . . thud. . . . It will never stop.

Standing there, my back shaped to the wall of the garage, I hear Jacob walking away. Cosco lies on his back, groaning very softly, his face bright red in the light that streams from the window.

I lift and drag Cosco up the steps and bump open the kitchen door and drag him to a chair. His father enters from another room, bent and gnarled and covered with sleep. His BVDs hang gray and limp from his knobby shoulders. He shakes his head. "Another fight," he says, shaking his head. "He ain't never gonna learn. . . ."

When I come into the kitchen the blood from Cosco has dried on my hands and arms.

Jacob and Poppa are sitting at the table. Poppa's mouth sags and his eyes, wide open, seem to see nothing.

"The hospital called," Jacob says. "Momma died."

The day we bury Momma an ambulance takes Poppa . . . mute as a stone . . . to the State Insane Asylum.

Two days later I walk Jacob back to Summer, to the bus station. He is on his way to Pittsburgh, to San Francisco, to the South Pacific.

At the bus station, as the driver calls for all to get on board,

237

Jacob puts an arm around my shoulders. "Benny, you ought to get out. Out of Sundown. Out of Summer."

I nod, agreeing. But I'm anxious for him to go.

"Do what you want with the house. Sell the goddamn place. Burn it down if you want to. I sure as hell don't ever want to see it again." He glances behind me, to the faces of the men on their way to the mills, on their way home from the mills. "You know, it's chance, just chance, that men are going from Sundown, from Summer, to fight the Germans. It's just chance. They could just as easily be fighting *for* the Germans. *For* the Nazis." He breathes deeply and winces, as if the inhaled air had been too cold. "Get out. I don't know where you can go, I don't know if there's any place *to* go, but getting out of Sundown, out of Summer . . . that's the first step. The memories here are evil. They'll suffocate you before" . . . and he waves his hand at the crowd behind me . . . "even before *they* will."

"I'll get along."

Jacob climbs onto the first step of the bus. "Write to me. I'm not a very reliable correspondent but maybe I'll change. Let me know what happens to you."

"I will, Jacob."

He goes into the depth of the bus and the driver roars the motor. A window goes up and Jacob sticks his head out as the bus moves forward. "Go see Max," Jacob shouts. "Maybe . . . who the hell knows . . . maybe he's had the answer all along."

I wave goodbye and stand there until the bus turns down Main Street and disappears.

I move through the dark store. I sit alone in the dark, cold kitchen. The wind throws snow against the house, each small flake making its own delicate impact on the windowpane.

Upstairs in Rachel's room the door squeaks when I open it. The movement of my body stirs the dank, cool dust. I sit on

238

Rachel's bed and gaze through the window, across the store roof to the hills.

I sit at the kitchen table. The only sound now in the entire house is the creaking of the boards as they give before the wind.

Benny, you're free. . . .

About the Author

Chester Aaron lives in Berkeley, California. He has, in his time, moved furniture, hauled trash, and worked in steel mills. He served in World War II, in the infantry. He is a graduate of the University of California. He is chief of an X-ray department in a hospital in Berkeley, and is now well on his way into his next novel.